FORTUNE
AND GLORY

BY JANET EVANOVICH

FORTUNE AND GLORY

TANTALIZING TWENTY-SEVEN

A STEPHANIE PLUM NOVEL

JANET EVANOVICH

ATRIA PAPERBACK

New York   London   Toronto   Sydney   New Delhi

ATRIA
PAPERBACK

An Imprint of Simon & Schuster, Inc.
1230 Avenue of the Americas
New York, NY 10020

Copyright © 2020 by Evanovich, Inc.

First Atria Paperback edition May 2021

ATRIA PAPERBACK and colophon are trademarks of Simon & Schuster, Inc.

For information about special discounts for bulk purchases, please contact Simon & Schuster Special Sales at 1-866-506-1949 or business@simonandschuster.com.

The Simon & Schuster Speakers Bureau can bring authors to your live event. For more information, or to book an event, contact the Simon & Schuster Speakers Bureau at 1-866-248-3049 or visit our website at www.simonspeakers.com.

Interior design by Dana Sloan

Manufactured in the United States of America

1 3 5 7 9 10 8 6 4 2

Library of Congress Control Number: 2020945056

ISBN 978-1-9821-5483-7
ISBN 978-1-9821-5485-1 (pbk)
ISBN 978-1-9821-5486-8 (ebook)

For Carolyn Reidy
A remarkable lady who was always a champion
for me and Stephanie.

CHAPTER ONE

My name is Stephanie Plum and I'm a fugitive apprehension agent in Trenton, New Jersey. I'm not especially brave, so you would think I'd pretty much stay out of trouble. Unfortunately, I occasionally ignore the obvious signs of danger and stumble into something ugly with the potential for disaster. This was one of those times. I was in a tunnel under a strip club, and I was with my coworker, Lula.

"This is a bad idea," Lula said to me. "My nipples are all shrunk up and trying to hide inside my body. It's like what men's gonads do when someone comes at them with a butcher knife. Those suckers abandon ship and there's nothing left but an empty nut sack. Not that I know firsthand. I'm just sayin' what I hear."

Aside from being a bounty hunter, I think I'm pretty normal. I have shoulder-length curly brown hair that's usually pulled back into a ponytail, blue eyes from my mother's Hungarian ancestors, and a bunch of rude hand gestures from my father's Italian side of the family. My nipples aren't as smart or nearly as big as Lula's. They were currently snug inside my sports bra, going along for the ride, and not paying attention to much of anything.

"Not only that, but I think my hair's standing on end," Lula said. "Look at it. Is it standing on end? It feels like it. My scalp is all tingly. That's a for-sure sign that something horrible is going to happen to us."

Lula's hair is always a surprise. Some days it's lavender. Some days it's braided. Some days it isn't even Lula's real hair. Today it was a massive puffball of chemically induced black ringlets shot through with hot pink highlights and sprinkled with glittery tiny pink stars. It was awesome. The rest of Lula is equally awesome, as her bounty runneth over in booty and boob and everything else. Today she was packed into a yellow spandex mini bandage dress that was sized for a much, much smaller woman. I was in my usual uniform of sneakers, jeans, and girly T-shirt.

Lula and I were playing hooky from bounty huntering to track down Lou Salgusta, a mob guy who specializes in information extraction and revenge by barbecuing various body parts of his victims. He's one of six hit men who, years ago, bought a strip club called the Mole Hole. It's located in downtown Trenton, and it's famous for its cheap drinks, outstanding burgers, and mob-occupied back room. It was common knowledge that the six club owners each had a personal La-Z-Boy recliner in the back room, and the possession of one of those recliners was as good as, if not better than, being made.

Recently, Salgusta and one of his La-Z-Boy pals, Charlie Shine, decided my grandmother had the key to a treasure. They kidnapped

Grandma and me, and while we endured some terrifying moments, we were able to escape with minimum damage. Problem is, Shine and Salgusta still want the key to the treasure, and we saw them murder a man in cold blood while we were captive. So, there's incentive for Salgusta and Shine to capture us again, persuade Grandma to give them the key, and then kill us.

"I know it's a righteous undertaking to protect your granny," Lula said, "but we aren't exactly that *Die Hard* guy."

"John McClane?"

"No, Bruce Willis. I'm guessing you don't even have a gun. I'm guessing your gun is home in your brown bear cookie jar."

She was right about the gun, and she was right about us not being Bruce Willis. Unfortunately, I can't let any of that stop me, because I love my grandma, and I will do whatever it takes to protect her. And as I see it, the only way to protect her is to track down Salgusta and Shine and get them behind bars.

Twenty minutes ago, I got a call from my mom, who'd gotten a call from Margie Wisneski, who'd gotten a call from her alcoholic brother that he was having his midmorning pick-me-up at the Mole Hole, and that Lou Salgusta had just walked in and gone straight to the back room.

Lula and I rushed to the scene, but the back room was empty when we arrived. Margie's brother was still at the bar and swore that Salgusta went into the back room and didn't come out.

"There's gotta be a secret way out of that room," Lula said. "That's the way it always is in the gangster movies. You've got to have a way to sneak out when the bulls show up. That's what they used to call the police. I know all about this because I got the classics movie channel on my TV package."

We returned to the back room and looked around. Six La-Z-Boy chairs. A monster safe. A card table with four folding chairs. Big-screen TV. No windows or doors other than the door opening to the barroom.

After several minutes of searching, we found a trapdoor hidden under a rug. We opened the door, climbed down a ladder, and stood squinting in the dim light of an escape tunnel that was approximately six feet high and three feet wide. It was encased in concrete and lit by a single bulb that was about thirty feet in front of the ladder.

Lula and I were now standing under that bulb. The tunnel changed from concrete to dirt at this point. It was supported by wood posts at regular intervals and it narrowed slightly.

"I'm going back," Lula said. "No way in hell am I going to squeeze myself into that dirt tunnel. First off, it's going to smudge up my dress. And second, it's the tunnel to death and doom."

"I imagine you got the death-and-doom message from your nipples?"

"Don't underestimate my nipples. I got nipple radar. When they talk, I listen."

Lula turned and huffed back to the ladder. She climbed the ladder and stopped at the top.

"This here door's closed," she said.

"You followed me down. Did you close the door?"

"Yeah. I didn't want anyone to know we were down here. I didn't count on it being so hard to get open again."

"Maybe there's a latch somewhere. A button to push," I said.

"I'm feeling all around and I don't see no button."

"Are you sure you can't push the door open?"

"Would I be standing here on this freaking ladder if I could get the freaking door open?" Lula said.

I replaced Lula on the ladder and tried the door. No luck. I climbed down the ladder and pulled my cell phone out of my pocket. No bars. I looked down the corridor at the dark, dirt tunnel of death and doom.

"Guess what?" I said.

"I don't like 'guess what.' And I don't like the way this place smells," Lula said, following me to the end of the concrete.

"It smells like dirt."

"Exactly," Lula said. "There's no other smells besides dirt, and that would indicate that we're underground with no windows or anything. Like we're in a tomb. You see what I'm saying?"

"We aren't in a tomb. We're in a tunnel that Lou Salgusta just used so it has to go somewhere."

Okay, truth is, I was every bit as creeped out as Lula. I didn't like being underground. It was claustrophobic. The air was heavy with dirt and damp, and I had to keep reminding myself that I wasn't suffocating. Even worse was the thought that Lou Salgusta might be waiting at the other end. I wanted to capture him, but I wasn't confident that I could do it under these circumstances.

I tapped my phone's flashlight app. "Stay close behind me and don't use your phone," I said to Lula. "We should save your battery."

"Do you want my gun, being that you're first in line?"

"Sure."

I took the gun from her not so much for self-defense as to make sure Lula didn't panic and accidentally shoot me in the back.

We walked a short distance and the tunnel curved. The single lightbulb disappeared from view and there was only blackness in front of us and behind us.

"I can't see what I'm walking on," Lula said. "It feels squishy and I hear water dripping."

Water was dripping from the top of the tunnel and the dirt underfoot was muddy. I could see men's footprints in the mud. Salgusta, I thought. Maybe someone else. Hard to tell in the dark. The tunnel came to a T-intersection. I flashed the light in both directions and saw nothing but endless dark tunnel. I went right, following the footprints.

"There's something dropped on my neck," Lula said. "I can feel it crawling. It's one of them big tarantulas. Lord help me, I got them all over me!"

I turned and flashed the light on Lula. "I don't see anything. I think you're just getting dripped on."

"It was on me and then it jumped off."

I directed the light to the ground and a small rat scurried away.

"Holy hell," Lula said.

I bit into my lip to keep from screaming and moved forward.

"I bet there's snakes up ahead," Lula said. "That's the way it is with Indiana Jones. First the tarantulas and rats and then the snakes. Where's the end of this freaking tunnel? I want to see the light. Where the heck is the light?"

"Hang on," I said. "I'm following footprints."

"I think we must be coming to the end because I smell something different," Lula said. "It doesn't smell like just dirt anymore. It smells like kerosene or gasoline or something."

I'd noticed the smell when we turned the corner a while back.

I didn't think it was a good sign since we were following a man whose best friend was an acetylene torch.

"What's those red dots in front of us?" Lula asked.

I flashed the light at the dots. "Rats," I said.

"Shoot them!"

I wasn't going to waste bullets on rats. I was saving them for whatever more horrible, more ferocious creatures might be lurking in the dark. Alligators or a slimy mud monster or Lou Salgusta.

I saw a flicker of light far down the tunnel. Another flicker eerily illuminated a smiling face, and WHOOOSH, the face disappeared behind a curtain of fire. Flames licked at the ground in front of a monstrous fireball and raced toward us.

I turned and shoved Lula. "Run!"

We ran blind in the dark, my flashlight beam bouncing around. A swarm of rats were also running for their lives, squealing beside us. I stepped on one and kicked another out of the way. Lula was huffing and puffing in front of me.

"Run faster!" I yelled. "I've got a wall of fire behind me."

We reached the intersection, made the turn, and the fire roared past us. We were bent over, catching our breath and I thought I heard footsteps, far off in one of the tunnels.

"We need to get to the trapdoor," I said to Lula. "Get moving."

"What happens when we get to the trapdoor?" Lula asked.

"We open it."

The dirt was dry underfoot in this part of the tunnel and the single bulb was visible in front of us. We passed under the light and I stared up at the wood door.

"Stand back," I said to Lula.

I emptied the clip into the door where I thought the latch was located. The door was pocked with rounds, and I could see through a couple of holes I'd drilled in the wood. I climbed the ladder and pushed, but the door didn't budge. I heard the scuff of shoes and muffled speech. I banged on the door and yelled for help.

The trapdoor was wrenched open and a young guy in a black Mole Hole T-shirt looked down at me. "What the heck?" he said, taking my hand, helping me out.

Lula was right behind. "No kidding, what the heck," she said. "You gotta fix that door. Bad enough you got a creep-ass tunnel down there, but your door don't even work when you want to get out. I got ruined Via Spigas, and I gotta take this dress to the cleaners. You know how much they charge to clean a dress? And on top of that, there's fireballs and rats down there, and I'm pretty sure I got the rat cooties on me." She tugged her skirt down over her ass and looked at the guy who helped me out. "You're the bartender, right? I want one of them man-eater burgers with extra fries and a chardonnay."

"Not a good idea," I said. "There might be someone following us, and I'm out of bullets."

"Yeah, but I really need a burger," Lula said. "I'm about having a heart attack. I need something to calm myself. I need meat and grease and cheese."

I could identify. My blood pressure was just a couple of notches below stroke level, but a burger wasn't going to do it for me. I wanted to get out of the Mole Hole. I needed air. I needed distance from the smiling face of Lou Salgusta.

"We can get a burger on the way to the office," I said. I looked at the bartender. "Thanks for the help. We appreciate it."

"Yeah, no problem. I wouldn't have heard the gunshots, but the music shut off between sets." He looked down at the open trapdoor. "I didn't know there was a tunnel."

I turned to go and almost bumped into a woman who was standing behind me. She was my height and about my age. She was exotically pretty, with long brown hair and large almond-shaped eyes. She was dressed in black. Black Louboutin combat boots with signature spikes covering the toes. Black skinny jeans. Black tank top with a black, Loro Piana Traveller jacket. Her lipstick was perfectly outlined just like her eyes.

"Did I hear you say there was a tunnel?" she asked.

"This here is the tunnel from hell," Lula said.

The woman moved closer and studied the ladder. "What's down there?"

"Mostly mud and rats," I said.

"Interesting," she said. "A tunnel under a strip club. If you'll excuse me, I think I'll investigate."

"And fire," I said. "Did I mention the fire?"

She was already halfway down the ladder.

"Hey!" I yelled at her. "The tunnel is dangerous. You shouldn't be exploring down there."

She disappeared from view, her boots echoing on the concrete for a short time, and then there was silence.

"Do you know her?" I asked the bartender.

"Never saw her before," he said.

"She's not from Jersey," Lula said. "She doesn't talk right. She sounds like Eliza Doolittle. And she's a crazy lady, but she got good taste in purses. She had a Fendi mini backpack hanging from her shoulder. I always wanted one of them."

Lula and I were splattered with mud and smelled of gasoline. We left the back room, walked through the dimly lit barroom, and went out the door. We stood blinking in the bright sunlight.

"I need to get out of these clothes before I got spontaneous combustion going on," Lula said.

CHAPTER TWO

I dropped Lula off at the bail bonds office on Hamilton Avenue. Her car was parked at the curb, and my cousin Vinnie's Cadillac was parked behind her. Vinnie's name is on the store front sign. Vincent Plum Bail Bonds. And on some more or less official papers it looks like Vinnie owns the business. Truth is, his father-in-law, Harry the Hammer, owns the business, and he also owns Vinnie.

Traffic was light, allowing me to do the drive from the bail bonds office to my apartment building in less than fifteen minutes. I had the windows open, hoping the gasoline smell wouldn't linger in the upholstery. I was driving a blue Honda CR-V that wasn't brand-new, but it was new to me.

I live in a boring but adequately maintained three-story apartment building on the outskirts of Trenton proper. My one-bedroom apartment is on the second floor and looks out at the parking lot. It's not a scenic location but it's quiet with the exception of the dumpster collection twice a week. I share the apartment with a hamster named Rex. He lives in an aquarium on my kitchen counter, and he sleeps in a soup can. Until very recently I sometimes shared the apartment with an on-again, off-again boyfriend, Joe Morelli. He's a plainclothes Trenton cop working crimes against persons. Our relationship is currently in the off-again stage, so these days it's just me and Rex.

Rex is mostly a nighttime kind of guy, but he peeked out of his soup can when I walked into the kitchen.

"Here's the deal," I said to Rex. "I didn't find Charlie Shine, but I did find his partner Lou. He tried to set me on fire, and he got away, but as you can see I'm perfectly okay. Except for my sneakers that smell like gasoline."

Rex retreated into his den, so I assumed he didn't feel compelled to know the details of my ordeal.

I dropped an apple slice into his food dish, and I tossed the sneakers into the trash. I needed new ones anyway.

———

My parents live a couple of blocks from the bail bonds office in a residential chunk of Trenton called the Burg. I grew up in the Burg and I feel comfortable there, but it's not where I want to live. The Burg is a lot like Rex's glass aquarium. Small and enclosed and open for everyone to see in. I can't get away from my past in the Burg. Not that my past is so terrible. It's more that I'd like to be judged on my future . . . whatever that might be. Since I don't have a good grip on my future, I'm stuck in the Burg and its surrounding neighborhood, which is another way of saying I'm halfway to who-knows-where.

My parents still live in the house where I grew up. It's a small house on a small lot. The house is painted mustard yellow and brown, not because anyone likes the colors but because it costs too much money to change. There are three small bedrooms upstairs plus a bathroom. Living room, dining room, and kitchen downstairs. Narrow front porch running the width of the house. Small stoop in the back off the kitchen door. Single-car detached garage.

My maternal grandmother lives in the house, too. She moved in when my grandpa Mazur succumbed to years of schnitzel and Marlboros and took up residence in heaven. At least we hope it's heaven. She was at the front door when I parked at the curb. Possibly checking the weather or maybe experiencing a moment of Grandma ESP that told her I was driving down the street.

"Just in time for lunch," she said when I walked up to the house. "It's Monday so that means leftover roast chicken. Your mother made it into chicken salad. And we have little rolls from the bakery."

Food is important in the Burg. It's the glue that holds everything together. News travels through the bakery and the deli. Bread is blessed at the church. Charities are funded at bake sales. Families still sit at the table for dinner whether they like it or not. Adult children are bribed into visiting their parents with the promise of pineapple upside-down cake, lasagna, fried chicken and biscuits, Virginia baked ham. Cultural appropriation is a good thing here. Polish housewives share recipes with their Italian neighbors. Kielbasa, macaroni and red sauce, Cozido a

Portuguesa, enchiladas, burgers, goulash, pot roast, pirogi, pad thai. We eat it all. The American melting pot is alive and healthy in Burg kitchens. Even death prompts an outpouring of food. Liquor flows at the after-burial reception and the buffet table holds a disturbing number of noodle casseroles.

My father was in his chair in front of the television in the living room. He's retired from the post office and drives a cab part-time, mostly taking a few regulars to and from the train station. He had a sandwich and a soda on a tray table, and he was tuned in to QVC. Grandma and I tiptoed around him and joined my mother in the kitchen.

"I'm glad you're here," my mother said to me. "Your grandmother is talking crazy again about going off on a treasure hunt. You have to speak to her. She won't listen to me."

At some point in time, my mother and grandmother reversed roles. My mother is now the voice of maturity and reason and my grandmother is the rebellious family member who is happy to throw caution to the wind and dye her hair flame red.

"They aren't crazy ideas," Grandma said. "And that treasure is my legitimate inheritance. My honey, Jimmy, left it to me. He was Keeper of the La-Z-Boys' Keys, and he left the two keys to me."

"He didn't leave the keys to you," my mother said. "He put them under his chair cushion, he died, one of his mob buddies stupidly gave you the chair, and by dumb luck we found the keys. And now I'm left with that horrible chair in my living room."

The chair was Jimmy's ancient Mole Hole La-Z-Boy recliner. My father loved it.

"Anyway, Stephanie promised she would help me find my treasure," Grandma said.

"Whatever the keys unlock belongs to the six men named on the keys. Not just to Jimmy," my mother said. "He was only *one* of the six La-Z-Boys."

The two keys appeared to be identical and weren't normal house keys. They were five inches long with a slim barrel handle. Double-sided teeth were cut into one end of the handle and a one-inch square was at the other end. The names of the six La-Z-Boy owners were engraved in the square. We'd checked with Google and determined that the keys most likely opened a safe.

"I get his share of the treasure," Grandma said. "It doesn't matter we were only married for forty-five minutes before he had the heart attack. His will said I got just about everything. And on top of that there's only three of the people named on the keys that are still alive, and two of them are going to jail for murder as soon as Stephanie can find them. The third is Benny the Skootch, and he's not in good shape."

This was all true. Three of the La-Z-Boy owners had died, and their chairs remained unoccupied in the back room. Two of the remaining mob guys, Lou Salgusta and Charlie Shine, were wanted for the murder Grandma and I witnessed. Charlie Shine was also in violation of a bail bond Vinnie had written on him over a year ago.

I hung my messenger bag on the back of a kitchen chair. I got a plate and a knife and fork and took my place at the small square table. Grandma sat next to me and my mom sat across from me.

"I think the treasure is here in Jersey," Grandma said, taking a roll. "I can't see them putting it far away. I did some checking, and it's not like any of the six men were world travelers. What we have to do now is find the safe that goes with the keys."

"That sort of safe usually has a combination lock that works in conjunction with the keys," I said. "And we don't know the combination."

"Yes, but you got Ranger," Grandma said. "And Ranger knows how to open everything."

Ranger is the other man in my life. His given name is Carlos Manoso but he goes by Ranger. He's former special forces, former bounty hunter, and on a few memorable occasions I've slept in his bed. He currently owns Rangeman, a high-end, under-the-radar security firm. And Grandma is right. Nothing stops Ranger when he wants entry.

I made myself a chicken salad sandwich and took some potato chips from the bag on the table. "Do you have any ideas about where this safe might be located besides New Jersey?" I asked Grandma.

"Not exactly," Grandma said, "but I got a lot of feelers out. And I'm doing what you said about not telling anyone I found the keys. I'm just making it sound like I'm curious."

"This is stupid," my mother said to Grandma. "You're going to get kidnapped again. Salgusta and Shine are going to burn our house down. You need to get rid of the keys. If you don't want to give them to Salgusta or Shine, you should give them to Benny. Maybe he'll give you some of the treasure."

"No way," Grandma said, "but I'll hand some of the treasure over to Benny when I find it, being that he's the one who was nice enough to give me Jimmy's old chair. I was thinking Stephanie should talk to him and maybe he'll spill the beans about the safe. He's on a lot of meds. He might not know he's giving up the secret."

I had to give credit to Grandma. She was a master schemer.

And she could be right about Benny. He was in his golden years that weren't entirely golden. He had heart issues and weight issues. It took two wise guys to get him out of his La-Z-Boy. He was on prescribed meds and I suspected recreational meds, not to mention he liked a good cigar and never passed up a glass of whiskey. The names on the keys were all geriatric or dead hit men who were mostly okay guys when they weren't whacking someone. This was true about Benny.

"I hear Benny is at home all depressed," Grandma said. "He used to meet up with all his cronies at the Mole Hole, but now they're either dead or hiding out. He'd probably be happy to have a visitor. I could even go with you. I'm real clever at worming information out of people."

My mother did an eye roll and made the sign of the cross.

"I'll stop in after lunch," I said to Grandma. "I'll go alone this time. If I can't get anything out of him, we'll bring you in next time."

"Sounds like a plan," Grandma said. "I have stuff to do anyway. I have follow-up phone calls to make. Jean Mulanowski said her nephew is a pit boss at one of the casinos in Atlantic City, and he told her that Jimmy was a regular. Her nephew is checking to see if Jimmy gave a local address. We're thinking he might have kept a second apartment there."

Originally, I thought I'd be pretty good at finding a treasure. After all, my real job is finding people and dragging them back to jail. People, treasure, what's the difference other than the payoff? Finding skips has me living paycheck to paycheck, if I'm lucky. My thinking is, the treasure has to be worth a lot more. Unfortunately, it's also turning out to be more difficult to find.

When I go after people, I already have a file full of clues assembled by the bond agency. Home addresses, work addresses, names of relatives, a picture. In the case of the treasure, I have to go find the clues before I can put it all together and actually go on the hunt. Then there's the danger factor. Most of my skips are dangerous, but not usually at the same level as Shine and Salgusta. Grandma and I were lucky to survive our last encounter with them, and I was pretty certain the only thing keeping Grandma and me alive and untortured up to this point is that Shine and Salgusta can't figure out how to snatch us. They used to have a bunch of wise guys working for them in the past, but not lately. And if they confided their plans to the wrong person, it would spread like wildfire through the Burg. It would be told to the second cousin of a first niece of a friend's brother who goes to church with his butcher's son, who happens to be a cop. This could result in not only jail time but also no treasure for Shine and Salgusta. So, I'm thinking they're being careful right now, but it's only a matter of time before they come after us.

CHAPTER THREE

I stopped at the bakery and got a box of freshly filled cannoli. If there's one thing a cardiac patient craves its full-fat ricotta cheese in deep-fried pastry. Steak and fried onion rings would be a second. I drove to Benny's house and parked at the curb. A purple Kia was in the driveway. Benny's wife, Carla, had late-stage Parkinson's, and I thought the Kia probably belonged to Carla's caregiver.

I rang the bell, a young woman answered, and I told her I'd come to talk to Benny.

"Who's there?" Benny yelled from another room.

"Stephanie Plum," I yelled back.

"He's watching television in the den," the woman said. "Just walk straight back."

The den was a small room that had been tacked onto the living room. Benny was wedged into a club chair positioned in front of a large flat-screen TV. A leather recliner was next to him. A tiger-striped cat was curled up in the recliner.

Benny smiled when he saw me, his eyes instantly focusing on the white bakery box.

"Cannoli," I said.

"You're gonna kill me," he said. "Are they fresh filled?"

"Of course."

"Hand them over," he said. "You want one?"

"No. I just had lunch at my mother's house." I looked at the cat. "I'm guessing the cat is in your chair."

Benny took a cannoli out of the box. "Yeah, he's an old guy. I don't like to disturb him when he's sleeping."

"I heard you weren't going to the Mole Hole anymore."

"None of the guys are there," he said. "It's not the same. And I hear it smells like dead rat roast."

This tells me that Benny is getting some real-time reporting from someone at the Mole Hole.

"I followed Lou Salgusta into the tunnel and he tried to cremate me," I said. "I managed to get away. The rats weren't so lucky."

Benny finished off the first cannoli and took a second. "Trust me, if Lou really wanted to kill you, you'd be dead. He was probably just playing around."

"So, you know about the tunnel?"

"We all knew about the tunnel. It's been there for years. I used it a bunch of times. We had plans to make improvements but never got around to it."

"Is that where Jimmy hid the treasure?"

"In the tunnel? No. There's nothing down there but dirt."

"I don't get why the keys are so important. If you know where the treasure is kept, why don't you just get it some other way. A locksmith or something."

"I knew there was a catch to the cannoli," Benny said. "You want to know about the treasure, right?"

"I'm curious."

"The freaking thing is boobytrapped. You try to get at the treasure without using both keys, and it'll look like Hiroshima. Stupid idea." He wiped his mouth with the back of his hand. "Where'd you get these? Italian bakery? I can always tell. Best cannoli in Jersey. It's the ricotta they use."

"Hiroshima is big."

"No shit. Excuse my French. Nobody ever thought the keys would get lost. Jimmy was Keeper of the Keys, and he was supposed to always have the keys with him." Benny ate half of another cannoli. "The keys weren't on or in Jimmy, so that means your granny has them. It's the only explanation. She was with him when he checked out. We looked everywhere. We x-rayed his corpse, he should rest in peace."

"This treasure must be worth a lot of money."

He finished the third cannoli. "Let's just say I could retire real nice on it."

"And you know where it is?"

"Not exactly. I got a clue. All six of us got a clue."

"Why such an elaborate scheme to protect the treasure?"

Benny shrugged. "We can't be trusted. We're all killers. We got no sense of remorse. I mean, it's not like any of us would kill for no reason. We got to have a good reason. Like it would have to be a job or something."

"Or a treasure."

There were three cannoli left in the box.

"I'm going to eat just one more," Benny said. "And yeah, like a treasure. It was put away as a kind of retirement fund. Mostly because it was too hot to fence when we got it. I'd tell you what my clue says but it wouldn't do you no good since you don't have the keys, right?"

"Right."

"Besides, that would be too much information for just a box of cannoli. More information would have to be moving into the sexual favors area."

"Eeuuw," I said. "Get real."

Benny scooped a glob of cannoli filling off his shirt. "I just said that for old times' sake. I wanted to see how it would feel."

"So? How did it feel?"

"Not as good as I remember. I was something in my day. You won't tell my wife, will you?"

"No. I won't tell her. You should share the last cannoli with her."

"Maybe," Benny said.

"One last question. And I think I already know the answer. Obviously, *someone* knows the location of the treasure."

"The guy who stashed it away," Benny said.

"The Keeper of the Keys?"

"Bingo. You got it. Jimmy. He was the guy we all trusted. He hid the treasure a bunch of years ago and gave us our clues. He even gave himself a clue. He got the last clue. I'm thinking it probably was the combination for the lock. You gotta stick the keys in and then you need the combination."

"And now he's dead."

"Yeah. Dumb fuck. Who would have thought he'd go like that?"

"When someone dies, what happens to his clue?"

"The clues get put in the Mole Hole safe . . . if we can find them. It was like a ritual. We drank some whiskey. We talked about old times. We spit on the floor and put the clue in the Mole Hole safe."

"Why did you spit on the floor?"

"Men do these things. Like I said, it was a ritual. Like retiring the dead SOB's chair." He looked at the two cannoli left in the box. "I might have to eat these."

"Three of the six treasure owners have died," I said. "And I'm guessing you only have two clues in the safe. I'm guessing Jimmy's clue is missing along with the keys."

"I'm not saying, but you could be right. Look, here's the deal. The clues were more like a fun game. Truth is, if we wanted to find the treasure we could. We could just put all our clues together. And besides, some of the guys probably followed Jimmy and figured it out. I couldn't be bothered. For that matter, we could have gotten the keys from Jimmy if we really wanted. All we had to do was kill him. None of us did any of this because the treasure was basically worthless hours after we got it. It was hotter than hot. The booby trap was set so the treasure would be destroyed if someone got stupid greedy before enough time had passed."

"Has enough time passed?" I asked.

Benny shrugged. "Hard to say."

Leaving Benny with cannoli crumbs and powdered sugar on

his shirt, I let myself out and drove to the office. As far as bail bonds offices go, this one's okay, but it's not going to get a spread in *Architectural Digest*. It's basically a storefront. The front room has an ugly brown Naugahyde couch against one wall, and two uncomfortable plastic orange chairs are positioned in front of a large metal desk on the other side of the room. A bank of rarely used file cabinets line the back wall. There's storage in the room behind the file cabinets, and a coffee station just inside the rear exit. My cousin Vinny hides out in a private office located behind the metal desk. Anyone wanting to beat the crap out of Vinnie has to get around the desk and through his locked door. Connie Rosolli, the office manager, sits behind the desk and keeps a loaded Glock nine in her bottom drawer. Vinnie is an excellent bail bondsman, but a slimeball in every other aspect of his life. Hence the security precautions.

Connie looked up from her computer when I walked in. She's a couple years older than me and a much better shot. She'd be a dead ringer for Dolly Parton if only Dolly had black hair and a mustache.

"I have three Failure to Appear files for you," Connie said to me. "One of them is a high bond. Vinnie is going to be all over you to bring him in."

If you get arrested and don't want to sit in jail until the court decides your ultimate fate, you pay my cousin to put up a bond for your release. If you don't show up for your court date and disappear off the face of the earth, Vinnie is out his bond money. If this happens too many times, not only is Vinnie in the red, but his father-in-law will amputate Vinnie's penis.

It's my job to make sure the *ifs* never get to the penis removal point. I make my money by finding the failure-to-appear idiots for Vinnie and dragging them back to jail. Currently, I was in desperate need of money. Rent was due, and I was two days away from searching the bottom of my bag for spare change.

Lula was on the couch. She'd changed her clothes and she'd added pink glitter to her eyelids for some afternoon glam.

"I already went through the files," she said. "We got a good one. George Potts. Remember him? He made national news a couple months ago when he got arrested for streaking down Hamilton Avenue and using the sidewalk in front of Tasty Pastry Bakery as a bathroom. He blamed it on bad weed and a gluten allergy."

I looked at the other two. Arnold Rugalowski, one of the fry cooks at Cluck-in-a-Bucket, was caught on camera putting fried roaches in his ex-wife's bucket of Clucky Chicken. She was insisting it was attempted murder, and he said it was a hate crime. The third FTA was the high bond. Rodney Trotter had been giving silicone butt implants in the back of his fifteen-year-old VW bus. His slogan was *we come to you and you get what you want.* After numerous complaints and an almost death, he was arrested for practicing butt enhancement without a license. The court set a six-figure bond because it deemed Trotter a high risk for flight.

"You look like a balloon someone just let the air out of," Lula said to me. "Are you okay?"

"The human race is doomed," I said. "How can we survive when the earth is populated by people like this?"

"These people aren't so bad," Lula said. "I've known lots worse. You gotta look at their whole picture. The Tasty Pastry Pooper was probably just trying to get happy with weed and a supermarket birthday cake, and it didn't work out for him. The cook at Cluck-in-a-Bucket fried the roaches. It's not like he was feeding them to his ex-wife while they were alive or something. And I don't know what to say about the butt injector. He shouldn't have been doing that. Anyways, the good news is that we're going to drag their sorry asses back to jail, where they'll have a chance to rehabilitate themselves."

"Do you really think serving time could help them?" I asked Lula.

"Hell no," she said. "They'll get gang raped and hooked on meth."

Connie held a half-empty box of donuts out to me. "This is why I get a box of donuts every morning," she said. "It's a box full of happiness."

I took a donut and shoved the files into my messenger bag. "I'm all about happiness."

"Me too," Lula said. "We should probably take the box with us in case our happiness runs out. We're going out after the bad guys, right?"

"Right."

CHAPTER FOUR

Lula followed me out of the office with the donut box under her arm. "Who's up first?"

"Rodney Trotter."

"Going after the big money," Lula said. "I like your style."

"No guts, no glory," I said. "Your car or mine?"

"I'm thinking you should drive on account of I just had my baby detailed. In case we get around to the streaker, and he still has gluten issues, I wouldn't want him in my backseat, if you see what I'm saying."

Lula drove a red Firebird that she kept in pristine condition. When she had her sound system cranked up it was enough to make birds fall out of the sky and your molars explode.

I got behind the wheel of the CR-V and handed the Trotter file over to Lula.

"It says here that he lives on Stiller Street," Lula said. "That's across town by the public housing projects."

I was having a hard time focusing on Trotter. My brain was stuck on Benny and the treasure. I drove over the railroad tracks and turned right, toward the train station.

"We're going the wrong way," Lula said. "You must be taking the scenic route."

"I want to ride past the Mole Hole. It's not that much out of the way."

"What do you expect to see there?"

"I don't know. Probably nothing."

"Are we going in?" Lula asked.

"Do you think we should?"

"I wouldn't mind. We could get some of those curly cheese fries. We left in a hurry this morning. You were all worried about what's-his-name."

"Lou Salgusta."

I was half a block from the Mole Hole and Lula leaned forward in her seat. "Look who's coming out of the titty bar," she said. "It's the crazy woman that went down into the tunnel."

I pulled to the side of the street and idled.

"She doesn't look singed or anything," Lula said. "Her hair isn't smoking. Hard to tell from this distance but her shoes don't even look muddy."

The woman walked through the parking lot and got into a black Mercedes sports car. She pulled out of the lot and I followed her.

"You think she's got something to do with the treasure?" Lula asked.

"I don't know. I think it's weird that she mysteriously showed up and went down into the tunnel."

"Yeah, who does that with their Fendi backpack and Louboutins? Those Louboutins didn't even look like knockoffs. They looked like they were made out of real quality leather."

The Mercedes took a right turn, drove two blocks, and took another right. It sailed through a yellow light, and I got the red.

"I think she made you," Lula said.

"Yep."

"Not her first rodeo," Lula said.

"Yep, again."

Twenty minutes later I was on Stiller Street. Narrow, two-story, redbrick row houses lined both sides of the street for three blocks. The brick was grimy with age. Paint was blistered and peeling on window trim. Front yards were postage stamp size, and most were neglected. It was easy to find Trotter's house. His van was parked at the curb.

"This isn't much of a neighborhood for a doctor," Lula said. "You'd think he'd have a nicer house. I'm guessing he does a lot of pro bono butt jobs."

"He isn't a doctor," I said, parking behind the van. "He's a con man."

"Even more reason why he should have a certain lifestyle. He doesn't have any overhead. He just has a lame-ass van to service. And he doesn't have to buy malpractice insurance. He probably don't have to fill out any Medicare forms, either, since it's a questionable cosmetic procedure."

Lula and I crossed the small yard, I rapped on Trotter's front door, and a woman answered. Hard to tell her age. Somewhere between fifty and infinity. Her face was deeply lined and artificially tanned. Her lips looked like they might explode at any minute. A self-rolled joint was stuck between the lips. She was wearing flip-flops and a magenta tent dress that came to mid-calf.

"Mrs. Trotter?" I asked.

"Yep."

"I'm looking for Rodney. I'd like to speak to him."

"He's in the kitchen having a late lunch."

The living room was dark and cluttered. Too much furniture. Stacks of newspapers. Giant box-store-size jars of snacks. Pretzel nuggets, dill pickles, Hershey miniatures, popcorn, Twizzlers, Cheetos, beef jerky. A gruesome collection of taxidermied animals. Squirrels, cats, foxes, skunks, a small pig, a weasel.

"The snack jars I get," Lula said, "but what's with the creepy dead animals?"

"Rodney says taxidermy relaxes him after a hard day of surgery," the woman said. "It's his hobby."

The kitchen was just as cluttered as the living room. Boxes of cereal were stacked on the counters beside jugs of vinegar, family-size jars of peanut butter, badly stuffed rodents with their teeth bared, loaves of bread, and bags of cookies.

A thin man with balding black hair and excessively bloodshot eyes was at the kitchen table. He was wearing a tight silky black shirt, and he was drinking Jose Cuervo tequila without benefit of a glass or straw.

"Hey, sweetie," he said, eyeing Lula. "You looking for a booty job? I got an opening this afternoon. Soon as I'm done with lunch."

"First off, I'm not your sweetie," Lula said. "Second, do I look like I need *any* work? My booty is perfect just like the rest of me. And even if I *wasn't* perfect, I wouldn't let a drunk punk-ass like you touch me."

"Sticks and stones," he said.

"Rodney Trotter?" I asked.

"Yeah. How about you, cutie? You looking to get beautified? I got a special going this week on lips." He squinted at the woman. "Hey, Ma, show her your lips."

His mother did duck lips at me and shuffled off into the living room.

"I could give you lips like that," Trotter said.

"Gee, hard to pass up, but no," I told him. "I'm looking to take you downtown to reschedule your court date."

"No can do. I got a big day ahead of me."

His eyes rolled back in his head, he fell off his chair, and crashed to the floor.

"Hunh," Lula said. "You think he's dead?"

"Not yet," I said. "I think he passed out from too much lunch."

"This man should *not* be practicing medicine," Lula said. "He's a mess. He shouldn't even be practicing fake medicine."

"Mrs. Trotter!" I yelled. "We have a problem."

The woman came into the kitchen and looked down at Rodney. "Sometimes he takes a nap after lunch," she said.

"We could drag him out, throw him into your backseat, and turn him over to the police," Lula said to me. "Problem is, the police might not want him being that he's unconscious. They've been getting picky about that lately."

I pulled cuffs out of my back pocket. "We can secure him and let him sleep it off at the office."

I reached for his wrist. His eyes blinked open and he scrambled away from me.

"That was a short nap," Lula said.

"Get away from me," Trotter said. "I know my rights. I'm a doctor."

"You aren't no doctor," Lula said, "and you got no rights. You signed them away when you got bonded out of jail."

Trotter lurched to his feet and grabbed a large syringe off the kitchen counter. "One step closer and I'll inject you."

"What the hell is that?" Lula asked. "It looks like something you'd use on a horse."

"Tools of the trade," he said. "I can work miracles with this baby."

"This is ridiculous," I said. "Put the syringe down."

"Get out of my house or someone gets this in their face," he said. "I'll make your nose look like it should be a balloon in the Macy's Thanksgiving Day Parade."

"You want me to shoot him?" Lula asked.

"No!" I said. "We don't shoot people."

"*Sometimes* we shoot people," Lula said.

"Not this time. He isn't armed."

"He looks armed to me," Lula said. "He's threatening to rearrange my nose with butt filler."

"Don't get too close to him," I said. "Let me handle this."

"How are you going to handle it? You going to let him pump up your nose? I'll tell you how I'm handling it. I'm leaving. If I can't shoot him, then I'm out of here. Adios. Au revoir. Sayonara."

Lula and I backed out of the kitchen, not taking our eyes off Trotter. We hurried through the living room, left the house, and jumped into my car. Okay, Stephanie, I told myself, so this wasn't your finest hour, but you'll have another chance to capture him. It's all about dogged perseverance, right?

"That was a disappointing experience," Lula said. "I need to elevate my endorphins. I say we go after the Cluck-in-a-Bucket fry cook, on account of I could try out those new donuts everyone's talking about. They're calling them chicken nuts because they fry the dough in the same oil as the fried chicken. I'm thinking some of those chicken nuts could take my endorphins to a whole new level. Besides it's a real innovation in the world of fast-food frying. And you know I'm all about innovating."

I pulled away from the curb. "Onward to the chicken nuts."

CHAPTER FIVE

Cluck-in-a-Bucket is five minutes from the bail bonds office on a good day. Ten minutes if church is getting out or if there's a funeral procession leaving the funeral home on Hamilton. It was twenty minutes from Trotter's house.

We got to Cluck-in-a-Bucket after the lunch rush and before the dinner rush. There were a few cars in the parking lot. No cars in the drive-thru line.

"I'm feeling good about this," Lula said. "This is gonna be a win-win. We capture the fry cook and we get chicken nuts as a bonus."

I'd be happy with just a win. I wasn't sold on the chicken nuts. I parked the car and got out and arranged my gear. Cuffs in jeans right-hand back pocket. Car keys in jeans left-hand back pocket. Pepper spray in right-hand sweatshirt pocket. Fake badge and legitimate right to apprehend papers in left sweatshirt pocket. Illegal stun gun left in car. Cell phone and credit card in sports bra. Lula kept her equipment in her purse. Lula rarely had pockets.

"Things could happen fast after we start the apprehension process with Arnold," Lula said. "So, I'm suggesting we get our chicken nuts first. I'll just step up like I'm an ordinary customer and then as soon as I get my nuts, we can make our move." She fished her wallet out of her purse. "What kind of nuts do you want? Regular or extra spicy?"

"I'm going to pass on the nuts."

"What? No nuts? You gotta try the nuts. It's just *wrong* not to try the nuts."

"I'm not in a mood for nuts."

"This is about that fight you had with Morelli, isn't it? It's the nuts association."

"That's ridiculous. It's not about Morelli. And it's definitely not about his . . . you know."

"His nuts."

"Yes, his nuts. It's not about his nuts. Morelli's nuts are just fine, thank you."

"Well, you gotta miss them."

"Could we please move on from this."

"Just sayin'," Lula said.

I cut a look at Lula and decided my chances of walking away with no nuts were small to none.

"Okay," I said. "I'll try the chicken nuts. I want the plain."

"Yeah, but it's all about the extra spicy," Lula said.

I felt my eyes narrow and my teeth clench. "Then get me the extra spicy."

"Good choice," Lula said. "I'll be right back."

I hung just inside the door while Lula went to the counter. Lula was right. I missed Morelli. I missed his dog, Bob. I missed his big-screen TV. I missed the comfort and security of being in a relationship. I missed hearing about his day and cuddling next to him in bed at night. I missed his playful sexiness and the heat that came with the play. I wanted to end the standoff, but I didn't know how to resolve the problem that caused the argument.

When Grandma found the keys, I told her I'd help her find the treasure. From that moment on, it's been a battlefield with Grandma and me on one side and the rest of my family plus Morelli on the other side. All of their objections are valid. Ownership of the treasure isn't clear. Much of the search will most likely fall into the gray zone of legality. And there are psychopaths involved, so it will be dangerous. Maybe even fatal.

Morelli's parting shot was that he didn't want a relationship with Indiana Jones. Okay, I get that because I have similar feelings about having a relationship with a cop. It's dangerous work and the hours aren't always great. My problem is that while Morelli made the statement to get a point across, he hit on a squelched desire. I'm realizing that I'm a closet Indy. For much of my childhood I was convinced I could fly. I broke my arm trying. I wanted to be Wonder Woman, Buffy the Vampire Slayer, and Princess Leia. None of that worked out for me. I ended up selling bargain-basement lingerie when I graduated from college, and now I'm tracking down a man who fried roaches and fed them to his ex-wife. Transitioning into Indiana Jones has a lot of appeal. Indy never had to eat chicken nuts to save the day. Monkey brains, yes, but not chicken nuts.

Lula put her order in for extra spicy nuts and waited at the counter. A couple of minutes later the counter girl handed Lula a giant bucket of nuts and Lula motioned for me to step forward.

"I can take it from here," Lula said to me. "I know I'm just the assistant agent, but I got a good grip on this one."

She popped a donut into her mouth and looked like she was in rapture.

"Omigod," she said. "This is the best donut ever. This is like having an orgasm in my mouth. And not someone else's either. Like it's *mine*."

The counter girl took a step back. "That's gross."

"Well, obviously you don't know a lot about orgasms," Lula said. "I gotta talk to the fry cook. I gotta compliment him."

"He's in the back," the girl said. "He's pretty busy right now."

"Hey, fry cook!" Lula yelled. "I gotta talk to you."

A big guy in a grease-stained white T-shirt appeared and stepped up to the counter. He was over six feet tall and built like a bear. He was balding and the hair he had left was pulled into a ponytail. He had a two-day beard and bloodshot eyes.

"You got something to say about my nuts?" he asked Lula.

Lula looked back at me. "Is he the one?" she whispered.

I nodded, yes.

"Are you Arnold Rugalowski?" Lula asked.

"Yeah," he said. "So what?"

Lula tucked the bucket of nuts under her arm and fished around in her purse. "Hold on," she said. "I gotta get my equipment."

Lula's purse had the capacity of a small suitcase. Lula could never find anything in her purse.

"Maybe I can help," I said, moving closer, offering Lula my cuffs.

"Thanks," Lula said, taking the cuffs, turning to Arnold. "We're bond enforcement agents, and we want you to come downtown with us, so we can reschedule your court date."

"Screw that," Arnold said. "And you're not getting my nuts, either."

He reached across the counter and grabbed the cardboard bucket Lula had tucked under her arm.

"Hey!" Lula said. "Those are mine. I paid for them."

Arnold flipped her the bird and walked back to his fry station.

"That's rude," Lula said. "I don't like his attitude. I want to see the manager," she said to the counter girl. "I demand to see the manager."

"He isn't here right now," she said. "It's just me and Arnold. Do you want to talk to Arnold again?"

"Damn right I want to talk to Arnold," Lula said. "Hey, Arnold!" she yelled. "Get your butt out here and bring my nuts with you."

Arnold stepped up to the counter. "You want your nuts? Try this on for size."

He took a donut from the bucket and threw it at Lula. It hit her in the forehead and was followed by a second that hit her left boob.

"Ow!" Lula said. "Stop that."

"Make me," Arnold said.

Lula fished around in her purse, found her Glock, and fired off a shot that took out an overhead sign advertising Clucky Nuggets.

The counter girl ducked behind the counter, and a handful of people who had been sitting in booths ran out of the building.

Arnold reached under his greasy T-shirt and grabbed the gun he had tucked under his waistband. "Dumb, fat bitch," he said. "Eat this."

Lula shrieked, panicked, and threw her gun at him, and we ran for the car. Arnold unloaded a couple of rounds that missed Lula and me but took out my side mirror.

I chirped the tires getting out of the lot and headed for the office.

"He said I was fat," Lula said. "Can you imagine?"

"That's what bothers you about that whole fiasco?"

"That's not all. I'm bothered that I never got my chicken nuts, even though the one I ate didn't live up to my expectations."

"What about the orgasm in your mouth?"

"Hunh, I suppose you never lied about a orgasm? I was being complimentary. And I'll tell you another thing. They should do something about gun control in this state. They let just any bat-shit crazy idiot carry a gun."

"*You* carry a gun," I said.

"That's different. I'm almost a police officer. I'm a quasi-law-enforcement person."

"You realize you left your gun back there?"

"Yeah, I'm gonna have to replace it. I'll detour to the hair salon on Stark when I go home today. Lolita Sue always has a nice collection. I get all my guns from her."

"You don't get them at a gun shop?"

"Hell, no. You gotta fill out all those forms and go through a bunch of crap. All I do with Lolita Sue is give her a couple bucks."

I dropped Lula at the office, and I called Ranger.

"I need you," I said to him.

"Babe," Ranger said. "I'm your man."

"I don't need you *that way*. I need you to help me break into a safe."

Okay, that was sort of a fib. Every woman I knew lusted after Ranger. Including me. He was six feet of hard-muscled perfection. He was magic in bed. And he had a magnetic pull that was beyond the physical. On the flip side, he wasn't a candidate for marriage, and he had a code of conduct that didn't necessarily conform to the national norm. I'd decided a while ago that it was best to ignore and deny Ranger-lust.

"I have a lot of skills," Ranger said. "Safecracking isn't one of them."

"But you know someone."

"I do."

"I'm on the hunt for the La-Z-Boys' treasure. Supposedly there are clues locked up in the safe at the Mole Hole."

"There's a little Italian bakery on Henry Street," Ranger said. "Carlotta's."

"Meet me in the lot behind the bakery at ten o'clock tonight."

"Okay, but . . ."

The Man of Mystery disconnected.

I thought about the files in my bag. Potts, Rugalowski, and Trotter. It was midafternoon. I could make another try at a capture. Potts was the obvious choice. He was guilty of a nonviolent crime. And he was a first offender, so he wasn't up to speed on the system. When I told him that I was merely taking him downtown to get a new court date, he might actually believe me. There was the gluten issue, but he'd probably have clothes on, so an accident wouldn't be an entire disaster. Plus, I kept a shower curtain in the back for blood and other body fluid emergencies. My bounty hunter skills are lacking, but at least I'm prepared for fugitive leakage.

CHAPTER SIX

Potts was thirty-seven years old and living with his parents in a house on Porter Street. A spouse wasn't listed on his bond application. His parents put up the bail bond money. He was unemployed.

Porter Street was about a mile from the bonds office in a neighborhood very much like the Burg. Small houses, nonexistent front yards, and backyards big enough to hold a Weber grill and a trash can. Mostly blue-collar, two-income families or retirees who had paid off their mortgage.

I parked across from the Potts house and watched for a while. A Ford Escape was in the driveway that led to a single-car garage. A rusted-out Sentra was at the curb. I was guessing everyone was home. Not my favorite scenario. I hated to make apprehensions that involved parents. It always felt sad that they had to see their kid led away in cuffs. It didn't matter that the kid was forty-two or that the parents were relieved to see him taken away. It still felt sad to me. If it was my child, I would be destroyed. Even Rodney Trotter's mother, in her La La Land pot-hazed delusion, had to shed a tear at having her son locked up.

I crossed the street and rang the Pottses' doorbell. A skinny guy with a large nose and mousey brown ponytail answered.

"George?" I asked.

"Oh jeez," he said. "I know who you are. How did you find me?"

"You gave this as your address," I told him. "It's on your bond application."

"Oh yeah. I forgot about that." He stepped outside and closed the door behind him. "So, what's up?"

"You missed your court date. You have to reschedule."

"Did they tell you I have PTSD?"

"No. Were you in the military?"

"No. College. It was a bad trip."

"Okay, but you still need to reschedule."

"Here's the thing. I don't want to involve my parents. They're sort of freaked-out about me. My mom won't go to the bakery anymore because . . . you know."

"I do," I said. "I know. That was an unfortunate emergency."

"Yes! OMG, you understand. That's so amazing. Thank you."

"Sure, but you still have to reschedule your court date."

"I get it," Potts said. "How do we do this?"

"I can take you to the courthouse and get you re-bonded."

"That would be cool. That would be amazingly cool. And we don't have to involve my parents?"

Here's the dilemma. If I say his parents won't be involved, it's not a fib, but the reality is he won't get out of jail unless he finds someone else to post his bond. If I tell him the whole story, he probably won't get in my car.

"What do you want to hear?" I asked him.

"Something good. Like you want to come in and hang out in my room with me."

"Not going to happen."

"I have a PlayStation and a big tub of cheese puffs. They're made from corn and the cheese dust is lactose free."

"No. Never."

"That's harsh. Never is a long time."

"Are you going downtown with me, or do I have to get your parents involved?"

"Wow," he said, "you play hardball."

I pulled cuffs out of my back pocket and clapped one on his wrist, and he squealed like a pig.

"Get it off! Get it off!" he said, jumping away. "I don't like it. I'm feeling anxiety. I'm feeling panic. I'm feeling faint. Call 911. I need a doctor. I need a paper bag. I need a joint."

"I haven't got any of those things," I said. "Do you want me to get your mother?"

"No! Not my mother. I'm feeling better. I just need a moment. You surprised me. I'm not good with surprises."

"I should put the other bracelet on you," I said.

"Is that necessary?"

"They like it at the police station. It's a security thing."

He held his hand out, so I could put the cuff on him. "I guess you never know who's going to be dangerous," he said.

"Exactly."

"I'm not very dangerous. I'm mostly fearful and I have allergies."

I led him across the street and got him settled into the backseat of my car.

"I'm allergic to cats and bananas and garlic and marigolds and wool and macadamia nuts and wheat gluten and cucumbers," he said. "There are other things, too. There's a long list of things I'm allergic to, but I'm not allergic to peanuts. For instance, I could have a peanut butter sandwich as long as it's on gluten-free bread." He was silent for a long moment. "Do you think they have gluten-free bread in prison? I get the poops if I eat wheat bread."

I turned onto Hamilton Avenue and glanced at Potts in the rearview mirror. "Hopefully you won't have to go to prison," I said. "You were accused of a nonviolent crime, so maybe you'll just get community service."

"That would be awesome," he said. "I'm all about community service."

"Do you volunteer anywhere?"

"No, but I think about it sometimes. I wanted to volunteer at the zoo in Philadelphia, but it turned out I was allergic to giraffe dander. And they're very big when you get up close. I'm not comfortable with animals that are bigger than me."

"You aren't having any allergic reactions now, are you?" I asked. "Like gluten?"

"No. I'm okay. I'm a little apprehensive, but that's normal for me. Did I tell you I have PTSD?"

"Yes."

"It makes me apprehensive."

Having Potts in my car was making *me* apprehensive.

"Do you mind if I hum?" he asked. "Humming helps to settle my stomach."

I checked him out in the mirror again. "You have a stomach problem?"

"It happens when I get apprehensive. I get a nervous stomach."

I was less than ten minutes away from the courthouse and police station. If I stopped to get the shower curtain out of the back, I'd add at least three minutes. Best to drive faster and take a chance he wouldn't spew before I pulled into the parking lot, I thought.

"Go ahead and hum," I said.

"Sometimes my humming bothers people," he said.

"Not me," I told him. "Hum all you want."

After seven minutes of listening to tuneless humming I thought letting him throw up in the car might have been a better choice. I sped into the lot across from the municipal building, slid into a parking slot, and jumped out of the car. I stood for a moment, enjoying the sound of traffic.

Court was still in session, so I took Potts directly to the judge. If the judge had the time and inclination to see him and Potts could make bail, Potts could avoid spending the night in jail.

———

Connie was alone when I walked into the office.

"I have a body receipt for Potts," I said.

Connie's eyebrows raised a little. "Didn't he want to get bailed out again?"

"He refused to call his parents, and he had no one else he could ask."

"There's more," Connie said. "I know you. You have that look."

"What look?"

"The look like you want to poke your eye out with a sharp stick."

I slumped into the uncomfortable plastic chair in front of her desk. "I put up his bail."

"Excuse me?"

"It was small. I put it on my credit card. I couldn't just leave him there. The man is a car crash. He has all these allergies and insecurities. And he has PTSD."

"Jeez. Don't drive past the Humane Society on your way home. You'll go home with a box of kittens."

"He hums," I said to Connie. "Parts of songs. Over and over. And sometimes he hums nothing."

Connie took my body receipt and wrote out a check for the capture. "My Uncle Big used to hum like that," she said. "One day he was humming, and someone shot him . . . twelve times."

"Because he was humming?"

"Maybe, but he was also trying to hijack a truck full of sneakers."

"Is he still humming?"

"You don't hum after taking twelve gunshots," Connie said. "Not ever."

I stuffed the check into my bag and headed out. I stopped at the door and looked back at Connie. "You haven't, by any chance, seen a woman my age and my height, dressed in black, with freshly ironed long brown hair and perfectly applied fake eyelashes on her big brown eyes?"

"Gabriela?"

"You know her?"

"She was here earlier today. She wanted information on Charlie Shine. She knew we bonded him out."

"Do you know her last name? Who is she?"

"She didn't give a last name. Just Gabriela. She didn't say much. She's looking for Shine, and she knew we were, too."

"What did you tell her?"

"That he was in the wind. She already had his police file. I'm guessing she's a PI or maybe an insurance investigator. Shine probably has a bunch of people looking for him."

I left the office wondering why Gabriela was interested in Shine. It didn't bode well. If she found him before I did, I'd be out bond money and the chance to extract information about the treasure's location. Even worse, what if Gabriela wasn't actually after Shine, but the treasure? What if she was out to steal the treasure from underneath Grandma and me?

CHAPTER SEVEN

I left my apartment at nine thirty and drove to Henry Street. I was meeting Ranger in a parking lot, and I expected to take part in a burglary. I had no further information. I wasn't sure of the dress requirements, so I went with basic black. Black sweatshirt. Black T-shirt. Dark jeans. Black sneakers.

A Rangeman SUV was already parked in the bakery lot when I arrived. There was a Rangeman driver behind the wheel, and Ranger and his tech guy, Ramone, were standing beside the SUV, waiting for me. Both men were in black fatigues without the Rangeman logo. Both men were wearing black ball caps. No logo.

Ranger was wearing a utility belt that held a Maglite, a knife, and a gun. Possibly the belt held other tools of his trade, but I couldn't identify them. Ramone had a small backpack slung over one shoulder. I'd watched Ramone apply his skills on a couple of other occasions, and I knew he had various gizmos and probably explosives in the pack. He was a crack shot, an electronics genius, a master safecracker, and, like most of Ranger's *specialists*, Ramone was comfortable on both sides of the law.

"Hey," I said by way of greeting.

"Hey," Ramone said.

Ranger gave a barely perceptible nod.

"What's the plan?" I asked Ranger.

"This bakery is owned by Benny the Skootch's cousin, Emelio. It's mostly used to launder money, and it has no security beyond a locked door. There's a tunnel exit in the basement. We can use it to get into the Mole Hole back room. Less complicated than going through the front or back door of the Mole Hole after hours."

"Have you ever been in the tunnel?" I asked Ranger. "There are rats in the tunnel."

"And?"

"*Rats! Big rats!* Lots of them."

"Babe," Ranger said.

Depending on the tone, *babe* could have many different meanings with Ranger. This babe was said with the slight hint of a smile. I amused him.

"Maybe not so many rats," Ramone said. "I understand there was a fire down there."

Ranger moved to the bakery's back door, inserted a slim pick, and the lock clicked open.

"Stay close behind me when we're in the tunnel," Ranger said. "Ramone will watch your back."

We walked through a small storeroom filled with racks of white bakery bags and unassembled white bakery boxes, large jars of food coloring, multicolored sprinkles, granulated sugar, powdered sugar, cinnamon sugar. The storeroom led to a room with a couple of refrigerators and a workbench.

"Where do they bake things?" I asked.

"In Carteret," Ranger said. "It all gets trucked in and they do some decorating here."

"That's disappointing," I said. "I always imagined Carlotta dusted in flour, baking bread and cupcakes before the sun came up."

"It gets worse," Ranger said, opening a door and shining his light on a flight of stairs that led to the basement. "There's no Carlotta. There's just Emelio and a couple minimum-wage cannoli fillers."

I followed Ranger down the stairs to a crude cellar that housed an ancient-looking water heater and furnace. Ranger opened another door, and we stepped into an offshoot of the Mole Hole tunnel.

I looked at the roughly carved dirt that was supported by wood beams and occasionally rebar, and I gave an involuntary shudder.

"This is safe, right?" I asked Ranger.

"Probably on a level with driving the Jersey Turnpike," Ranger said.

Ranger had the big Maglite beam focused a good distance ahead of us. I had my little pocket light shining on the ground in front of my feet. I could hear Ramone close behind me. So far, no rats, bats, giant spiders, or insane arsonists.

We reached a T-intersection, and Ranger turned to the left.

"You've been in this tunnel system before," I said to Ranger.

"Years ago, when I was working as an agent for Vinnie, I tracked a couple skips down here."

I flashed my light on a support beam and saw that it had been superficially charred. This was the part of the tunnel Lou Salgusta had set on fire. Ranger made another turn, we passed under the overhead light and stood in the concrete passageway that led to the trapdoor.

"We need to kill the lights," Ranger said. "Ramone has infrared goggles, and I have a penlight."

He went up the ladder, found the hidden spring-latch that had eluded Lula and me, and quietly opened the trapdoor. I followed. Ramone came last, wearing the goggles.

"Someone made Swiss cheese out of this trapdoor," Ramone said.

"That would be me," I told him. "I couldn't find the latch."

Ranger wrapped his hand around my wrist, and I got a rush. His hand was warm, and I could feel him close beside me in the total darkness. I was basically blind in the absence of light, but Ranger had vision like a cat. He'd grasped my wrist, so he could guide me across the room to the safe. I heard Ramone move past us and stop.

"Whoa," Ramone said. "This is old-school. I don't need equipment to open this. I could stand a foot away and hear the tumblers."

Minutes later the safe creaked open and Ranger flicked the penlight on. There were two bricks of what I suspected was cocaine on the top shelf. The second shelf held stacks of money neatly held together by paper wrappers. The third shelf was a jumble of porno magazines, a TV remote, a half-eaten Snickers bar, and a cardboard cigar box.

I took the box out and flipped the lid open. There were two

pieces of paper in the box. They were each folded in half. The message on one was *ACE it*. The other message was *Philadelphia*. Each piece of paper had a number on the bottom. *ACE it* was #1 and *Philadelphia* was #3.

"Is this it?" Ranger asked.

"I don't know," I said. "I expected to find two clues, and I guess these are the clues, but they're disappointing. I was hoping for pieces of a map."

I used my phone to take photos of the clues. I put the clues back in the box and put the box back in the safe.

Ramone closed the safe and spun the dial. Fifteen minutes later we were back in the bakery parking lot. Ranger loaded Ramone into the Rangeman SUV and waved them off.

"I'm riding with you," Ranger said. "I had my car dropped at your apartment."

"Thinking ahead?"

"Babe," Ranger said.

This was a noncommittal *babe*. It could mean that he wanted to talk. It could mean that he was being protective and wanted to see me safely to my door. Or it could mean that he had his cargo pants pockets stuffed full of condoms.

Ranger took three calls while I drove. I parked next to his Porsche 911 Turbo, and he put his phone away.

"Break-in at the home of a high-end client," he said. "They weren't home when it went down. Three men with ski masks. Parked in the driveway in a stolen car. One of them was dumb enough to remove his mask before driving away, and we have him on an exterior camera. The police can take it from here."

"Inside job?"

"Probably. They took cash. Knew where to find it. I suspect they also took drugs, but the homeowner isn't going to report a drug theft."

We crossed the lot and Ranger followed me into the building. We took the elevator to my floor, walked the length of the hall, and Ranger inserted a key in my door lock. This was no surprise. He'd installed my security system, and truth is, he could have easily opened my door without a key.

I flipped the light on, and Rex stopped running on his wheel and blinked at us. I took a couple of Froot Loops from a box on the counter and dropped them into Rex's cage.

"Would you like something to drink?" I asked Ranger. "Water, wine, beer? Froot Loops?"

"Pass," Ranger said. "We need to talk."

Damn. That was my least favorite of the three options.

"I know the basic facts about the keys," Ranger said. "Jimmy was Keeper of the Keys. He died. The keys disappeared. Supposedly the keys are needed to open a safe that contains something valuable."

I nodded. "Those are the facts."

"And I know that Grandma has the keys."

I narrowed my eyes at him. "You planted a listening device on me again."

"Babe," Ranger said. "You told me."

"Oh yeah. Sorry. I forgot."

"I want to know what's happening *now*. Starting with today when you visited Benny."

"How do you know about Benny?" I closed my eyes and held my hand up. "Never mind. Erase that question. I know the answer."

Early in our relationship Ranger decided it was his job to keep me alive. Placing a GPS locator on my car turned out to make his job goal more realistic.

"Benny told me about the two clues in the safe," I said. "He also said that if you try to open the safe without the keys it's Hiroshima."

"What about the combination? There's usually a combination lock in conjunction with keys."

"Benny didn't say much about that. He thought Jimmy's clue, the last clue, might be the combination."

"You have two clues," Ranger said. "*Ace it*. Labeled as #1. And *Philadelphia*. Labeled as #3. Do they mean anything to you?"

"No. Only the obvious. *Ace it* could refer to the playing card. Or it could mean total success. Like I aced the test. And *Philadelphia* is Philadelphia."

"Babe, you need the rest of the clues. What about Jimmy's clue?"

I squelched a grimace. "It's missing."

"It wasn't in the chair?"

"Not *in* the chair or *under* the chair. Not in his apartment, his office, his car, or any of his body cavities."

"Do you have plans to get the other three clues?"

"I have to capture Lou Salgusta and Charlie Shine. And I have to bargain with Benny the Skootch."

"Once you capture them, how are you going to convince Salgusta and Shine to give you their clues?"

"In the words of Indiana Jones, 'I'm making it up as I go.' Do you have any ideas?"

"I do," Ranger said. "You're going to like them."

"Do these ideas involve Salgusta and Shine?"

"Not even a little."

I was pretty sure I knew where this was going. Ranger had kept his distance, romantically speaking, while Morelli and I were a couple. Now that Morelli was out of the picture, it was game on for Ranger.

"You look like you're about to have a panic attack," Ranger said. "Not the reaction I was going for."

"Yeah, caught me by surprise, too."

That got a smile. He reached out, pulled me close, and brushed a kiss across my neck, just below my ear. A second one lingered.

"How's the panic level?" he asked.

"All-time high."

"With good reason," Ranger said.

"How about you? Are you feeling panicky?"

His hands slipped under my T-shirt. "Panic isn't included in my emotional package."

His hands were warm, leaving a heated trail as they moved up my rib cage to my breasts. We kissed, our tongues touched, and my fate was sealed. I'd been here before with Ranger, so I knew the deal. He'd just put a match to the fuse that was going to send me off like a bottle rocket. *Zzzzing! Blam!!!*

CHAPTER EIGHT

"**B**abe," Ranger said, "I'm heading out. What's your plan for the day?"

I propped myself up on one elbow and squinted at him in the dark. "Plan? What time is it? Am I awake?"

"It's five o'clock and I'm late," Ranger said. "The morning briefing and roll call is five thirty. Text me when you're up and can talk."

I gave him a thumbs-up and pulled the quilt over my head. I didn't have a plan for *anything*, much less for my day. And as for talking, if he wanted to discuss what just happened between us my comments would be *Wow, Holy Cow, Damn Skippy,* and *Omigod.* I had other thoughts, but I'd keep them to myself. In fact, I intended to work at pushing the other thoughts out of my head. The other thoughts had to do with love and commitment and who the heck was this guy, anyway? And why wasn't he tired?

I dragged myself out of bed when the sun came up. I showered, dressed in my usual uniform of jeans and T-shirt, gave Rex his breakfast, and made coffee for myself. I put the coffee in a to-go cup and headed for the office.

I called Grandma on the way and told her about the two clues. "Do they mean anything to you?" I asked her.

"Not a thing," Grandma said. "I don't think Jimmy was crazy about Philadelphia. And he was more of a slots guy than a card guy."

"Keep thinking about it," I said. "Hopefully we can get a couple more clues."

"Better sooner than later. My list of things to do with the money is growing."

Connie was unlocking the door when I arrived. "Whoa," she said. "This isn't something I see every day. Are you up early for a reason? Or have you not been to bed yet?"

"I need to find Shine and Salgusta, and I need to be the one on the hunt, not the other way around. Problem is, I don't know where to begin."

Connie handed me a box of donuts, opened the door, and we stepped inside.

"Begin by having a donut," Connie said. "Start with the good stuff."

I put the box on her desk and took a donut. "Any other ideas?"

"If it's the treasure you're actually interested in, ask yourself, what would Indy do?" Connie said.

"Indy always comes through. Me not so much."

"Indy has what you have, perseverance," Connie said. "Most of the time you don't know what the heck you're doing, but you stick with it, and eventually you get lucky."

"I haven't got a lot of time to get lucky on this. Salgusta and Shine are also after the treasure, and they have two extra clues that I don't have."

"Shine has been like the invisible man," Connie said. "Everyone knows he's here, but no one has seen him. And with good reason, he's being invisible. There's an outstanding warrant on him for tax evasion, among other things. Plus, he's now a murder suspect. Salgusta keeps circling back to the Mole Hole. Never stays long. No pattern to his visits. Have either of them made a move on Grandma?"

"You mean since they kidnapped us a while back, and we escaped? No."

"That kidnapping had to have been horrible."

I nodded.

Horrible didn't begin to describe it. It was terrifying, and I still had an occasional nightmare about it.

"Any ideas about where these guys are staying?" I asked Connie.

"No, but Shine likes the ladies. Last time he was hooked up with a pro. Lula might be some help there. Salgusta pretty much creeps out everyone. I don't know who would harbor him. Especially since he's also a suspect for the murder you witnessed."

"Can you get me information on recent credit card use? It might lead me to a neighborhood."

"You want me to hack into his accounts?"

"Yeah."

"Okay," Connie said. "Not a lot going on here. I have some extra time. You'll visit me in jail, right?"

"I'll bring you lasagna on visiting day."

The front door banged open and Lula swung in. "What's going on here?" she said. "Did I miss something? Did Stephanie eat the Boston creme donut?"

"No," I said. "I ate a maple glazed and a jelly donut. I left the Boston creme for you."

"I appreciate it," Lula said, "but that's worrisome. First one here always gets the Boston creme. What's up?"

"I wasn't in a Boston creme mood," I said. "I have a lot on my mind."

Lula took the Boston creme. "Like what?"

"I need to find Lou Salgusta and Charlie Shine."

"Good luck with that one," Lula said. "Last time we tried to catch Salgusta we almost got roasted. I'm not going after him no more. And I'm not going into that tunnel again, either."

"Okay," I said, "but we could look for Charlie Shine. Connie thinks he might be shopping around for a new girlfriend. Do you still have friends on the street?"

"I know a couple of the older girls, but it's been a while since I was a professional satisfier," Lula said. "Still, I guess we could ask around tonight."

I looked at Connie. "Do you have anything else?"

"He's not with his wife in the Burg," Connie said. "That's definite. I'm thinking he's hanging somewhere close, but not in Trenton."

"Unless he's with a new honey," Lula said.

Connie and I nodded agreement.

"So, what are we gonna do now?" Lula asked

"We can look in on Rugalowski and Trotter," I said.

"I'm not excited about that," Lula said. "I don't like them. I especially don't like Arnold Rugalowski and his stupid nuts."

"We're going to try Rugalowski at home this time," I said. "I'm hoping he'll be more receptive to getting re-bonded."

"He don't look like he even got a home," Lula said. "He looks like he lives in his ten-year-old Chevy Nova. I'm guessing the ex-wife got the home."

I pulled his file out of my bag. "He gives a home address of 43 South Clinton Street."

Lula tapped it into her phone. "That's a weird address," she said. "It don't look like there's any houses. It's only got a cemetery on one side and some government offices on the other."

I looked over at Connie.

"I didn't write the bond," Connie said. "Vinnie wrote the bond."

"Is Vinnie coming in today?" I asked.

"Vinnie is in Vegas," Connie said. "Poker tournament."

I hiked my messenger bag higher onto my shoulder. "Let's see if there's a ten-year-old Chevy Nova parked on South Clinton."

"I guess I could go along with that," Lula said.

I drove a short distance down Hamilton Avenue, turned onto South Clinton, crossed over the railroad tracks, and followed Clinton to the cemetery. There were some cars parked at the curb alongside the cemetery, but none of them looked like they were home to a fry cook.

"He could be camped out inside," Lula said. "This is a cozy cemetery. It's got lots of trees, and I can see from here that they keep the grounds nice."

I parked behind one of the cars.

"Hold on here," Lula said. "What are you doing?"

"I'm going to walk around and see if he's camped out behind a tombstone."

"I'd just as leave stay here, thank you. Cemeteries bring me down. And on top of that I'm not looking forward to seeing the roach cooker. I got a bad feeling about him."

"Okay," I said. "You stay here and guard the car while I prowl around the cemetery. Make sure the roach cooker doesn't carjack us."

"You didn't believe in my nipple radar, either, and look where that got us," Lula said.

I left Lula in the car, found the entrance gate, and meandered around, following paths, listening for activity. I walked up a small hill and saw a solitary figure on the other side. It was a slim woman dressed in black. She was very still, staring at a headstone on a relatively new grave. It was Gabriela. She turned as I crested the hill and glanced my way. She did a small nod of acknowledgment and returned her attention to the simple granite marker.

I walked downhill and joined her. The name on the headstone was Julius Roman. He'd been one of the six La-Z-Boys. He'd recently been killed execution-style and one of the clues in the Mole Hole safe had been his.

"A relative?" I asked Gabriela.

"No," she said. "And you?"

"No."

"But you knew him."

"We met shortly before he died," I said.

"I understand he was killed. Gunshot. Deliberate."

I nodded. "Yes. Was he a close friend?"

"No," she said.

"Are you here looking for someone who knew Julius or are you looking for something else?"

"Just looking."

She turned and walked away, following a path that led in the opposite direction from where my car was parked.

After ten more minutes of wandering around, looking for Rugalowski, I was back behind the wheel.

"How did that go?" Lula asked.

"I didn't find Rugalowski, but I ran into Gabriela."

"Who?"

"The woman in black with the Fendi bag. More and more I'm thinking she's after the treasure. She was at Julius Roman's grave."

"What was she doing there?"

"Nothing. Looking at the gravestone."

"Did she have a shovel?"

"No," I said. "This time she had a Hermès purse."

"I always wanted a Hermès purse. They're real classy."

"I didn't know you were into classy."

"You bet your ass," Lula said. "I'm all about it."

I backtracked down Clinton to Hamilton and drove past Cluck-in-a-Bucket. An aging Chevy Nova was parked in the lot.

"Looks like he's got the breakfast shift," Lula said. "Probably people coming in for their morning nuts."

I made a U-turn, swung into the lot, and idled next to the Nova.

"Now what?" Lula asked.

"Now you're going to look in his car to see if he's asleep in there."

Lula got out and looked in the car.

"Nobody here," she said, "but this car is a mess. It's full of crumpled-up beer cans and dirty clothes. And there's a bunch of ratty magazines."

"Porno?"

"Mostly *Guns and Ammo* and Food Network." Lula got back into my CR-V. "You aren't planning on another takedown attempt while he's working the fry station, are you? I couldn't come up with a lot of enthusiasm for that."

"No. I want to get him after hours. I'll have Connie do some research on his schedule and maybe she can find an address that isn't a cemetery."

"That leaves the butt guy," Lula said. "It used to be that we went after carjackers and armed robbery guys, and now we got a bunch of creepers."

I was with Lula. I couldn't get excited about another face-to-face with Rodney Trotter. I had treasure on my mind.

"I say we go back to the office and see if anything good came in this morning," Lula said. "A killer or a serial rapist. Something normal."

———

"Sorry," Connie said, "I haven't got any new skips, but I made a couple phone calls while you were gone, and it looks like Charlie Shine is definitely in town. Marge Russo saw him yesterday. She said she was crossing the street and he drove past her. He was wearing a hat pulled down low and dark sunglasses but she was sure it was him. And Loretta Bettman saw him over the weekend.

She said he was behind her at the Dunkin' drive-thru. Both times he was alone and driving a white Kia."

"Has anyone seen Salgusta?" I asked Connie.

"My mom and my aunt Cookie think he's hanging out in the tunnel," Connie said. "They said there are a bunch of exits, and one of the exits is at the Hotel Margo."

"I know that hotel," Lula said. "It's got good hourly rates. When I was in the customer happiness business I frequented that hotel. It gave a special discount if the customer was mob."

"Anything else?" I asked Connie.

"No," Connie said. "That's all of it."

"Good enough," I said. "I'm going to take a look at the Margo."

"I guess I'll tag along," Lula said. "It'll be like one of them nostalgia trips."

CHAPTER NINE

The Margo was in a sketchy neighborhood four blocks from the Mole Hole. It was three floors with six cubbyhole bedrooms on each of the top two floors and five bedrooms and a minuscule lobby on the ground floor. There was on-street parking in front of the Margo and a small parking lot behind it. A white Kia was parked on the street two doors down. I took a photo of the plate and sent it to Connie.

"This could be your lucky day," Lula said. "Or maybe not."

I parked across the street from the Kia and Lula and I walked over to the Margo. The small lobby was dimly lit. It contained two worn-out armchairs and a reception desk. There was no one at the desk.

"You gotta push the buzzer on the desk," Lula said. "And then

Andy comes out. He's got an office in a broom closet behind the desk."

Lula pushed the buzzer and a small old man shuffled out of the broom closet.

"Hey," he said to Lula. "Long time, no see."

"Been busy," Lula said. "I want to show my protégé around. Any rooms occupied?"

"Seven, nine, and twelve," Andy said. "The rest are open."

"How about Charlie Shine?" Lula asked. "Is he in one of them? I saw his car outside."

"Haven't seen him," Andy said, "but you know how it is. Healthier not to look too hard."

Andy went back to his broom closet and I followed Lula down the hallway.

"They never lock the doors here," Lula said. "Mostly because they lost the keys and they never got replaced." She paused at door number one. "Do you want to check out all these rooms?"

"Might as well," I said.

Lula opened the first door and a huge rat scurried across the room and hid under the bed.

"Maybe it's not necessary to check *every* room," I said.

"Yeah," Lula said. "They're all pretty much the same."

"Just because Andy hasn't seen Shine today doesn't mean Shine isn't here," I said. "He could be using this to access the tunnel and go somewhere else."

"I don't like where this thinking is going," Lula said. "I'm worried it's leading to looking for the tunnel, and then it could lead to us going *into* the tunnel and possibly *dying* there. And you know how much I hate the thought of dying. And besides this,

you don't even know if that Kia belongs to Shine. It could belong
to anybody."

"I'm not going into the tunnel," I said, "but I wouldn't mind
finding it. There's a door at the end of this hallway that's different
from the others. I bet it goes to a mechanical room."

I opened the door, flipped the light switch, and stared at steel
stairs leading down to a poorly lit jumble of decrepit machinery
and hoarded junk. Truth is, I don't like mechanical rooms. They
conjure up images of explosions and scalding hot steam escaping
from ruptured corroded lead pipes wrapped in cancerous
asbestos.

"You aren't going down there, are you?" Lula asked.

"No," I said. "Maybe."

"*Maybe?* Are you shitting me? That's sick. There's no maybe
going down in that hellhole."

"It's just a mechanical room," I said. "And there might be a
door to the tunnel down there."

"No way. No how. You try to go down those steps, and I'll
shoot you with my new gun."

"That makes no sense at all."

"It wouldn't be a fatal shot," Lula said. "Maybe I'd just pretend
to shoot you. Like I could say *Bang!*"

"Okay, give it the nipple test."

"Say what?"

"Stand on the first step and see what your nipples say. You've
got nipple radar, right?"

"Damn right I got nipple radar."

I made a sweeping gesture toward the stairs. "So, stand on the
first step and give it the nipple test."

"I guess I could do that, but you move back in case I gotta get out into the hall real fast. I don't want to have to knock you over."

Lula crept onto the first step and froze.

"Well?" I asked.

"Shush," she said. "I need quiet to concentrate. I need to give them a minute to go sensory."

I stared at my watch. "It's been three minutes," I said. "What's the nipple verdict?"

"I got nothing."

"Not even a tingle?"

"Nothing," Lula said. "Zero. It's like I got a systems failure. Like my nipples are out to lunch."

"You might not be close enough to the danger," I said. "Try going down a couple more steps and see if that does anything."

Lula crept halfway down the stairs and stopped.

"Now what?" I asked her.

"I hear something," Lula whispered. "It's like someone's singing the *Snow White* song. *Hi ho hi ho, it's off to work we go.* Only it's muffled so I can barely hear it, and it doesn't sound like there's a lot of dwarfs singing it. I think I'm only hearing one dwarf."

I moved next to Lula and listened. "You're right," I said. "Someone's singing the Seven Dwarfs' song. It's coming from somewhere in the basement."

I squeezed past Lula and went to the bottom of the stairs. The singing was coming from somewhere deep in the bowels of the basement room. The lighting was dim, and I had to weave my way around discarded hotel furniture, crates of plumbing fixtures, storage tanks filled with God-knows-what, water heaters, a furnace that looked like it belonged in a crematorium, and bales of what I'm pretty sure was weed. I inched around a stack of boxes labeled EXPLOSIVES. No other information given. A small area had been cleared beyond the explosives. The floor of the area was littered with empty bags of chips, what looked like crushed Cheetos, crumpled fast-food burger wrappers, and french fry containers. A card table and a folding chair had been set in the middle of the area. The table was lit by a single, bare, overhead lightbulb. A man was hunched over the table. His back was to me, and he was singing the Seven Dwarfs' song, oblivious to the fact that I was standing a short distance behind him.

The man was Lou Salgusta, and he was laboring over his torture tools, oiling and sharpening blades and adjusting tension on pliers and clippers. I'd seen those tools not so long ago when he'd kidnapped Grandma and me.

I had an instant gut reaction of revulsion so strong it sickened my stomach. I heard Lula suck in air behind me, and I suspected she was in a similar state. My mind was telling me to bolt and run, but my body was frozen in place by the horror in front of me.

Salgusta obviously sensed our presence because he turned in his chair and calmly stared at us.

"Unexpected visitors," he said. "How convenient. I have a new knife that I believe will be superior at flaying the skin off a human being. Who would like to be my first test case? It might be uncomfortable in the beginning, but eventually I believe the brain will shut down from the trauma."

Lula gagged and vomited up a half-digested Boston creme donut.

I jumped away in time to miss most of the splatter and worked at mustering some bravado.

"I thought you were retired," I said to Salgusta. "Have you decided to take on another job?"

"I'm getting these ready for you and your granny," he said. "As you know, she has something I want."

"We've already been through this," I said. "Grandma doesn't have what you want."

"Then she knows where to find it. And if she's forgotten, I'm going to help her remember."

"I need a wet wipe," Lula said, searching through her purse. "I know I got one in here somewhere."

Salgusta grabbed one of his knives, and before I could react, he threw it at Lula and impaled her purse.

"Hey!" Lula said. "What the heck is wrong with you? You stuck a knife in my handbag. This here's an original Louis Vuitton knockoff."

"Sorry," Salgusta said. "I was aiming at your heart, but you moved at the last minute." He picked up another knife. "Let's see if I can be more accurate this time."

Lula hauled her gun out of her purse and aimed it at Salgusta. Her eyes were practically popping out of her head and her gun hand was shaking. "Put the knife down, or I'll blow a hole in your head," she said.

Salgusta threw the knife at Lula, and Lula fired off a bunch of shots at Salgusta. The knife missed Lula's head but sliced into her massive puff ball of curls. All of her shots missed Salgusta.

I didn't have a knife or a gun, so I ducked behind a couple of bales of weed. "Everyone *stop*!" I yelled. "*Just stop!*"

Salgusta grabbed a flamethrower he had leaning against the card table and blasted a stream of fire at me. It missed me but it hit the stack of weed, and *whooooosh*, the weed went up in flames. The burning bales crackled and popped, and sparks shot out, setting off satellite fires. A line of fire licked along the floor toward Salgusta. I grabbed Lula by her purse strap and yanked her toward the stairs.

"Time to go!" I yelled.

"Fuckin' A," Lula said, scrambling after me.

We reached the stairs and there was a series of small explosions. We were halfway up the stairs when the big one blew, shaking the building. *KABLAAAAM!*

We stumbled into the hall and saw that smoke and flames were billowing out of the small lobby area. I opened the nearest bedroom door, and Lula and I ran in, climbed out the window, and dropped to the sidewalk.

Andy, two naked old men, and three women in ho clothes were standing in the middle of the road, mouths open, eyes wide. One of the men had blood streaming from a gash in his forehead. Sirens were wailing a couple blocks away and a Trenton PD car angled to a stop at the curb. A second car followed.

I knew the cop in the second car. He gave me a short wave, and I tried not to cringe when I returned the wave. This was going to get back to Morelli.

The Rangeman number buzzed on my cell phone.

"Babe," Ranger said. "Your car is in a red zone."

"The Margo sort of got blown up, but I'm okay," I said.

"Good to know," Ranger said. And he disconnected.

"That was a hideous experience," Lula said. "And I think I might have a knife stuck in my hair."

I pulled the knife out and handed it over to her.

"Am I bleeding?" she asked.

"Not that I can see," I said.

Lula felt her hair. "I got a lot of product in my hair today. I was going for a certain look."

A big chunk of Lula's hair fell off her head and floated down to the ground.

"Damn," Lula said. "I hate when that happens."

CHAPTER TEN

Connie looked up when we walked in. "Oh boy," she said, eyeing Lula's hair.

"We had an incident," Lula said. "Are there any of those donuts left? I lost mine."

Connie moved the donut box to the edge of her desk. "Help yourself."

"If you don't mind, I'm gonna take the box and go home," Lula said. "I've had an upsetting day."

Lula left and I slouched in the chair in front of Connie's desk. "This was bad," I said. "We blew up the Margo. I guess technically Lou Salgusta blew it up."

"When you say you blew it up . . . exactly what does that mean?"

"Explosion. Smoke. Fire. Big crater where the Margo used to be."

"Wow. And Salgusta?"

"Don't know. I'm hoping for the worst."

"Was anyone hurt?"

"No. Not seriously. A bunch of people got a contact high from the weed burning and one of the customers slipped going down the stairs and cracked his head."

Connie's attention shifted to the door. "Uh oh," she said. "Morelli's here, and he doesn't look happy."

I'd been dreading this. The Margo fiasco wasn't going to help smooth things over with us. If anything, it was going to reinforce his position that I was a nut case. Morelli started out as a wild kid and turned into a more or less sane adult. I started out as a more or less normal kid and lately I've become a walking disaster.

I gave up a sigh and turned in my seat. "Hey," I said to Morelli. He crooked his finger at me. "I'd like to see you outside."

I did an eye-roll at Connie and joined Morelli on the sidewalk. If you dressed Morelli up in a suit, he looked like a gangster. If he was undercover and required to wear khakis, he looked ridiculous. Today he was wearing his usual outfit of black running shoes, dark jeans, a blue button-down shirt, and a black blazer. Today he was *hot cop*. He was lean and muscled, with black wavy hair, a constant five o'clock shadow, and testosterone to spare. His father was an abusive, womanizing drunk. His grandmother is batshit crazy. Morelli is none of those things. Morelli is a good cop, and until recently he'd been a good boyfriend.

"I just came from what's left of the Margo," Morelli said. "I was told I missed you by a couple minutes."

I leaned into him a little. "You smell smoky," I said.

"I smell like burnt weed. Do you want to explain this to me?"

I shook my head. "No."

"Do it anyway," Morelli said.

"I was pretty sure that Charlie Shine's car was parked by the Margo, so . . ."

Morelli went to his eyes-narrowed cop face. Never a good sign.

"If you want me to keep going, you're going to have to get rid of the scary cop face," I said.

"Not gonna happen," Morelli said. "Keep going anyway."

I went to my own eyes-narrowed, don't-mess-with-me face. "Fine," I said. "Whatever. Lula and I went to the Margo to check things out. We opened the basement door and heard someone singing the *Hi Ho Hi Ho* song."

"What's the *Hi Ho Hi Ho* song?"

"The Seven Dwarfs song."

I sang the song for him and he cracked a smile. When Morelli smiled it was like puppies and fresh-baked, warm chocolate chip cookies. His brown eyes got soft and dark, and I wanted to snuggle into him. The snuggle was usually followed by the desire to undress him. All things considered, this wasn't appropriate at the present time and place, so I kept my distance and told myself to get a grip.

"We went down to investigate, and it turned out it was Lou Salgusta singing," I said. "He got carried away when he saw Lula and me and accidentally set about six bales of weed on fire. The bales were next to some crates labeled EXPLOSIVES, and that was the end of the Margo."

"You're lucky it wasn't the end of *you*."

"We were already on our way out when the first explosion went off. Are you assigned to investigate the fire?"

"I'm investigating a homicide that took place at the Margo last week. I wanted to make sure the two incidents were unrelated."

"And?"

"Now that I've spoken to you, I don't see a connection," Morelli said.

"Always happy to help the police."

"If you wanted to help the police, you'd give up this crazy treasure hunt and give the keys to Benny."

"If the police want to help *me*, they'd get Salgusta off the streets. Keys, or no keys, he's convinced Grandma has information that he needs to access the treasure."

"And?"

"And she doesn't have that information. It wasn't passed on to her."

"Any more bad news?"

"I'm all out of Frosted Flakes."

"Tragic," Morelli said.

"That's just the tip of the iceberg."

"Your intentions are good but misdirected," he said. "You aren't helping. You're meddling. You're making things more difficult for the professionals."

"That's absolutely not true. I'm not meddling in police affairs. I'm pursuing my own investigation, and there is still an outstanding bond on Shine."

"Okay, let me put it another way. You're making things more difficult for *me*. I'm at my desk in the middle of paperwork and I get a call from dispatch that the Margo blew up and you were seen jumping out of a window."

"It was more of a short drop," I said. "Still it's nice to know you were worried about me."

"Worried doesn't cover it," Morelli said. "Mostly, I was really pissed off that I was so freaking worried."

His phone buzzed and he went into cop mode. "I have to go. Gang shooting in the projects. This is going to be a long day."

"Do you want me to walk Bob?"

"No." He took a moment to stare down at his shoe. "Yes," he said. "Thanks. I won't get home anytime soon. And besides, he misses you."

"I miss him, too," I said.

Morelli looked like he was going in for a kiss. He stopped himself midway and gave his head a shake like he thought he was an idiot. I understood this completely because I thought we were both idiots.

I watched him drive away and I returned to the office.

"I sent you a picture of the white Kia parked by the Margo," I said to Connie. "The manager said he hadn't seen Shine, but it would be easy for Shine to walk through the lobby to the cellar door and not be noticed."

"And the tunnel entrance would be in the cellar," Connie said.

"Probably in the area where Salgusta was working. Unfortunately, that lead is now a dead end. Were you able to run the Kia plate?"

"It's a rental. Rented to Lester March. Bogus address and driver's license with Shine's picture on it."

"I don't suppose you have anything else for me?"

"No, but I'll keep digging," Connie said.

I left the office and drove past Rodney Trotter's house. His van wasn't parked at the curb, so I kept going. He was undoubtedly trolling neighborhoods, looking for women who wanted bigger butts, keeping an eye out for roadkill he could take home and stuff.

I gave up on Trotter and went to Morelli's house. It was within minutes of my parents' house, in a very similar neighborhood. The layout of the house was almost identical to my parents' house. He'd inherited the house from his Aunt Rose, and he was gradually making it his own, modernizing the kitchen and swapping out Rose's dining room furniture with a billiards table.

I opened the front door and Bob galloped the length of the house and slammed into me. He was a big, shaggy, orange-haired beast with soft brown eyes that were a half-shade lighter than Morelli's. I gave him a hug and told him he was a good boy.

"So here I am, back again," I said to him. "Right now, it's just to take you for a walk, but then we'll see how it goes."

I checked out the living room. It was way too neat. No pizza boxes or empty soda cans on the coffee table. No shoes that had obviously been kicked off under the coffee table.

"What's with this neat house thing?" I asked Bob. "And look at *you*. Have you been to a groomer? You're all fluffy and you don't smell like a dog."

I marched into the kitchen. No dirty dishes in the sink. No coffee cup rings on the counter. Not that Morelli was a complete slob, but he wasn't Felix from *The Odd Couple*, either. I looked in his fridge. No fresh lasagna from his mom, so she hadn't stopped in to clean his house. And then I saw it. A bottle of Chardonnay. There was only one explanation. The son of a bitch had a new girlfriend. And she was a Chardonnay drinker. Ick! Gross.

"And he's got you all spiffed up for her," I said to Bob. "That's so disgusting."

I was being indignant in front of Bob, but the truth is my stomach was in a knot and I had an ache in my chest. Morelli and I split up and I knew there was no reason why he shouldn't see other women. That didn't make it any less painful. Especially when I'd just gotten all gooey over his smile.

I hooked Bob up to his leash and walked him up and down a bunch of streets. I brought him back to Morelli's house, gave him some dog kibble and fresh water, and left. Good deed well done.

I drove home on autopilot, surprised when I ended up in my parking lot. I took the elevator to the second floor, the doors opened, and I saw George Potts, aka the Pooper, sitting on the floor in front of my apartment. I closed my eyes for a moment and wondered if life could get any worse. Of course, it could get worse, I told myself. You could get run over by a truck, or catch the plague, or get head lice.

Potts jumped up when he saw me in the hall. "Surprise," he said. "Are you surprised? I saw your picture on social. The one with you jumping out of the window of the burning hotel. It went viral. You're famous. Anyway, I got worried about you, so I thought I'd come be like, you know, a bodyguard."

"I didn't jump. I dropped," I said. "And it's nice that you were worried about me, but I'm really in no danger."

"That's not what social is saying." He leaned forward and sniffed. "You smell smoky . . . like weed."

I unlocked my door and stepped inside. "Thanks for stopping by," I said. "Don't forget you have a court date coming up."

Potts opened his mouth to say something, and I closed and locked the door before he uttered a word.

I waited a minute and looked out my security peephole. He

was still there, staring at my door as if it would open at any minute and he'd be invited in. Don't encourage him, I told myself. Eventually he'll go away.

I stripped, threw my smoky clothes in the laundry basket, and took a shower. I dried my hair, got dressed in new clothes, and went to my front door. I looked out the peephole and I didn't see Potts. Hooray. I put my ear to the door and listened. Someone was humming. Dear God, Potts was still there, sitting with his back to the door, in my peephole blind spot.

I made myself a peanut butter and potato chip sandwich for dinner. Rex came out of his soup can den to get a potato chip and I told him not to worry about Potts.

"I'm almost positive he's harmless," I said to Rex.

I called Lula and made arrangements to pick her up at her house at seven thirty.

"That's a good time," Lula said. "Some of the ladies start work early to service the geriatric losers who need to be home in bed by nine o'clock."

I checked my email and spent some time rereading the file I had on Charlie Shine, hoping I'd missed something that resembled a clue. At seven o'clock I stopped reading, grabbed my messenger bag and a sweatshirt, and went to the door. I made a fast promise to God that I'd go to church if I opened the door and Potts wasn't there. I looked out my peephole and saw Potts. He was marching back and forth in front of my door.

"You can kiss that promise good-bye," I said to God.

I opened my door and Potts stopped marching.

"Now what?" he asked.

"Now I go to work and you go home."

"No way," he said. "I'm sticking to you like glue. I've made up my mind. You saved my life by putting up my bond and now I have to save yours."

"I didn't save your life," I said. "You would have managed."

"No, no, no. I would have died. I had a premonition. Did I tell you I get premonitions? It's a curse. They're always terrible."

"Do they come true?"

"I don't know, they're usually about people in Slovenia."

"Do you have relatives there? Do you know anyone there?"

"No. That's why it's so odd. Sometimes my premonitions are local and then I just avoid the situation. Like once I had a premonition that I was going to get run over by a clown on a motorcycle, so I stayed home, and it didn't happen."

"Smart."

"Yeah. So, where are we going? Are we going out after some real bad guy? Like a murderer?"

I locked my door and headed for the stairs. "Just doing some research."

"I'm good at research. I'm like a Google pro."

My plan was to take the stairs fast, sprint across the lot to my car, get in, and lock the doors before he could reach me. I was halfway down the stairs when he suddenly catapulted past me and rolled head over teakettles to the bottom.

He was flat out, on his back with his eyes open and unblinking.

"Holy crap," I said. "Are you okay?"

"I think I'm okay," he said. "I need a minute. Do you see any bones sticking out like they're broken? Do you see any blood?"

"No."

"I can wiggle my toes in my shoes, so I'm not paralyzed. And look, I can move my fingers."

"Those are all good signs," I said. "I have to go now. I'm meeting someone."

"What about my head?" he asked. "Did I hit my head?"

"Yeah, lots of times. All the way down."

"I could have a concussion."

He stood and swayed back and forth. "Am I swaying?" he asked.

"Yes."

"That's good because I'm trying to sway."

I looked around. "Do you have a car here?"

"No. I had my friend Morgan drop me off. I thought I'd be going in your car, being that I'm protecting you."

"Wrong."

"Here, look at this. I'm walking. And I'm talking. I was afraid I might black out. I did that once at the dentist office. And while I was out, I peed my pants."

"You aren't going to do that now, are you?"

"I don't think so, but I might be a little dizzy. I'll feel better when I get to your car and I can sit down."

I was doomed. I was never going to be rid of him. This is what happens when you try to be nice. You find out your ex-boyfriend has a new girlfriend and you get stuck with George Potts.

"Get into the backseat," I said. "I'll drive you home."

"You can't do that. I'm supposed to be with you. I took an oath."

I looked at him in my rearview mirror. "An oath?"

"Yes. An oath to protect you. It was a blood oath, too. I stuck my finger with a pin and swore to protect you." He shivered. "Bad things happen to you if you break an oath."

"I really don't need protecting," I said.

"Of course, you need protecting. Social media says you're a hot mess. Who are you meeting? I know it isn't a date because you said you were going to work. It might be awkward to bring me along on a date, but I could be useful on a work assignment. I have excellent powers of observation. And besides, I won't get out of your car if you take me home. I'll kick and scream until I have an asthma attack. Did I mention I sometimes have asthma attacks?"

No surprise there. Why leave out asthma from his many ailments.

"Okay. Fine. Have it your way. I'll take you with me, but you have to *not move from the backseat*, and *no talking*."

"No problem. My lips are sealed. Look what I'm doing. I'm zipping my lips. *Zip!* Did you see that? Did you see me zip my lips?"

I told myself to relax my grip on the wheel and stay calm. Lula and I would cruise Stark Street, talk to a couple of women about Shine, and go home. Easy peasy.

CHAPTER ELEVEN

Lula was waiting on the sidewalk in front of her house.

"What's going on?" she asked, getting in and buckling up. "Is that the pooper in the backseat?"

I looked at Potts and he made a zipper motion across his mouth.

"It's George Potts," I said. "He's riding with us. It's a long story, not worth telling. Are we going to Stark Street?"

"I'm thinking we start at the train station. A couple of the girls hang out for the late commuters. They're usually on Grimly Street."

I crossed the railroad tracks, drove past the train station, and turned left onto Grimly. A plus-sized hooker wearing pink sweats and black patent leather platform stilettos was standing on the corner.

"Do you know her?" I asked Lula.

"No," Lula said. "I never got in with the train station girls."

I pulled over and lowered my window. Pink Sweatsuit walked over and looked in at Lula and me.

"I don't usually do girls," Sweatsuit said. "They take too long. I make exceptions if you want to pay by the hour or go electric."

I waved a twenty at her. "I'm looking for a friend. Maybe you've seen him." I replaced the twenty with Shine's photo.

"Nope. Never seen him," she said. "Not for a twenty anyways." She looked into the backseat. "Is that Georgy Potts back there? Hey, Georgy, how's it going?"

Potts looked at me and I pretended to unzip my lips.

"Hey, Leticia," Potts said.

"All the girls been missing you, honey. Where you been? How's your asthma?" Leticia turned her attention to me. "He has PTSD. I hope you're taking good care of him."

"The best," I said. "He's special."

"You bet your ass he's special," Leticia said.

Potts leaned forward. "So, have you seen this guy? We'd really like to get in touch with him."

"Sure, just for you, Sweetums. He's got a thing for Patches. She's good with the older folks. She usually hung on the corner here with Jody and me, but I haven't seen her in a while. You might try Lizzy on Stark. Lizzy and Patches were tight."

"Thanks," Potts said. "You're the best."

"Don't be a stranger," Leticia said, taking my twenty, stuffing it into her pocket.

"That girl has no curbside manners," Lula said when I drove away. "I would never have approached a prospective client like that."

"She's nice when you get to know her," Potts said. "She has a cat named Kiki."

Lula turned in her seat and looked at Potts. "Are you a regular or something?"

"No," Potts said. "I mostly only have sex with myself. Before the bakery pooping incident, I had a job delivering pizza and the ladies were big pizza eaters. Sometimes I would run errands for them when they had an emergency or a special request . . . like chocolate syrup or a package of frozen hot dogs. That was a tough one because hot dogs aren't usually frozen. And once Samantha forgot her paddle and I had to buy her a spatula at the grocery store."

"That Samantha is a trip," Lula said. "She's been around for a long time. That's on account of she's a specialist. Specialists like her got a longer shelf life than an ordinary service provider."

"Do you know Patches?" I asked Potts.

"No, but I know Lizzy. She used to work the train station."

"Do you know Lizzy's corner on Stark?"

"No," he said. "I would never deliver on Stark Street. It's too scary. I went there once, and I accidentally ran over a big rat. It was so big I thought it was a cat, so I got out to see if I could help. And while I was looking at the squished rat, someone stole my car."

"Yeah, you gotta give it to the Stark Street boys," Lula said. "They're fast. Did you get your car back?"

"No. The police said it probably got taken apart right away."

Lula added, "There's good money to be made on auto body parts."

I drove through town and turned onto Stark Street. The first two blocks of Stark are okay, with small businesses on the ground floor and apartments above them. After that it deteriorates.

"I'm not comfortable," Potts said. "I'm feeling anxious. I might have a panic attack coming on."

"Keep a watch out for Lizzy," I said.

"I can't see. My vision is blurry," Potts said. "I'm pretty sure I'm having an ocular migraine."

"Maybe we should take him to the hospital," Lula said.

"What does Lizzy look like?" I asked Potts.

"She's black. I think she said that she's from Haiti. And she had dreads with beads in them."

"There she is," Lula said, pointing to three women clustered on a corner. "And I know the other two hookers."

I pulled over and Lula stuck her head out the window. "Hey, ladies," she said. "How's business?"

They trotted over and Lula introduced us. "This is Lucy, and this is Sharon," Lula said. "We shared a corner together just before I retired from the profession."

"We heard you got hurt real bad," Lucy said. "Are you okay?"

"I'm good," Lula said. "I'm working in bail bonds now. We're looking for a guy. Charlie Shine. Any of you know him?"

"Patches was spending time with him," Lizzy said. "She talked about him a lot. I got the idea he was an older gentleman with a lot of money, but I never got to see him."

"Do you know where we can find Patches?" I asked.

"Usually she's across the street," Lizzy said, "but she hasn't been showing up."

"It's been a week since we've seen her," Sharon said. "We're a little worried."

"Have you tried to get in touch with her?" I asked.

"She isn't answering her cell phone, and Lizzy went to see her, but no one answered the door."

Lizzy looked into the car. "Is that Georgy in the backseat? Hi, honey, are you doing okay?"

"I'm a little light-headed," Potts said.

"No doubt from that PTSD you got," Lizzy said.

"If you give us Patches's address, we'll look in on her," I said.

"Sure," Lizzy said. "She got a room on Parker Street. Second floor. You can't miss the building. It's got a big red peace sign painted on it still from the seventies."

"I'll let you know if we see her," Lula said.

"Appreciate it, honey. You stay well."

I drove away and Potts started humming.

"What's he doing?" Lula asked.

"Humming," I said. "He hums when he has anxiety. It keeps him calm."

"It's annoying," Lula said. "He's not humming a song or anything. He's just freaking humming."

"The alternative might be diarrhea," I said.

"How about the alternative be we chuck him out of the car and let him call Uber."

"I can hear you," Potts said. "You're making me more panicky. My heart is racing. I think I have tachycardia. I've got spots in front of my eyes and I might see an angel. There's something floating in front of the car."

Lula sat forward in her seat. "I don't see anything."

"It went away," Potts said. "It was there for a minute. It might have been one of those escort angels that take you to heaven."

"As long as it's not coming for *me*," Lula said. "I'm not ready. I got a hair appointment tomorrow."

Parker Street was two blocks away. The neighborhood wasn't the best, but it also wasn't Stark Street. It was mostly residential row houses that were two and three stories. Occasionally there would be a small bar on a corner or a small grocer in the middle of a block. There was the usual gang graffiti on the buildings, but the buildings weren't pockmarked with bullet holes. I found the peace sign building and parked at the curb.

"Are we going in this building?" Potts asked.

"Yes," I said. "Do you want to wait in the car?"

"By myself?"

"Yes."

"I guess I can't protect you if I wait in the car."

Lula cut her eyes to me. "He's protecting you?"

"He took an oath," I said.

"Oh boy," Lula said. "Hah!"

"It's true," Potts said. "I would give my life for her. She's been nice to me."

Lula went serious. "That's heavy," she said. "Sort of stupid, but heavy."

Potts nodded. "Exactly."

"Okay then," Lula said. "Let's do it."

We all got out of the car and walked to the building. The door was unlocked and led to a tiny lobby with some mailboxes. There were two names for the second floor. Tim Windrow in 2A and Alice Smuther in 2B. We took the stairs to the second floor, and I knocked on 2B. No answer. I knocked again. Still no answer.

"I don't like the way it smells here," Lula said. "I've smelled this smell before."

"I've never smelled it, but I don't like it," Potts said. "It's unpleasant."

I tried the doorknob and it clicked open. "Not locked," I said.

I pushed the door open and we all stepped inside. One medium-size room with a door leading to the bathroom. Kitchenette lining one side. Small table with two chairs. Queen-size bed against the far wall. Slept in and unmade. Dead woman sprawled on the floor. Probably been dead for a couple of days.

Potts looked at the corpse, his eyes rolled back into his head, and he crashed to the floor.

"He handled that pretty good," Lula said. "At least he didn't poop himself. Not yet anyways."

I called 911 and reported a possible homicide. It looked like the woman had been shot in the chest and the head, so I was pretty sure it wasn't self-inflicted. We grabbed Potts by his ankles, dragged him into the hall, and shut the door.

"I guess we gotta wait for the police," Lula said. "I hope this all doesn't take too long. I've got some stuff lined up on my TV. I've been binge-watching *Game of Thrones*. This is my second time around, but I still like it. Not to mention if I stay here much longer, I'm going to throw up."

Potts opened his eyes. "What?" he said.

"Stay down and relax for a couple of minutes," I told him. "You fainted."

"I had the craziest dream while I was out. I thought I saw a dead woman with blood all over. It was horrible."

I gave Lula the keys to my car. "I'll stay here, and you can go home. I'll pick my car up tomorrow. Take Potts with you and drop him at his parents' house on Porter Street."

"How will you get home?"

"I have options."

"I bet," Lula said. "Probably involve a happy hour. Or at least twenty minutes." She pulled Potts to his feet and pointed him at the door. "Time to go," she said. "Auntie Lula is driving."

———

I moved from the second floor to the lobby, where the air was better. Two uniforms arrived and I sent them upstairs. I knew plainclothes would follow. I was hoping it wasn't Morelli. I gave up a sigh of relief when Tom Schmidt walked in. I went to high school with Tom. He graduated into plainclothes a year after Morelli. He was a good cop. Not as talented as Morelli, but he was honest, and he cared about the law.

"Looks like you're pulling the night shift," I said to him.

"Yeah, lucky me. What do we have here?"

"A very dead body in 2B. The name on the mailbox is Alice Smuther. I was looking for a hooker going by Patches. I don't know what Patches looked like but I'm guessing she's lying on the floor upstairs."

"Do you have anything else that's interesting to tell me?"

"She was servicing Charlie Shine. Do you have anything interesting to tell *me*?"

"No, but I saw your picture online and you looked real cute jumping out of the hotel window."

"I didn't jump. I *dropped*. Big difference. Huge difference."

"Did you remove anything from the crime scene? Are your fingerprints all over everything?"

"No. And no. I can leave now, right?"

"Yeah. I know where to find you."

I went outside and called Ranger. "I need a ride," I told him. "I'm on Parker Street. Just look for all the squad cars and EMT trucks."

"This is the homicide that just got called in?"

"Yep. Dead hooker. Close friend of Charlie Shine."

The line went dead. I hoped that meant he was on his way.

Seven minutes later, Ranger snaked his way through the cluster of cars and trucks in front of the peace symbol building and picked me up.

"Thanks," I said. "Lula didn't want to wait for the police, so I loaned her my car."

"I'm guessing this has something to do with the treasure hunt. Were you able to look around before the police arrived?"

"No. She'd been dead awhile. The smell was really bad. I'm surprised her neighbor didn't investigate."

"You don't go looking for trouble in this neighborhood," Ranger said. "Tell me about her."

"I knew Shine liked the ladies, so Lula and I talked to a couple of her hooker friends earlier tonight on Stark Street. They gave us the address."

Ranger left Parker Street, turning toward the center of the city. "Is it important that you get home tonight?"

"No. Rex has lots of food and fresh water."

———

Ranger owned a stealth office building that was located on a quiet side street in the middle of downtown Trenton. The façade was brick and low-key. A small gold plaque by the impact glass front door had a single word on it. Rangeman. The man at the desk in the modest lobby was armed and dressed in Rangeman black. The interior of the building was high-tech and more secure than the White House. The heart of the operation, the control room, was located on the fifth floor. Ranger's lair was on the seventh floor. His clients were for the most part wealthy businessmen who for one reason or another needed personalized security services that went beyond the norm.

Ranger drove into the underground garage that housed the fleet cars and Ranger's personal cars. He parked in his slot next to the elevator and reminded me that until we were in his apartment, we were on an audio and video security feed. I'd been in the building many times before. Sometimes with Ranger and sometimes without Ranger when he'd been off-site and I needed a safe haven.

We went directly to Ranger's apartment, which occupied the entire floor. When he bought the building, he'd turned it over to a design firm. He was probably sleeping with the designer at the time, because the color palette and furnishings were perfect. Simple, modern, comfortable. White walls. Furnishings in black, gray, brown, and cream. Elegantly masculine. Small state-of-the-art kitchen. Everything kept immaculate by his housekeeper, Ella.

I followed him to the kitchen.

"What would you like?" he said. "Wine?"

"Red."

He took a bottle of Pinot Noir from the wine cooler and

selected two glasses from the above-counter display. "Prowl through the fridge if you're hungry," he said. "Ella usually has some late-night food in there."

I pulled out a tray with dried fruit and nuts and cheese, and I set it on the counter. Ranger lived well. This hadn't always been the case. When I first met him, his address was a vacant lot.

"Let's move this into my office," he said. "I'll do a search on Alice Smuther."

I took the cheese tray and my wine and followed Ranger.

The apartment consisted of a hallway leading to the kitchen, a small eating area off the kitchen, and a living room with comfy couches. Ranger's office was in the master bedroom area off the living room.

I set the cheese tray on his desk and pulled a chair up next to him. He typed Alice Smuther into his search program, and we sat back and waited for the information.

She was relatively clean for a hooker. A few arrests for solicitation. That was it. She was twenty-six years old. Grew up in Atlanta. Migrated north when she graduated from high school. Had a bunch of short-term minimum wage jobs and then turned to prostitution. Ranger pulled her driver's license up and I was pretty sure it was the woman on the floor.

"She owned a ten-year-old Range Rover," Ranger said. "Here's her plate. If it's not parked on the street close to her building, Shine might be driving it."

"Do you have any other ideas?"

"Yes. Let's move this into the bedroom."

Oh boy.

When I spend a night in Ranger's bed the sex is always great, but honestly, his sheets are equally orgasmic. They're gloriously soft and as smooth as glass because Ella irons them. His pillows are perfect. His comforter is perfect. When he turns the light off, the room is dark and quiet and cool. The cool never lasts very long. Ranger is hot in bed.

CHAPTER TWELVE

I was dragged out of sleep by the sound of the shower running. The bedroom was dark. My cell phone read 5:00 a.m. I fell back asleep and when I woke up it was twenty-five minutes later, and I could hear Ranger moving around the room. I switched the bedside light on and saw that he was already dressed. Usually Ranger wore the same cargo pants and Rangeman logo shirt that the rest of the men wore. He was in a suit today. Black and custom tailored. Black dress shirt. Black striped tie.

"Nice," I said. "Sexy in a successful-businessman sort of way."

"New corporate client meeting this morning. Don't think he'd be happy if I came dressed ready for a SWAT ambush." He strapped his watch on. "Stay as long as you like. Ella will bring your breakfast up at eight o'clock. If you want it sooner, you can call her. Rafael will pick your car up this morning and leave it in the garage for you. Try not to jump out of any windows today."

"*Dropped!* I *dropped* out of the window."

I rolled out of bed at seven thirty and shuffled off to take a shower. This is an experience second only to being in Ranger's bed. The tiles are gleaming white, his showerhead is perfect and not encrusted with lime, and he has unlimited hot water. And the best part is that Ella makes sure he's supplied with Bulgari green shower gel and shampoo. I've never gotten a full-on orgasm just from smelling Bulgari green, but I've had some decent rushes. The scent evaporates almost immediately on me but mysteriously clings to Ranger. This explains the reason for the rush.

My hair was still damp when I went in search of breakfast. Ella had obviously tiptoed in when I was in the shower because the tray was already on the kitchen counter. Coffee, cream, and croissants with jam. Plus, smoked salmon with a dollop of caviar and crème fraîche, if I was in need of protein. Some toast points for the salmon. Assorted fresh fruit. No Frosted Flakes.

I planned my day while I ate. I would make a fast stop at my apartment to check on Rex and change clothes. Then I'd give Connie the information about the car and have her feed it to her network of gossips and snoops. There were two open FTAs and there was Grandma and the treasure. I was getting nowhere fast on all this stuff, but as Yoda says, "Do or do not. There is no try." So, I was all about the *do* today.

It was almost nine o'clock when I left Ranger's apartment. I took the elevator to the garage and found my car. It had been detailed and the keys on the dash were attached to a Rangeman key fob. I looked into the security camera pointed at me and said, "Thank you."

I rolled into my building's parking lot a half hour later. I took the stairs and found Potts, sound asleep, stretched out in a sleeping bag in front of my apartment door. I carefully inserted my key, opened my door, and stepped over Potts. I closed and locked the door and looked out my peephole. Couldn't see Potts. That meant he was still asleep on the floor. Yay.

I changed my clothes, pulled my hair up into a ponytail, and gave Rex a piece of croissant from breakfast.

Potts was still asleep when I opened my door to leave. I stepped over him again, closed and locked the door, and sprinted down the hall to the stairs. I got to the stairs and looked back at him. He hadn't moved. Crap! What if he was dead? I watched him for a minute and saw him move. Okay! Not dead.

———

Lula was surfing the net on her phone when I walked into the office. Connie was reading a Nora Roberts page-turner.

"What's new?" I asked.

"I have a positive ID on the dead hooker for you," Connie said. "No surprise. Alice Smuther. AKA Patches."

"I did some research last night," I said. "She owned a gray Range Rover." I handed Connie a slip of paper. "Here's the plate number. Pass it on to your network of snitches."

"You think Shine killed her and took her car?" Lula said. "That's not smart to be driving around in someone's car after you drill two holes in them."

"People aren't always smart," I said. "Shine has gotten away with a lot of horrible things. I suspect he feels above the law after all these years."

Charlie Shine was the La-Z-Boy dandy. He wore flashy jewelry, drove flashy cars, and enjoyed abusing beautiful young women. He was a ruthless killer who left his calling card of a bullet in the forehead and another in the chest. In his prime, he supplemented his wet work business with a variety of illegal activities, including but not limited to white slavery, gaming, pushing drugs, and extortion. He was frequently charged with crimes but never convicted. Witnesses always recanted or disappeared. Evidence vanished.

"What do you want to do? Do you want to ride around and look for him?" Lula asked.

"No. I want to see if Trotter is home. I have a responsibility to Vinnie to bring him in, and I need the capture money. We can keep our eyes open for the gray Range Rover on our way across town."

"I guess I'm game for that," Lula said. "Maybe we can lure Trotter into your car with the promise of roadkill. We can tell him we saw a nice bloated dead possum on the side of the road, and he can have it if he comes with us. In case that doesn't work, we should take the giant can of bear Mace we got in the back room."

I hiked my messenger bag higher on my shoulder and headed for the door. "I'm hoping he'll be more reasonable before lunch."

"What about breakfast? You think he doesn't drink breakfast?"

"Maybe, but I have a new attitude. I'm going to be the ball-breaker I want to be."

"Who said that?" Lula asked. "Was that AC/DC? They had a lot of songs about balls."

"I don't know. It just popped into my head."

"I noticed you got a bunch of those things popping into your head lately. Motivational sayings. We should choose one and make business cards. Like how about *Stephanie and Lula, Apprehension Agents. We do epic shit.*"

I liked it. Might not be accurate but it was something to work toward.

Lula followed me out and pulled up when she saw my car. "Hold on. Your car is clean. It's all shiny and the inside looks clean, too. There's something wrong here. Your car is never clean. It wasn't clean when I drove it home."

I got behind the wheel. "It's clean sometimes."

"It wasn't even clean when you bought it."

She buckled in, leaned close to me, and sniffed. "Ah hah! I know that smell. That smell is delicious. You smell like Ranger. Holy cow, you spent the night with Ranger, didn't you? And that's why one of his muscle men picked your car up this morning. And they got it detailed! Girlfriend, you must have done something special for that man last night."

I pulled out into traffic. "I called him to give me a ride home from the crime scene."

"See, now that's an invitation."

"It wasn't an invitation. I needed a ride."

"You could have called Morelli."

"We aren't a couple anymore."

"Yeah, but you're friends. And you know you're going to be a couple again. You break up and get back together all the time. You been doing it since you were five years old."

"This is different. He has a girlfriend."

"Already? That's just wrong."

"Exactly!"

"Everybody knows there's a period of time to be observed," Lula said. "It's common courtesy. How do you know about this?"

"He had to work late, so I offered to walk Bob."

"Now that was real nice of you. No reason Bob should suffer because you and Morelli aren't getting along."

"Anyway, I let myself in and I immediately knew something was going on because the house was clean."

"Like how clean?"

"Really clean."

"Maybe his mama came and cleaned up."

"That was my first thought, but when I went into the kitchen and looked in the fridge there was no Mama Morelli food there. No lasagna. No vodka rigatoni. No ricotta cake. And here's the clincher." I paused for effect. "He had Chardonnay chilling in his fridge."

"What? Are you shitting me? Chardonnay? Morelli isn't no Chardonnay drinker."

"I think it must have been in there for his girlfriend."

"The bitch. I bet she's a blonde, too."

"Yes! And thin."

"Chardonnay drinkers are always skinny blondes," Lula said. "With fake boobs. Not that I would want to talk bad about someone wanting to enhance their body. Just sayin'."

"You drink Chardonnay."

"Yeah, but I don't like it. I just like the way it sounds . . . I'll have a *Chardonnay*. Someday I might get a dog. It would be one of those Chihuahua dogs and I'd name her Chardonnay."

Here it is. You think you know someone and then next thing they tell you is that they want a Chihuahua named Chardonnay.

"Wait a minute," Lula said. "This isn't the way to Trotter's house."

"I'm taking the scenic route," I said.

"This isn't the scenic route," Lula said. "There's nothing scenic about Trenton. You're heading for the Mole Hole. I thought we weren't treasure hunting this morning."

"I can't help myself. I'm just going to do a drive-by. See if the gray Range Rover is parked in the lot."

I drove past the train station and turned onto the Mole Hole street. No gray Range Rover in the lot, but there was a black Mercedes sports car there.

"Gabriela," I said.

"Maybe she got a job on the pole," Lula said. "Pick up some spare change."

"Maybe she's down in the tunnel," I said.

"No way are you getting me back in that tunnel. Don't even think about it."

"No problem," I said, cruising past the Mole Hole. "I don't want to go back into it, either. At least not from the Mole Hole side. I want to take a look at the Margo."

"I saw it on the news this morning and there isn't much left."

The street was open to traffic but the sidewalk in front of the hotel was cordoned off with crime scene tape. A squad car and two sedans were angled against the curb. One of the sedans was an unmarked Trenton PD car. The other sedan had the fire marshal sticker on it. I didn't see anyone by the cars, so I assumed they were prowling through the rubble. I thought there was also a good chance that Gabriela was on the scene, following the tunnel from the Mole Hole to the Margo. She was pursuing something that was clearly important to her. I didn't know why or what.

I cruised past the Margo, turned at the corner, and drove to Stiller Street. I did a silent groan when I got there. Trotter's van was parked at the curb. While I really wanted to be all jazz hands and high-fives about breaking balls, the thought of a drunk Trotter and his elephant syringe was making it hard to get fully motivated.

"I say we need to fortify ourselves before we knock on Trotter's door," Lula said. "I guess I'm up for doing some shit, but if we want it to be epic I need a breakfast sandwich. Something with cheese and sausage. Or maybe egg and bacon. Or maybe I could get one of each and combine them and make a super sandwich."

"We wouldn't want the shit we do to not be epic," I said.

"Hell no. Ordinary shit is just shit."

"And if we're lucky, when we get back the van will be gone?"

"I guess that would be a possibility," Lula said. "It would be in God's hands."

I drove past Trotter's house and after a couple of blocks, I glanced at Lula. "Do you know where we're going to find your sandwich?"

"No," she said. "Does it matter?"

I turned toward the center of town, stopped for a light, and Charlie Shine and the gray Range Rover drove by on the cross street.

"Did you see that?" Lula yelled. "It was *him*."

By the time I could make a turn there were two cars between me and Shine.

"He's up ahead, going into the drive-thru lane at Dreamy Creamery," Lula said. "You can catch him at the drive-thru."

"What the heck is Dreamy Creamery?"

"Ice cream. And they got ice cream cakes, too. And shakes. And inside it's like an old-fashioned soda fountain."

I circled around to the front of Dreamy Creamery and idled at the end of the drive-thru.

"Here's the plan," I said. "As soon as he moves forward, the car behind him is going to move up to the window. Then Shine will have the building on one side, a two-foot curb on the other side, the guy behind him, and me in front of him."

"He got a sundae," Lula said. "I saw the girl hand it to him. It's ginormous. It's not even noon yet and he got a big-ass sundae. You got to respect a man for that."

"Here he comes," I said, pulling into the drive-thru lane and stopping where the building began.

"Now!" I said to Lula. "We got him."

Lula and I jumped out and ran at Shine. Lula was waving her gun and yelling like a crazy woman. I had cuffs and pepper spray.

There was a moment where surprise registered on Shine's face, and then he hunkered down over the wheel and gunned the engine.

"Holy crap," Lula said. "He's gonna ram you. He's going for ramming speed."

I dove over the curb, Lula flattened herself against the wall of the building, and Shine roared past us. He crashed into my CR-V and pushed it out of the exit lane and into the parking lot. He paused for three seconds, and then he took off down the road. A black Mercedes sports car appeared out of nowhere and followed Shine.

"What the heck!" I said. "Sonofabitch!"

"No kidding," Lula said. "He's got a problem with that old Range Rover. The air bag didn't inflate. I bet nobody paid attention to a recall notice."

"He wrecked my car."

"Yeah, we didn't see that one coming. Do you think that was Gabriela following him?"

"Yes!"

"She gets around," Lula said. "Do you think she's after our bounty money?"

"Worse," I said. "I think she's after our fortune and glory."

Customers were wandering out of Dreamy Creamery to see the wreck and take selfies.

"You should do something," Lula said. "Get a tow truck out here or phone Uber. I need to use the restroom."

"You aren't going to use the restroom. You're going in to get ice cream."

"Yes, but before I do that, I might wash my hands."

Rangeman control room called. Undoubtedly notified of the wreck by one of the many sensors surreptitiously placed on my car.

"Your front sensor is reporting a malfunction," he said.

"Long story short, my car has a crumpled front end."

"Can you drive it?"

"No. The hood is smashed up against the windshield."

"Are you okay?"

"Okay is relative for me."

"Do you need assistance?"

"Assistance would be wonderful."

I retrieved my purse from my car and went inside to get ice

cream. A fire truck arrived, followed by a cop car. Lula and I took our ice cream outside and said hello to the guys. The fire truck left, and the cop went inside to get ice cream.

A black Rangeman SUV rolled in and Tank got out.

"I'll take it from here," he said. "Wayne will drive you home . . . or wherever."

Lula went back to the office, and I went to my parents' house to borrow a car.

"Look who's here," Grandma said. "Miss Celebrity! You're all over the internet. YouTube and everything. The phone hasn't stopped ringing."

"Why me?" my mother asked. "Mary Jo Krazinski's daughter works in the bank. A teller. *My* daughter jumps out of hooker hotel windows."

"I didn't jump," I said.

"Of course you jumped," Grandma said. "It was a beauty. You came out of that window like you were shot from a cannon. Some bystander got it all. Lula backed out after you. I don't like to speak bad about anyone, but it wasn't a pretty sight. It was like Winnie the Pooh getting stuck in the rabbit hole, if Winnie the Pooh was wearing a red thong."

"I thought I dropped," I said to Grandma.

"Nope," she said. "You jumped."

She pulled the video up on her cell phone.

"This is horrible," I said. "My hair is a mess, and I look fat."

"It's these T-shirts you wear," Grandma said. "They're all washed out and they don't give you any shape. You need some pretty clothes."

"I can't afford to buy clothes. I have to buy a new car."

"You can buy whatever you want when we find the treasure," Grandma said.

My mother brought bread and deli ham and provolone cheese to the little kitchen table. I set my messenger bag on the counter and got mustard and mayo from the fridge.

"I'm not moving as fast as I'd like on the treasure hunt," I said. "Every time I get a lead, it ends in disaster."

"I got a good lead at the grocery this morning," Grandma said. "I was in line next to Dottie Clark and she was talking about her son the fireman and how he got called out to the Lucky Lucy Café last night. Seems that it suddenly filled up with smoke and dust and that the smoke set off the fire alarm. She said it was odd that it happened right after you blew up the Margo."

"I didn't blow up the Margo," I said. "Lou Salgusta blew up the Margo."

My mother sucked in air. "Lou Salgusta was there?" She made the sign of the cross. "He's a maniac. He burns his initials onto people's private places. And then he kills them."

Grandma went to the fridge to get pickles. "Maybe he died in the blast. Did they bring in any cadaver dogs?"

"I don't know," I said. "I haven't heard anything about a search and recovery effort."

Grandma brought bread-and-butter pickles to the table and added them to her sandwich. "I know the boys' secret escape tunnel ran to the Margo. So maybe the tunnel also went from the Margo to Lucky Lucy. They're only a couple blocks apart."

I paused with my sandwich halfway to my mouth. "You know about the tunnel?"

"Jimmy told me about it. He said no one used it much anymore and it needed some repair, but it was still an important part of the La-Z-Boy club. I figured it just went between the Mole Hole and the Margo, but maybe it goes to lots of other places. And maybe one of those other places has the safe with the treasure. So, if we can't figure out the clues, I say we investigate the tunnels. We should just go down there and follow all the different tunnels to see where they end up."

My mother looked like she was trying to decide between booze or Xanax. I understood her dilemma. Her thankless job was to be the voice of reason and maturity in a family of oddballs. My father keeps his head down and wills himself to be invisible, occasionally barking for more hot gravy at the dinner table. My sister Valerie is married to a very sweet man who seems to be incompetent at everything other than keeping her pregnant. And then there's me and Grandma with Superhero Derangement Syndrome.

"I'm told the tunnels are in bad shape," I said to Grandma. "I don't think we should go in them, but I can get Ranger to map them out for us."

The part about Ranger was a fib. I didn't feel comfortable asking Ranger to map the tunnels. I put it out there because I didn't want to push my mother off the ledge.

"I guess that would be okay," Grandma said.

I finished my sandwich, ate three chocolate chip cookies, and stood to leave. "I'd like to borrow the Buick," I said.

The Buick is a '53 baby blue and white Roadmaster monster that was left to Grandma when her brother passed. It sits unused in the garage because Grandma has a lead foot and lost her license, but can't bring herself to sell the car.

"Where's your CR-V?" my mother asked.

"I had a fender bender," I said. "No big deal, but I'd like to use Big Blue while my car gets fixed."

"Sure, you can borrow it," Grandma said. "And you can drop me at the hair salon. I'm getting my nails done. I'm thinking about going midnight blue."

CHAPTER THIRTEEN

The hair salon was a block from the bail bonds office. I dropped Grandma off and checked in with Connie. Lula was absent. Potts was present. He jumped up off the couch when he saw me.

"Thank goodness you're safe," he said. "I don't know how I missed you. I spent the whole night in front of your door. And then when it was almost lunchtime and you weren't answering when I knocked and yelled, the super came to see what was wrong. So, he went in to make sure you weren't dead, and that's when I found out you weren't there. How did you get past me?"

"You were asleep," I said. "I stepped over you."

"From now on I'm not going to sleep," he said. "Never."

"If you didn't come soon, I was going to lock him in the storeroom," Connie said. "He won't leave. And he hums."

"Anything new?" I asked Connie.

"Angie Mackie told my mom that she saw Lou Salgusta come out of Carlotta's Bakery yesterday afternoon. She said he was carrying a flamethrower and limping. And Lula just cracked a tooth. She was trying to open a beer bottle with her teeth. She's at the dentist."

"Why was she trying to open it with her teeth?"

"We had pizza delivered for lunch, and Lula found a couple beers in the fridge, but we couldn't find the opener. She said she saw a guy open a beer bottle with his teeth once. I bet her a dollar she couldn't do it. And she cracked her tooth."

"Did she get the bottle open?" I asked.

"Not with her teeth. She popped it open with a screwdriver." Connie handed me a computer printout. "This is the latest on Charlie Shine. He's using his credit card at restaurants and grocery stores. He's staying away from places where he would be recognized. Not shopping at Giovichinni's. He's moving around but he never seems to go out of the greater Trenton area. At least not with his Charlie Shine ID. There are gaps between credit card expenditures, so it's possible he's using a bogus ID as well."

"Thanks," I said to Connie. "I'll take the printout. Maybe I can see a pattern. Grandma's at the hair salon. I'm going to see if she needs a ride home."

"Take the hummer with you."

Potts followed me out and stopped when he saw the Buick.

"This is your car?" he said. "I mean, you're really driving this Buick? It's a classic. I've never seen one of these in person."

I hated the Buick. I only borrowed it when I had no other choice. It was a bulbous sow, lumbering down the street, grunting and wheezing. I felt like Betty Rubble when I was behind the wheel, wrestling the beast around corners.

I opened the back door for him, and he sprawled across the seat.

"Wow," he said. "This is huge. It's like a bedroom back here."

I drove a block, parked in front of the hair salon, and called Grandma. No answer. I left Potts in the car and I went into the salon. It wasn't big. Dottie and Irene Hurley had their own styling stations and they also did nails. They were younger than Grandma, but not by much.

"Edna left with Ruth Kuleski," Dottie said. "She got a quick nail color change, and Ruth drove her somewhere. Edna said she was going on an adventure. And Ruth said she was going to have lunch with her daughter."

"An adventure?" I asked.

"That's what Edna said. Off to find a treasure."

Crap!

I ran out of the salon and took off for the Mole Hole. I forgot about Potts in the backseat. I crossed over the railroad tracks and he started humming.

Double crap.

"Where are we going?" he asked.

"The Mole Hole. I need to check on something."

I pulled into the lot and skidded to a stop. "Stay here," I told Potts. "I'll be right out."

I marched into the bar and stood for a moment, letting my eyes adjust to the dim light. Two girls were working the poles and the bar was packed with lunchtimers. I approached one of the bartenders and asked if an older woman had come into the bar.

"There's an older couple in the booth to the right and a single woman is halfway around the bar."

I scanned the bar and spotted Grandma. She was eating a burger and watching the stripper directly in front of her.

"One more question," I said to the bartender. "Have you seen Charlie Shine today?"

"No one sees Charlie Shine," he said.

"How about Lou?"

"Salgusta? Never heard of him."

"Anyone in the back room?"

"Some furniture movers. It's getting redecorated."

I walked around the bar to Grandma. All the stools were taken so I sidled up next to her.

"Looks like a good burger," I said.

"It's excellent," she said. "And this young lady on the pole is amazing. She can do an upside-down and a split. And she can do a full squat to get money stuffed into her G-string. I wish I could do that. My knees aren't what they used to be. What are you doing here? Did you come for lunch?"

"No. I'm here because I thought you might be here."

"I came to investigate the tunnels, but I thought I'd have a burger first. The Mole Hole makes the best burger in town."

"Finish your burger while I peek into the back room. We can't access the tunnel if the room is occupied."

I walked around the bar and opened the door to the back room. The La-Z-Boy recliners were gone and had been replaced by five leather club chairs. There was a thick cream-colored rug on the floor and a new big-screen TV on the wall. The rickety card table had been replaced by an elaborate dark wood poker table and six poker table chairs on casters.

Two men in T-shirts and jeans were arranging side tables by

three of the club chairs. Two forty-something chunky men in suits were leaning against the far wall, arms crossed over their chests, eyes focused on me.

"This is a private party," one of the suits said. "This isn't a public room."

"I'm looking for Charlie and Lou," I said. "Have you seen them?"

"Maybe," he said. "Who are you?"

"Stephanie Plum."

He smiled and looked over at the other suit. "This is our lucky day, Ed. Just when we're wondering how we're going to snatch Stephanie Plum, she brings herself to us."

"Yeah, lucky us," Ed said. "Unlucky her."

The door pushed open behind me, and Grandma stepped in. "I thought I'd give it a peek, too," she said.

"Well, what have we got here?" Ed asked.

"I'm Edna," Grandma said. "Who are you?"

"I'm Ed. And this is Chick."

The other suit nodded and smiled at Grandma.

"This is a very nice room you have back here. I like the decorating," Grandma said. "Although, I'm guessing Benny will miss his La-Z-Boy."

"I'm thinking we have Stephanie Plum's granny here," Ed said.

"Yeah, we hit the jackpot," Chick said. "It would be good if you two ladies would move away from the door."

"Actually, we're going to be heading out," I said. "Nice meeting you."

Both of the suits pulled guns and the two guys in jeans moved to the back of the room. I heard Grandma take in a sharp breath, and I wrapped my hand around her wrist and gave it a fast squeeze.

"Step away from the door," Ed said. "There's people who want to talk to you and Granny."

My heart was running at double time, beating so hard I had blurred vision. Bad enough I had stumbled into this—now I had Grandma in their crosshairs.

"Who wants to talk to us?" I asked.

"People," Ed said. "You got a hearing problem?"

"That's rude," Grandma said. "The La-Z-Boys would never talk to a lady like that."

I was calculating the distance between Grandma and me and the open door and the time it would take the gorilla in a suit to pull the trigger. Probably he wouldn't kill us because *people* wouldn't like that. On the other hand, *people* might think I was expendable. Grandma had the key to the treasure. I was most likely just a pain in the ass. So, they might be willing to kill me and run down Grandma. I was about to turn and drag Grandma through the door when Potts burst in.

"Here you are," he said. "I got worried when you didn't come right out. So, I came to see if you were okay."

Potts spotted the two goons in suits and his eyes got wide. "Oh b-b-boy," he said.

"What the heck," Ed said.

Without a thought in my head, I acted on the distraction, spun Potts around, and shoved him toward the door. "Run!"

"What?" he said.

"RUN!"

Ed yelled to the two guys in jeans to grab us, but we were already out of the room, rounding the bar. Potts stumbled into a waitress, carrying a tray full of food, and everything flew off the tray and crashed onto the floor.

"Oh jeez," Potts said to the waitress. "I'm so sorry."

"No time," I said, grabbing him and shoving him through the room and out the door.

I stuffed Grandma and Potts into the Buick, jumped behind the wheel, and stomped on the gas pedal. The two suits stood squinting in the sun, watching us chug down the street.

"Did I save you?" Potts asked.

"Yes," I said. "Absolutely."

"Were those real guns?"

"Yes, again."

"That caught me by surprise," Grandma said. "I know I'm in a dangerous situation being that everyone thinks I hold the key to the treasure, but I wasn't expecting to be kidnapped by two men in suits. They looked so respectable."

"They looked like thugs to me," Potts said. "Of course, they already had their guns out when I came in, so that might have something to do with my first impression. I thought they looked like mob guys in those old Al Capone movies."

"You could be right," Grandma said. "I wasn't thinking about Al Capone. I was thinking about the La-Z-Boys. They wore more comfortable clothes that had some elastic in the waistband."

"Elastic waistbands are excellent, especially if you have intestinal issues," Potts said.

"Who are you?" Grandma asked Potts.

"I'm Potts," Potts said.

I brought Grandma home and suggested she not share this adventure with my mother.

"No problem," Grandma said. "I have enough problems getting out of the house as it is."

I returned to the office and left Potts outside, guarding the door.

"I stopped in at the Mole Hole," I told Connie. "The back room was getting a makeover. New chairs, new rug, and a poker table. New goons."

"Who ordered the makeover?"

"I don't know. I was hoping you knew."

"I haven't heard anything."

I set my messenger bag on the floor and sat in one of the chairs in front of her desk. "There were two young guys moving furniture around. Looked like wiseguy wannabes. And there were two guys in suits. Ed and Chick. They were in their forties. Chunky. Looked like muscle. They said someone wanted to see me and Grandma, and the two morons pulled guns on us."

"Grandma was with you?"

"I caught up with her there. Anyway, Potts came bumbling in and created enough chaos that we were able to get out."

"It sounds like someone is reorganizing the La-Z-Boys," Connie said.

"Or someone is taking over the La-Z-Boy territory."

"I'll call Mom," Connie said. "She'll find out what's going on. We haven't got as much inside pull since Uncle Jimmy died, but we're still in the network."

I looked toward the front of the office. I could see Potts standing at attention, super alert.

"I can't get rid of him," I said. "He won't go away."

"No good deed goes unpunished," Connie said. "And while we're on the subject of good deeds, it would be good for my end-of-the-month balance sheet if you could snag Trotter."

———

Potts was sitting on the edge of the Buick's backseat, looking over my shoulder.

"Where are we going? Is it going to be dangerous? Should I have a gun? Do you have a gun?"

"We're going to Stiller Street. And no, no, and no."

There was a good chance that Trotter would be home for lunch. It didn't go well last time I approached him, but I was better prepared this time. I knew what to expect. And with any luck at all, he'd be passed out.

I turned onto Stiller and parked behind Trotter's van.

"Is this it?" Potts asked. "What should I do? Should I go in first and make sure it's safe for you? I'm okay with taking a bullet. Just in case, I'm wearing a medical bracelet that has my blood type."

"Wait in the car. I won't be long."

"You said that last time, but you didn't come out right away."

I walked to the door and rang the bell. I had my stun gun in one pocket and cuffs in another. Potts was behind me.

"I know you said to stay in the car," he said, "but bodyguards in the movies are always close to the bodies they're guarding. Besides, I could be helpful. I could tell this person about my positive experience with the bail bonds system."

"No. No talking. I do the talking."

The door opened, and Trotter's mother squinted at me. "Do I know you?"

"Stephanie Plum," I said. "Is Rodney home?"

"He's in the kitchen, eating a late lunch. He had a big procedure this morning."

I stepped around her and threaded my way through the hoarded groceries and stuffed dead animals. I could hear Potts wheezing, following in my footsteps.

"I need my inhaler," he said. "Did I tell you I was claustrophobic? Do I smell formaldehyde? I'm pretty sure I smell formaldehyde."

If he crashed to the floor and his lips were blue and his eyes were rolled back in his head, I'd drag him out to the sidewalk and call 911. Otherwise I was going to ignore him.

"I don't like these dead animals," he said. "They aren't smiling. They don't look happy. When I'm laid out, I want to be smiling. Not a big smile like the joker. Just a little smile, like I know a secret."

Trotter was at the table when I walked into the kitchen. There was a half-eaten sandwich and a half-empty vodka bottle in front of him.

"Hi," I said. "Remember me?"

"Yes, I remember you. Go away."

"If you would come with me to get re-bonded, you would never have to see me again. It would take a half hour."

"I'm not wasting a half hour on bogus charges. I'm a renowned dermatological enhancement specialist. I have a wait-list of customers." He reached down, took a tackle box off the floor, and opened it. "The syringes in this box are filled with my unique enhancement formula. If you go away, I'll give you one free of charge."

"What would I do with it?"

"Inject it somewhere. Blow up your lips. Puff up your cheek bones. Inject it in the pencil dick standing behind you and he'll have a custard launcher the size of a horse."

"I appreciate the offer," I said, "but we aren't in need of a syringe, and you're going to have to check back with the court. Because you failed to appear for your first date, you're now officially a felon."

"Screw the court. I have a business to run."

He threw a syringe at me and I jumped away. The syringe missed me and tagged Potts in the thigh, sticking in him like a dart in a corkboard.

"Omigod, omigod, omigod," Potts said, staring down at the dart. "What should I do? Should I take it out? I'm afraid to touch it. I'm paralyzed with anxiety."

I grabbed the dart and yanked it out.

"I think my leg is going numb," he said. "I'm having one of my allergic reactions. I'm having a panic attack. Is my face getting blotchy? It feels blotchy. Next thing my tongue will swell up and I'll choke to death."

"Has that ever happened?" I asked him.

"All the time," he said. "Except I don't usually die."

"What exactly was in the syringe?" I asked Trotter.

"Nothing. It was empty. Look at the syringe."

"I need air," Potts said. "I need to get out of here. Where's the door? Everything is going black."

He staggered into the living room, knocking over a stack of Ritz cracker boxes, a taxidermied groundhog that was missing a leg, and a tower of toilet paper.

"That was a mean thing to do," I said to Trotter.

"Bite me," he said. "And anyway, I was aiming for you."

I caught up to Potts on the sidewalk. He had his finger on his jugular, taking his pulse.

"There was nothing in the syringe," I said. "You just got stuck."

"Are you sure? I could feel the serum going into me."

"I have the syringe. It was empty."

"My heart is racing," he said.

"No doubt. Get in the car and I'll buy you some ice cream. Do you like soft-serve?"

"Yeah. I like when they swirl the chocolate and vanilla together."

"Me, too."

CHAPTER FOURTEEN

Connie looked up from her computer when I walked into the office. "Where's your new best friend?"

"He had a tough afternoon. I bought him ice cream and took him home. Any news from your mom?"

"Yes. None of it good. Charlie Shine arranged the back room remodel. It's primarily for some bad guys he brought in from Miami. He felt like he needed new muscle to run his operation."

"He has an operation?"

"Apparently he's coming out of retirement. My mother thinks he's two cans short of a case. I think he needs money to hire lawyers to keep him out of jail."

"Do we know what the operation includes?"

"The usual. Prostitution. Extortion. Old-school stuff. Plus, I don't know what Jimmy had stashed away, but the word is that

Shine wants it bad. And there are people who think the only reason the two witnesses in Shine's murder charge are still alive is the fact that one or both of them holds the road map to the La-Z-Boys' treasure."

"Grandma and me."

"Yes."

"You're right," I said. "This isn't good news."

The big takeaway from Connie's news was that Shine now had the ability to grab Grandma and me. He had henchmen.

"I don't suppose you have a body receipt for Trotter?" Connie said.

"No, but I'm making progress. Have you heard anything from Lula?"

"The tooth she cracked had already been capped, so they popped it off and gave her a temporary. She would have come back to work, but she also chipped a nail and had to wait for an appointment with her nail tech."

I looked down at my nails. They weren't chipped but they weren't wonderful, either. Maybe Morelli would have liked me better if I got a manicure once in a while. Probably the blonde had perfect nails. Probably she always chose lavender nail polish.

"Ugh!" I said.

"It was only one nail," Connie said.

I blew out a sigh. "I'm heading out. Things to do."

I had to get Shine and Salgusta off the street, and I had to get those freaking clues. Question was how? What would Indy do? He'd enlist professional help. I wasn't sure Lula, Potts, and Grandma Mazur fell into the category of professional, but I knew two people who did.

If it wasn't for the blonde, my first choice would be to go to Morelli. He had mob snitches. He was street-smart. He had all the self-defense skills I lacked. He was a cop, and law enforcement resources were available to him. Plus, he was sane. The fact that he was incredibly hot and sexy ordinarily would be in his favor, but would be a distraction right now.

Ranger had all the same skills as Morelli, but he was rogue. His karma path didn't always follow the letter of the law. This was a strike against him, but he got points for not having a blond girlfriend. At least not one that I knew about. Truth is, I didn't know for sure that Morelli had a girlfriend. It was more of a dreaded suspicion.

I called Ranger and told him I needed more help.

"I'm committed until eight o'clock," he said. "I'm all yours after that. Is this going to involve a field trip, or can we talk at Rangeman?"

"Talking at Rangeman would be good."

It was midafternoon. I wasn't up for spending more time with Trotter, and I couldn't get excited about tracking down the gun-toting fry-cook, Arnold Rugalowski. It was too early to mooch dinner at my parents' house, so I headed for home.

I took a detour after two blocks, thinking I'd drive past Morelli's house. See how it felt. Maybe convince myself that I was jumping to conclusions about the blonde. And even if my conclusions were correct, I needed to dial back on the indignation since I'd just spent time with Ranger. I needed to be open-minded about the situation, right? Cut Morelli some slack. Give him another chance to try to tolerate me.

I stopped in the middle of the road when I got to Morelli's

house. His car was parked at the curb and Gabriela's Mercedes was parked behind it.

"What the fuck!" I said. "What the fucking fuck!"

I sat there for a full minute, waiting for my heart to start beating again. I tapped my head with my index finger. "Think, think, think." She's somehow connected to the La-Z-Boys. She's looking for someone or something. It's possible that she's looking for the treasure. Morelli is a cop. She could assume he knows something. Or she could be a vampire and she came here to suck his blood and he's lying on his kitchen floor, half dead. I was leaning toward the vampire theory.

I drove to the end of the block and turned the corner. I parked, got out of the Buick, and cut through three backyards before I reached Morelli's. His kitchen was at the back of the house. He had a window over the sink and a window in his back door. I could faintly hear muffled talking. He had a small wooden table next to his Weber grill. I moved the table, so it was under the window, climbed up on it, and peeked into Morelli's kitchen.

Gabriela had draped her jacket over one of the two chairs at Morelli's small kitchen table. She was wearing a knee-length black pencil skirt, a silky black tank top that could pass for lingerie, and black strappy Chanel sandals that were trimmed in pearls and showed off her perfect pedicure and bloodred painted toes. She was casually lounging against the counter, a glass of white wine in her hand, laughing at something Morelli said. Morelli was close to her and he was smiling. The Chardonnay bottle was on the counter.

Bob was lying under Morelli's kitchen table, and he was looking like he couldn't believe this was happening. Like he wanted to choke on his own vomit. Okay, maybe it wasn't Bob that wanted to choke. Maybe it was me. I was really close to spewing all over Morelli's window.

I climbed off the table, returned it to the grill, and speed-walked back to the Buick. I kicked the beast's whitewalls a bunch of times, wrenched the door open, got behind the wheel, and burst into tears. By the time I pulled into my apartment building's parking lot I was pretty much done sobbing. Over the past couple of months, I'd acquired a laundry list of things worth crying about. My love life. My job. My apartment. My squint lines. My inability to cook, shoot, figure out streaming, understand the cloud, or complete any of the books recommended by Oprah. The list was endless. So hopefully the last twenty minutes of blubbering covered all the bases and I was good for another couple months.

The real bummer in all this was Gabriela. She was a double whammy. She had her hooks into my ex-boyfriend, and I was pretty sure she was trying to steal my treasure. The most annoying part to all this was that I knew next to nothing about her, and Morelli undoubtedly knew all sorts of things. He probably knew her last name and where she was living. And he probably knew why she was here. The obvious, intelligent, mature way to go about this was to simply have a conversation with him. Not at this precise moment, of course, but in the near future.

I marched up the stairs to my apartment and found Potts sitting on the floor, with his back to my door.

"I put a Band-Aid and some antiseptic on the hole where the dart went in and I'm back on the job," he said, getting up.

"How did you get here?"

"My mom brought me. She was going out to the market anyway."

I opened the door and Potts followed me into the kitchen. I gave Rex a pretzel, and I gave Potts a bottle of water. I turned the television on and gave him the remote.

"I have work to do in my bedroom," I said. "Don't move off the couch. If you decide to go home, leave me a note."

"I'm not going home. I'm here forever."

"You're a nut."

"I know," Potts said. "I can't help it."

I closed my bedroom door and flopped onto my bed. I didn't have work to do. I needed a nap before I tackled the Morelli-Gabriela connection.

Grandma called at 5:45 PM.

"Your mother made too much spaghetti," she said. "Do you want to come to dinner?"

I cracked my door and looked out. Potts was still there.

"Is your mother expecting you to be home for dinner?" I asked him.

"No, I told her I was working the night shift."

"Can I bring a friend?" I asked Grandma.

"You can bring an army. Your mother was hitting the hooch, and next thing, *poof*, we got two weeks' worth of pasta."

———

"This is getting serious," Potts said from the backseat of the Buick. "You're taking me to meet your parents. Do they know about us?"

I cut my eyes to the rearview mirror and glanced at him. "What's to know?"

"That I protect you. That we're life partners."

"We aren't life partners. I bailed you out of jail and now I can't get rid of you."

"Good thing, too. I already kept you from getting shot, and then I took a syringe in the thigh for you."

This is why I don't keep a loaded gun. I might have been tempted to shoot one of us.

CHAPTER FIFTEEN

Grandma was waiting at the door when I arrived with Potts.

"You remember George Potts," I said to Grandma. "You met him at the Mole Hole."

"I'm her bodyguard," Potts said. "It's my life's work to protect her. And we might eventually be a couple."

I kicked Potts in the shin.

"Ow!" he said. "Why did you do that? I have thin skin and my blood vessels are very close to the surface. I'm going to have a bruise. I might even get a hematoma."

"It was an accident," I said. "It was an involuntary action. And I didn't kick you hard."

"I'm very sensitive to pain because of my PTSD."

"PTSD is serious," Grandma said. "Where were you stationed?"

"Newark," Potts said.

Grandma nodded. "That explains it."

My father was already at the table. "It's after six o'clock," he said. "What's the holdup?"

"We were waiting for Stephanie and her guest," Grandma said.

My father looked up. "Guest?"

"This is George Potts," I said, seating him in the chair next to me, putting myself between him and my father.

My mother came in with two big bowls of spaghetti, and Grandma and I went to the kitchen to help with the rest of the food. Meatballs in red sauce, Italian bread from the bakery, a bowl of fresh grated Parmesan Reggiano, an antipasto platter, red wine.

Potts took a few pieces from the antipasto platter and passed on everything else. "I break out in hives if I eat tomatoes," he said. "And I'm allergic to hard cheese and gluten."

"Is that from the PTSD?" Grandma asked.

"No," Potts said. "It's genetic on my mother's side of the family. We're all allergy-prone."

"That must be terrible," Grandma said.

"It's a cross to bear," Potts said.

My mother poured herself a goblet of wine. "God bless," she said.

Grandma filled her wineglass, Potts and I passed on the wine, and my father kept his head down, forking in spaghetti and meatballs.

"This is very good antipasto," Potts said.

"You can take some home with you," Grandma said. "Where do you live? Are you local?"

"I live with Stephanie," Potts said.

Everyone stopped eating and looked at me.

"Pay no attention," I said. "It's the PTSD."

My father accepted that as a decent explanation and returned to his meatballs. My mother poured herself more wine. My grandmother wouldn't let it go.

"I understand some of those PTSD people are homeless," she said. "Are you one of those?"

"Potts lives with his parents on Porter Street," I said.

"That's a nice neighborhood," Grandma said.

My father picked his head up. "Cheese!"

I grabbed the bowl of cheese and passed it over to him.

"Have you had any luck getting the tunnels mapped?" Grandma asked me.

"I'm working on it," I said. "It might take a while."

"I don't know if I got a while," Grandma said. "I need us to find the treasure soon, so I can get to Hawaii during the whale season."

My father perked up at that. Undoubtedly calculating if he had enough money to get her on a plane.

"What tunnels? What treasure are you talking about?" Potts asked.

"There are tunnels under Trenton," Grandma said, "and we think there's treasure in one of them."

"I wouldn't put treasure in a tunnel," Potts said. "The tunnel could collapse and then you couldn't get to the treasure. And besides, I don't like tunnels. They don't have windows."

"That's something to think about," Grandma said. "Where would you hide treasure?"

"That's an interesting question. If I was a pirate, I'd bury it on an island or put it in a cave that led out to the ocean. If I was a king, I'd put it somewhere in my castle."

"Suppose you were a hit man for the mob?" Grandma said.

"In the old-time movies, it's always in a big safe," Potts said. "And the safe would be in the back room of a speakeasy or a strip club like the Mole Hole. I couldn't figure out where the money was all the time in *The Sopranos*. I think it must have been in the strip club sometimes or it could have been offshore. Or the money could be in a mobster's house. In the *Godfather* movie they had the house in Long Island, but it was in Staten Island in real life. Did you know that?"

"I didn't know that," Grandma said.

"110 Longfellow Avenue," my father said. "Do we have dessert?"

————

I got Potts settled into the backseat at seven thirty and drove him home, taking a detour past Morelli's house. Lights were on in the front room. His green SUV was still parked at the curb. The Mercedes was gone. I blew out a sigh and slumped in my seat a little.

"What?" Potts said. "When I sigh like that it always means something."

"It's my life," I said. "It's confusing."

"You don't look confused. You look like you have it all figured out. Except, and I don't mean to be critical, but you don't seem entirely suited to being a bounty hunter. You don't have a gun or anything. And you don't have a leather jacket. And bounty hunters on television are always kicking doors open, and I don't think you could do that in your sneakers. You'd break a bone in your foot."

"I guess I'm a bounty hunter by default. When I got out of college I worked in retail. I got laid off, and I couldn't get another job, so I blackmailed my cousin Vinnie into hiring me."

"What would you like to be? What's your dream job?" Potts asked.

"I don't know. I might want to be Indiana Jones."

"That wouldn't be my choice," Potts said. "He was always getting beat up and shot at and once a monkey tried to poison him. Of course, that doesn't sound too different than your current job, so I can see why you would find it appealing."

"What's your dream job?"

"I don't want a job," Potts said. "I had a couple jobs and I didn't like them. I like where I'm at now. I live at home and play video games in my pajamas. And now I'm your bodyguard. I got the idea from Banger Race. It's this video game about aliens disguised as geeks. And this one alien, Mugman, falls in love with a princess and realizes his life purpose is to be her bodyguard and protect her."

"So, you're Mugman?"

"I'm trying it on for size."

"How's it fitting so far?"

"It's not perfect."

"I'm not a princess," I said.

"That's okay. I'm not actually Mugman."

I reached Porter Street and stopped in front of Potts's house. "I'm staying with a friend tonight," I told him. "Do *not* sleep in front of my door."

"I could sleep in front of your friend's door," he said.

"I appreciate the offer, but I'll be safe with this friend."

"It's a boyfriend, isn't it? I bet he's really good looking and he has muscles."

"He's not a boyfriend. He's just a friend."

Truth is, I didn't know how to categorize Ranger. He was more than just a friend, but he didn't feel like a boyfriend. There were times when our relationship felt more like a marriage. There was an acceptance of personality that was sometimes lacking between Morelli and me. Maybe that was because Ranger and I had no illusions about a binding, long-term commitment. There wasn't as much at stake between us.

I waited until Potts disappeared inside his house before I drove off. I returned to Hamilton, cruised past the bail bonds office on my way to State Street, and I picked up a tail. It looked like a dark-colored SUV. I couldn't see the occupants. I called Rangeman control and asked if it was one of their cars. I was told that it wasn't, and I was patched over to Ranger.

"I'm pretty sure I'm being followed," I told him. "It's not like they're being subtle about it. They're right on my bumper."

"I can see you on my screen," he said. "You're about a half mile away. Go straight into the garage."

The car disappeared a block before Rangeman. The gate was already open for me. A Rangeman car was idling nearby. I slipped into the garage and parked in one of Ranger's spaces. I took the elevator to the seventh floor and let myself into Ranger's apartment. He was waiting for me in the kitchen.

"Calvin said you didn't have a tail when you pulled in," Ranger said.

"They cut away at Monroe Street."

"Any idea who they were?"

"Yes. That's why I'm here."

"I thought you were here for my sheets and my shower."

I smiled. "I've been found out."

"I'm having a late dinner. Ella left me a salad that would feed four people, if you want to join me."

"Thanks, but I had dinner with my parents."

"Wine?"

"Yes."

I sat across from him at his dining room table and sipped my wine while he ate.

"Talk to me," Ranger said.

"Charlie Shine's brought in some muscle from Florida. I ran across some of the new goons today. Apparently, I'm on their to-snatch list. Two of them had Grandma and me at gunpoint but Potts bumbled in and we were able to escape. I imagine they were the ones following me."

"Potts?"

"Long story short, he's sort of a sad sack that I captured and then bailed out. It was a small bond and I put it on my credit card. Anyway, he's latched on to me. Says it's his job to be my lifelong protector."

Ranger had stopped eating, with the fork halfway to his mouth.

"Is that a grimace I just saw on your face?" I asked him. "I've never seen you grimace before. This is a first."

"Why was he arrested?"

"It's not important."

"I think it's important."

"He had an accident in front of Tasty Bakery."

"What kind of accident?"

"It was personal."

Ranger leaned forward a little. "And?"

"He *pooped*! He *pooped* in front of Tasty Bakery. He's the *pooper*."

Ranger pressed his lips together and looked down at his plate.

"Now you're trying not to laugh," I said. "Go ahead and laugh. I know it's absurd. I'm stuck with the pooper."

Ranger grinned. "You said you needed help. Do you need me to get rid of Potts?"

"No. I have bigger problems than Potts. I was told the goons have orders to bring Grandma and me to Shine. The only way we'll be safe is if the treasure is found, Shine and Salgusta are dead or behind bars, and the hired help goes back to Florida."

Ranger nodded. "I agree. Are you making progress with the treasure hunt?"

"Grandma thinks the treasure is in one of the tunnels, and we should check them all out."

"I can send someone into the tunnels to make sure we aren't missing something, but I would be surprised to find the treasure there. There were four tunnel entrances years ago, and I don't know if the system has been enlarged since then. From what I saw when we were underground, the maintenance has been minimal."

"Where's the fourth entrance?"

"Cannon Street. The building used to be owned by Bobby Ragucci. He sold it and I'm not sure who took it over, but it's always been a deli on the ground floor and an apartment above it."

"Could the deli or the apartment contain a safe?"

Ranger took his plate into the kitchen, rinsed it, and put it in the dishwasher. "We can take a look."

"Now?"

"No. I want to send Rodriguez into the tunnel first. And I'll find out who bought the building from Ragucci."

"That leaves Shine, Salgusta, and Benny the Skootch. I need their clues. I can handle Benny but Shine and Salgusta are a problem. With Grandma's life on the line, I don't have time for dogged perseverance to get the job done. I could use some help taking them down and persuading them to hand over their clues. And I know you can be very persuasive."

"Babe," Ranger said.

CHAPTER SIXTEEN

Ranger was standing alongside the bed when I opened my eyes.

"You've got ten minutes in the bathroom and ten minutes to eat," Ranger said. "I want to be on the road in half an hour."

"Where are we going? What time is it?"

"It's seven o'clock. I've got Rodriguez in the tunnel. He went in at the Margo site and that's where he's supposed to exit. I have Tank waiting for him there. We're going to Ewing Township. Shine brought four guys in from Miami. Two are cheap labor and two are seasoned soldiers. They're staying in a house in Ewing. My source thinks Shine might be there, too. I want to take a look. I'll meet you in the garage."

I dragged myself out of bed and shuffled into the bathroom. By the time I stepped out of the shower I'd lost fifteen minutes. I towel-dried my hair, got dressed in the clothes I'd dropped on the floor the night before, and went to the kitchen. I shoved a bagel into my messenger bag, found a to-go mug and filled it with coffee, black, and took off for the garage.

Ranger was waiting by his Porsche Cayenne SUV. "I'm guessing from the wet hair that you needed more time."

"It doesn't dry in three minutes."

"Did you get breakfast?"

I pulled the bagel out of my bag and took a bite.

We got into his Cayenne and rolled out of the garage.

"I didn't see the Buick in your garage just now," I said.

"I had it returned to your parents' house. I'll give you a less conspicuous car. You're too easy to spot in the Buick. I could also run some security on your parents' house, but last time your father declined."

"And he would probably decline again, so let's concentrate on finding the treasure."

I ate my bagel and drank my coffee while Ranger drove. It was a beautiful fall day with the promise of blue skies and a warm afternoon. Not a lot of traffic on the road yet, but in fifteen minutes, there would be an explosion of people heading off to work and kids going to school.

We entered a neighborhood of moderately priced homes. Some older single-level ranches and some larger colonials. Ranger idled in front of a single-level ranch. Two vehicles were in the driveway. A blue pickup and a black Escalade. Shades were drawn in the house. Ranger drove to the end of the block, made a U-turn, and parked on the opposite side of the street, two houses down.

Ranger can go into a surveillance mode where I swear his heart rate drops to 20 beats per minute but he's still alert and focused. My heart rate was considerably higher, and I had a problem with focus. I was watching the house, but I was wishing I was wearing clean clothes. That led me to wishing I was wearing *new* clothes. And from that point I went to wondering what sort of clothes I should buy. I had no clue.

After a half hour of mind-numbing surveillance, the front door opened, and the two suits came out and got into the Escalade. No sign of the lesser wise guys.

Ranger let them get a sizable lead before following. They cruised through town, turned just before the train station, and continued on to the Mole Hole. They parked in the lot and went inside. There were no other cars in the lot.

We watched from a distance for a while. No one went in or out. No other cars entered the lot. I pulled the visor mirror down and checked out my hair. I was freak girl. I found a brush and a scrunchie in my bag and pulled my hair back into a ponytail.

"What do you think they're doing in there?" I asked.

"Playing cards, watching reruns of *Friends,* checking in with their wives back in Miami."

"Do you think they're coming out anytime soon?"

"Babe," Ranger said.

"Just sayin'."

Ranger called the Escalade plate and location in to his control room and requested that someone place a tracking device on the SUV. He turned the ignition key on the Porsche and put it in gear.

"Let's check back on the Ewing house."

———

No pickup in the driveway of the Ewing house. Shades were still down. No sign of activity. No street traffic. We were parked one house away, in front of a white colonial with black shutters.

"Let's take a closer look," Ranger said.

We went to the door and rang the bell. No answer. Ranger knocked. No answer. He picked the lock, and we were in. He closed and locked the door behind us.

"Bail bond enforcement!" he shouted. "Anyone here?"

Nothing.

We went room by room, looking for information that might lead us to Shine. The furnishings were basic and beige. It didn't feel like a house that had ever been a home. Possibly a safe house for the mob. Or maybe a rental property. There was very little in the fridge. Half-and-half for coffee. A loaf of white bread. Some provolone cheese slices and deli ham. Mustard. Leftover pizza. A six-pack of beer. Two tubs of ice cream in the freezer, coffee and chocolate.

There were four bedrooms. Two with bathrooms en suite. The other two were small and shared a bathroom. Suitcases and duffel bags were mostly unpacked and open on the floor. Beds were unmade in three rooms. The third room had a perfectly made bed.

"Military," Ranger said.

"It looks like they've only been here a couple days."

"My source told me they flew in on Monday. It wasn't clear if they were making a permanent move. The suits have families and houses in Miami. The other two guys are free agents. One of them is Shine's nephew."

We returned to the car and I buckled in. "Now what?"

"Now we wait to see where the suits take us," Ranger said.

"Do you think they wear suits all the time?"

"No. I think they didn't take a lot of clothes with them."

"My old friends Chick and Ed. Do they have last names?"

"Ed Gruman and Chick Rizer," Ranger said. "The nephew is Kenny Farmer. I don't have a name for the fourth." He pulled away from the curb. "Do you have any other leads you'd like to run down?"

"No. But I could use some backup bringing in an FTA. Last time I tried to apprehend him he stuck a syringe in Potts's leg. He lives on Stiller Street."

Ranger drove down Stiller Street and parked behind Trotter's van. I gave him the paperwork and he paged through it.

"This reads like bad fiction," Ranger said. "Who would be dumb enough to let this guy inject them?"

"Enough women to keep him in vodka and tequila."

He gave the paperwork back to me and we went to the door. Trotter's mother answered. She was wearing fluffy pink slippers and an orange-and-purple flowered tent dress that came to her knees. She had a cigarette stuck to her overinflated lower lip.

"We're here to see Rodney," I said.

"He's in the kitchen," she said, "but he's busy. He might not have time to be real social."

Ranger and I stepped around her, and I wove my way through the cluttered living room and dining room. Trotter was at the kitchen table, mixing up God-knows-what. There were measuring spoons and cups on the table, a large unlabeled canister of white powder, a large jug of canola oil, several smaller canisters, and a large mixing bowl with some glop in it.

"Hey, Trotter," I said. "How's it going?"

"What do I have to do to get rid of you?" Trotter said. "Shoot you? Stab you? Inject you with formaldehyde?"

"You're in violation of your bond agreement," Ranger said. "You need to come with us."

"Where'd you get the all-in-black pretty boy?" Trotter asked me. "He looks like he's auditioning for a television show."

Trotter scooped some glop up in a measuring cup and threw it at me. I didn't move fast enough, and I got tagged in the chest. I looked down in horror and another glob of the stuff hit me in the head.

"Stop it," I said. "What the heck is this stuff?"

"It's my special enhancement formula," Trotter said. "Flour, water, oil, cream of tartar."

"That's Play-Doh," I said.

"My proportions are different, and I added the oil," Trotter said. "My enhancement formula takes longer to set up, and it goes in smooth as silk. Problem is sometimes it hardens like concrete. You don't want to let it sit in your hair too long."

I put my hand to the top of my head. The gunk was already starting to solidify.

"Here's some more," he said, hurling another cupful of glop that caught me in the forehead and oozed down my nose.

"What the fuck!" I yelled at Trotter.

In my peripheral vision I saw Ranger move toward Trotter. "Stand back," I said to Ranger. "He's mine. He's going down."

"Oh, I'm so scared," Trotter said.

He barely got the words out of his mouth when I charged across the room, snatched him by the front of his shirt, and head-butted him. I gave him a shove. He wobbled backward and sat down hard. I called him a dumb-ass, dumped the remaining glop on him and hit him in the head with the bowl. His eyes went out of focus, and I clapped cuffs on him while he was still fuzzy-brained.

Ranger went full-on grin. "Babe."

"I have a headache," I said. "I never head-butted anyone before."

"Best display of female rage that I've seen in a long time. Maybe ever. I liked the part where you hit him with the bowl."

"Hair is important in Jersey. You don't dump glop in a Jersey girl's hair."

"No doubt," Ranger said. "You have me convinced."

He yanked Trotter to his feet and dragged him toward the front door.

"We're leaving!" I yelled to Mrs. Trotter. "Rodney is coming with us."

"Okay," she answered from somewhere in the house. "Have a nice day."

We got to the sidewalk. Ranger stowed Trotter in the backseat of the Porsche and opened the passenger-side door for me.

"I'm going to make a mess of your car," I said.

"Not a problem."

———

Ranger pulled up to the back of the police station and marched Trotter inside while I waited in the car. Ten minutes later, Ranger slid behind the wheel and handed me my body receipt.

"Do you want to come back to Rangeman and have me scrub you down?" he asked. "Or would you rather I take you home?"

"Home."

I needed to regroup. And there was a good chance that I wouldn't be able to get all of the enhancement gunk out of my hair and I would have to visit Salon Philip at the mall. Philip was a genius at cut and color. Hopefully he was also a genius at gunk removal.

Ranger left the police lot and joined the flow of morning traffic. "I talked to Rodriguez while I was in the police station," Ranger said. "He followed every offshoot and found three exits. The Mole Hole, the Margo, and the bakery. The fourth exit was cemented closed. Probably happened when Bobby Ragucci sold his property. Rodriguez said there's nothing down there but dirt and rats, but there might have been another tunnel near the Margo. There was a lot of debris and possibly a cave-in at one point. Beyond that there's no secret hideaway where there might be a safe."

"Grandma's going to be disappointed."

"Why is this treasure so important to her?"

"She has a bucket list."

Ranger stopped for a light and looked at me. "How about you? What's in your bucket list?"

I was stumped. I didn't have a bucket list. My bucket was empty. "I haven't gotten around to making a bucket list," I said. "Do you think that's a personal failure?"

"No. You're busy living every day. That's a personal triumph."

"It doesn't feel like a triumph. It feels like I'm moving through my life with no important goals or aspirations."

"What do you consider to be an important goal?"

"Being a doctor or a vulcanologist or a marine biologist or finding the Ark of the Covenant."

Ranger glanced over at me. "Is the La-Z-Boys' treasure your Ark of the Covenant?"

"Maybe not the equivalent of the Ark of the Covenant, but it would be moving in the right direction."

"One more reason why you need to find it."

CHAPTER SEVENTEEN

Ranger drove into the lot to my apartment building and stopped alongside a black Honda Passport.

"This is yours," he said. "It should be unlocked. The key fob is in the gun box under the passenger seat." He handed me a key. "This is for the gun box. The SUV has the usual tracking device plus a rear camera that allows us to see if you're being followed."

I got out, unlocked the gun box, and got the key fob. I locked the car and waved Ranger off. I went straight to my apartment, said a fast hello to Rex, shucked my clothes, and jumped into the shower. Twenty minutes later I was in the Honda Passport with a towel wrapped around my head, and I was on my way to Salon Philip. I called Connie from the road and told her I captured Rodney Trotter, but had a slight apprehension mishap, and was now booked into an immediate emergency appointment at the hair salon.

"I have my own emergency," Connie said. "Potts is on the couch. And he's humming. I'm going to put him in an Uber and send him to you."

"No! No, no, no, no."

Too late. Connie was already disconnected.

I reached Route 1 and took the exit to Quaker Bridge Mall. I parked by Macy's and walked through the mall with as much dignity as I could muster considering I had a towel wrapped around my head.

"Stephanie Plum," I said to the fashion-forward woman at the salon reception counter. "I have an appointment."

The woman looked at my towel. "Is this a color issue?"

"No," I said. "Play-Doh."

I removed the towel and the woman bit into her lower lip. I wasn't sure if it was to keep from laughing or gagging. She stepped from behind the counter and motioned to Philip.

"We need triage here," she said.

———

Potts arrived while I was in the shampoo area. He took a chair across from the reception desk and paged through the salon's magazines, occasionally looking up to make sure I wasn't being held at gunpoint. I was moved from the shampoo sink to Philip's chair, and Lula came in. She breezed past Potts and came straight to me.

"Connie said you had a incident," Lula said. "What's that about?"

"Ranger helped me apprehend Trotter, but before we got Trotter in cuffs I got some glop thrown at me."

"It was in her hair," Philip said. "We were able to get some of it out, but I'm going to have to cut the rest."

"How much are you going to cut?" Lula asked.

"A couple inches," Philip said. "Maybe four or five."

I got light-headed and little black dots floated in front of my eyes.

"She looks whiter than usual," Lula said.

"Deep breath," Philip said to me. "Put your head down between your legs. Don't worry. You're going to look terrific."

Potts rushed over. "I know CPR," he said. "Does she need CPR? And I have an EpiPen. I always carry one because of my allergies. Does she need an EpiPen?"

"I'm okay," I said. "I just had a moment."

"It happens here all the time," Philip said. "It's the *I'm going to cut all my hair off* syndrome."

"I can't look," Lula said. "I'm going out to the mall and get a big pretzel."

"I'll stay here," Potts said. "Just in case she needs my EpiPen."

"Okay, here we go," Philip said to me. "Close your eyes. Don't open them until I tell you."

I kept my eyes closed through the cutting and the styling. Mostly because I didn't want to embarrass myself by fainting or shrieking or jumping out of the chair before Philip was done. I heard the hair dryer cut off. Philip did some fussing with his magic fingers. And I heard Lula barge into the salon with her spike heels clacking on the tile floor.

"Omigod!" she said. "*Omigod!*"

"What? What omigod?" I asked. "Is it good? Is it awful?"

I opened my eyes. It was short. And kind of cute. Big curls and waves. He'd added red highlights.

I stared at myself in the mirror. "This isn't me," I said. "Who *is* this?"

"Girl, it's the *new* you," Lula said. "It's Super Steph. This is happy hair. Kick-ass hair without going yesterday's punk. Kudos, Mr. P.," Lula said.

"It's pretty," Potts said. "Can I touch it?"

"No," I told him. "Not ever."

I gave my credit card to the woman at the reception desk.

"You can't be going around in jeans and T-shirts anymore," Lula said to me. "That hair deserves better. You need a new look."

"She needs a black leather jacket," Potts said.

"Absolutely," Lula said. "With studs and bedazzle shit on it. And then she needs a black leather bra to go under it. Or maybe a red satin bustier."

"That would be hot," Potts said.

I took my card back and put it in my messenger bag. "I don't think I would be comfortable in a leather bra."

"You gotta see the whole picture," Lula said. "The hair is sexy in a sweet way. And then you pair it up with nasty clothes, and it says *Hey, look at me. I'm complex.*"

"I don't feel complex," I said.

"That's on account of you're in a transitional phase in your life what with the new hair," Lula said. "You leave it to Potts and me and we'll get you sorted out."

"I've got a lot of ideas," Potts said. "I've been reading the fashion and makeup magazines while I've been waiting."

I looked at Lula. "I thought Connie said you had a temporary crown in place of the one that got damaged."

"Yep. The cracked crown got popped off and the new temporary one got stuck on," Lula said.

"And it was in the front?"

"Yep."

"It's gone."

"Say what?" Lula felt around with her tongue. "What the heck!" She went to a makeup mirror and looked at herself. "Damn! I lost my temporary."

"I bet it got stuck in that big pretzel you ate," Potts said. "You probably swallowed it. So, you didn't actually lose it. You just have to wait until you poop it out."

"I can't wait," Lula said. "I'm unsightly. I got an image to protect. We're going to have to delay the makeover until I get another crown stuck on. It won't take long."

Lula hustled out of the salon, and Potts turned to me. "Now what? We could go shopping without Lula. Or we could wait for Lula. Or we could go to the car and make out."

"Not only will we never make out, but if you ever suggest it again, I'll shoot you."

"You don't have a gun," Potts said.

"Okay, then I'll have someone else shoot you."

"Just for suggesting we make out? That's extreme."

"You could punch him in the face," the receptionist said. "That might be more appropriate."

"I don't like to bleed," Potts said. "It gives me anxiety. I guess it would be okay if I got punched in the forehead."

An alarm went off on his phone.

"What's that?" the receptionist asked.

"It's past lunchtime. I get low blood sugar if I don't eat on schedule," Potts said.

"There's a food court in the mall," I told him. "You can get something to eat there."

"I can't eat at a food court because of my allergies," Potts said. "There's all kinds of cross-contamination. I break out in hives and I get diarrhea if I walk through a food court. Did I tell you I'm extremely sensitive to gluten? And they let anyone work at those places. I know for a fact because I got a job at a chicken place in a mall once. Anyway, I only worked there for a couple days because of the diarrhea from the gluten spewing out of the fry station. And that was when I moved back to my parents' house."

"I know someone who would shoot him," the receptionist said.

"I'll get back to you," I said to the receptionist.

I walked Potts out of the salon and through the mall to the Macy's exit.

"I don't see the Buick," Potts said.

"I have a different car. It's a loaner from a friend."

"Is it the guy you sleep with? The good-looking one with muscles?"

"Yes."

I unlocked the Honda.

"This is it? A Honda?" Potts asked. "It's nice but I expected you to perform at Porsche level. Maybe Mercedes. Boy, this is an eye opener. Where are we going for lunch?"

"Giovichinni's Grocery. You can get something from the deli, and we can eat at the office. I want to check in with Connie."

———

I got Potts settled onto the faux leather couch with his chicken wrap and Pepsi, and I took the chair in front of Connie's desk. I unwrapped my ham and cheese panini and opened a small tub of coleslaw.

"I like the hair," Connie said.

I nodded. "Thanks. I'm getting used to it."

"Lula called and told me she was back at the dentist."

"Her temporary popped off." I reached into my messenger bag, pulled out the body receipt for Trotter, and handed it to Connie.

"Vinnie's going to love this," Connie said. "This was a high bond."

"I'm going to love it, too," I said. "I need the money."

Connie wrote a check and slid it across her desk to me. "What are you buying with this?"

"Food. Clothes. Maybe a manicure. My rent is due. Any more information from your mom?"

"The latest gossip is that the La-Z-Boys are having problems. Lou Salgusta has gone from a successful sadistic killer to flat-out crazy, and Charlie Shine has decided he's Al Capone."

"What about Benny?"

"Benny is never seen. He's in his house, eating cheese ravioli and watching television with his cat. My mom said his wife was moved into a hospice facility yesterday. She's been sick for a long time."

"That's sad," I said. "I didn't know her, but everyone seemed to like her."

"My mom will miss her," Connie said. "They were friends for a lot of years."

I finished my lunch and Grandma called. "I need a ride," she said. "And I could use some help picking an outfit. Your mother is babysitting for your sister and can't take me. I'd go myself but they hid the keys to the Buick."

"What kind of an outfit?" I asked.

"Carla Skootch went into hospice yesterday, and she's not expected to last the night, so I need something to wear to the viewing. I want to look respectful for her. She's a nice lady and she put up with a lot over the years."

"Sure," I said. "I need to get some new clothes, too. When would you like to go?"

"Now would be good," Grandma said. "Your father is eating at the lodge tonight, and your mother won't be home from Valerie's house until late. Valerie and Albert had to go to some lawyer shindig."

"I'm taking Grandma shopping," I said to Potts. "Can I possibly do this without you tagging along?"

"No," Potts said. "I'm following you to the end of the earth."

"I won't be going that far," I said.

———

Grandma was waiting at the curb. And she was carrying her big black patent purse. This meant she was packing her .45 long barrel. It was frightening to think that she had the gun, but it was good to know she recognized the danger level.

She slid onto the passenger-side seat and buckled up. "I almost didn't recognize you," she said. "You have a new car and a new hairdo."

"The car is a loaner from Ranger. The hair is job related. An FTA threw some gunk at me and it got stuck in my hair."

"I like the new cut and color," Grandma said. "It's flirty."

Grandma turned and looked at Potts in the backseat. "What do you think?"

"I'd like to touch it," Potts said, "but she won't let me."

Grandma leaned close to me. "He's kind of a creeper," she whispered.

"It's that he has no filters," I said.

"I heard that," Potts said. "That's insightful. There was a time when people thought you were forthright if you said what was on your mind. It was a sign of good character."

"When was that time?" Grandma asked.

"Olden times," Potts said.

"Like in the good old days," Grandma said.

"Exactly," Potts said.

CHAPTER EIGHTEEN

I parked by the Macy's entrance for the second time today and everyone followed me into the store.

"I don't want to spend a lot of money, but I want something that looks expensive," Grandma said. "And I'm not family so I don't have to wear black."

Death was almost as important as food in the Burg, and life was often lived in such a way to ensure a good showing at the final event. If you joined a lodge or the mob, you got a crowd at your viewing. If you worked your way up to Grand Poobah of the lodge, you got a premier room at the funeral home. The church service was a comfort, but everyone knew it was the casket selection that really counted. Seven o'clock viewings relieved the tedium of after-dinner television. Morning funerals meant whiskey straight up was flowing immediately following the burial. It was all good.

Grandma found her way to the dresses and sorted through them. "I don't have a problem like some of the ladies my age," she said. "I don't have to worry about hiding a fat roll. I've always had good metabolism."

Grandma didn't have a fat problem, but she was a victim of gravity. She could walk forever, and she could lug the long-barrel around in the crook of her arm like the queen of England, but beyond that she had the muscle development of a soup chicken.

"This one is nice," she said, pulling out a cranberry A-line dress with a little jacket. "I like the color, and the skirt looks like the right length. I like when it hits just below my knee."

She found three other dresses and took them into the dressing room to try them on.

"She's a good shopper," Potts said. "She found what she wanted right away. What are you going to buy? Do you need a dress, too?"

I prowled through the racks. "No, I think I'm all set for viewings and funerals."

"Then you need better everyday clothes."

"The thing is, I'm comfortable in my jeans and T-shirts," I said. "They work for my job."

"Then just get nicer, newer jeans and T-shirts. In the magazines I read at the salon they dressed jeans and T-shirts up with jackets and cool boots." He searched around and found a black jacket that was a take on a motorcycle jacket. "This is good. It looks like something Indy would wear if he was a girl. According to the tag it's also abrasion-proof, rip-resistant, breathable, and has waterproof seams." He gave me the jacket and moved to a table with T-shirts. "Try the jacket with one of these shirts. The material is soft, and I like the plain round neck. It's supposed to be odor-shirking and fast drying. Try it in white."

I grabbed a pair of dark denim jeans and went to the dressing room. I had the jeans and white shirt on, and Potts came back with more jeans and jackets and sweaters and shirts. I worked my way through the stash and liked everything.

"What's your budget?" Potts asked. "We're in four digits."

"That's over my budget but everything looks great."

"If you take everything, you have a week's worth of clothes."

Grandma looked at the bundle of clothes in my arms. "You really need the clothes. I can't remember when you bought work clothes last. And you can even wear these on a date. If anyone ever asks you out."

"You need boots or flats," Potts said. "Maybe both. You can't wear these outfits with your sneakers."

By the time we got back to the car I was in a cold sweat and my stomach was sick. I'd blown the entire apprehension check, and I wasn't sure I was comfortable trading my hooded sweatshirt for tailored jackets and chunky sweaters. The ankle-high rubber soled boots and the black flats were keepers.

"I just got a text from your mother," Grandma said. "Carla Skootch passed this morning. The viewing is tomorrow with the burial on Saturday. Good thing I didn't wait to go shopping for a dress."

"I can't go to viewings and funerals," Potts said. "I'm allergic to carnations and there are always carnations in the flower arrangements. Mostly I get congested but sometimes I wheeze if there are carnations and lilies. Lilies are the worst. Most funeral directors know CPR and have defibrillators to counteract the lily reactions."

"I didn't know that," Grandma said.

"I read it somewhere," Potts said. "It might have been in the AARP magazine, or I might have seen it on YouTube." The timer went off on his phone. "I have to eat," he said. "I'm overdue for dinner. Are my lips blue? Am I pale?"

"You're always pale," Grandma said. "You need to get more sun."

"I can stop at Country Diner when I get off the highway," I said.

"That suits me," Grandma said. "I eat there sometimes with the girls after bingo. I like their rice pudding."

"I need a booth," Potts said. "I get agitated if I sit in the middle of a room."

"You've got a lot of rules," Grandma said.

"I know," Potts said. "I'm annoying. I can't help it."

"Of course, you can help it," Grandma said. "Make a list of everything you think is annoying and then stop doing all the things on the list."

"That's a good idea," Potts said. "You tell me when I do something annoying, and I'll put it on my list."

I turned off the highway and took Mitchell Street.

"What's that noise?" Grandma asked.

"It's Potts," I said. "He's humming."

"Good Lord," Grandma said.

"Is my humming annoying?" Potts asked. "It annoys some people."

"It annoys *me*," Grandma said. "Put it on your list."

"I don't know if I can stop humming," he said. "It keeps me calm. I hum during times of stress. Also, when I'm thinking. And I hum when I'm bored."

"How about if you hum on the side of the road, watching us drive away and go to the diner without you," Grandma said.

"That would be terrible," Potts said. "You wouldn't do that, would you?"

"Problem solved," I said, pulling into the lot to the diner. "Here we are."

We snagged a booth and gave the waitress our order.

"It doesn't seem to me that we're making much progress getting to my treasure," Grandma said. "We've got clues, but we only have two of them, and we don't know what they mean without the rest of the clues."

"I'm good with clues," Potts said. "What are they?"

"*Ace it*. And *Philadelphia*," Grandma said.

"I see your problem. Standing alone those clues aren't helpful. How many more clues are there?"

"Four more," Grandma said. "The six gangster owners of the Mole Hole each had a clue to a treasure."

"And you want their treasure?" Potts asked.

"One of the gangsters was my late husband," Grandma said. "I got a rightful claim on his share."

"That sounds fair," Potts said. "What's the treasure?"

"We don't know," Grandma said, "but we hear it's worth a lot of money. Three of the gangsters are dead, including my honey, Jimmy. The other two are scumbags who are trying to kidnap Stephanie and me."

"What about the last one?" Potts asked. "Will he give you his clue?"

"We're working on it," Grandma said.

"We should go talk to him," Potts said.

"His wife just died," I said.

Potts looked to Grandma and then to me. "Is that a problem?"

"I guess we could offer our condolences and work the treasure into the conversation," Grandma said.

Our food arrived. Turkey dinner with mashed potatoes and gravy for Grandma. A burger, no bun for Potts. Grilled cheese and fries for me. This is the joy of a Jersey diner. Something for everyone.

"What about the tunnels?" Potts asked. "Did you find any clues down there? Sometimes in the movies there are symbols etched into stones or brick walls or wooden beams."

"No luck with the tunnels," I said.

"My friend Morgan is the fry cook at the Lucky Lucy Cafe. He says there's an old, mostly sealed-up entrance to a tunnel in the basement, and when the Margo blew up it filled the entire café with smoke."

"I told you about that!" Grandma said to me. "Remember, I heard it from Dottie."

I had totally forgotten about the Lucky Lucy. I wasn't too keen on going back into the Mole Hole tunnel to look for symbols that had been carved into now charred wooden braces, but the hope that a tunnel entrance from the Lucky Lucy was still at least partially intact was enough to motivate me. "Do you think your friend would let us see the sealed-up entrance?"

"I don't see why not. He should be working until closing today."

I parked in the Lucky Lucy's small side lot and removed a giant Maglite from the driver door's pocket. Good for illumination and cracking skulls.

We walked around to the front and looked up. A large sign displayed the Lucky Lucy's name along with a logo of four playing cards, all aces.

"You think that's the *Ace it*?" Grandma said.

I didn't want to jinx anything, but I thought there was a pretty good chance.

"Only one way to find out," I said. "Let's talk to Morgan."

The Lucky Lucy had booths along the walls and a few tables in the center of the room. All mostly full.

A waitress noticed Potts. "Hey, Georgie. Looking for Morgan? He's in the kitchen."

Morgan was wearing an apron that covered a small portion of him. My guess was that Morgan ate more fried food than he served. His face was sweaty and greasy from standing over the fryer, and he was singing an unintelligible song to himself.

"Potts, my man," Morgan said, dumping a basket of fries out into a metal tray under a heat lamp. "What's up? You have a cutie and her grandma standing here. Dude, don't ask me to play wingman on this one."

"Nah, it's cool. I was telling Stephanie and her grandma about the tunnel entrance in the basement," Potts said. "Is it okay to show them?"

Morgan jerked his thumb toward the back of the room.

"Basement door is through the storage closet. I'd go with you, but I have to put some burgers together."

I led the way past tubs of lard and gallon jugs of mayonnaise. A roach the size of a hamster peered at me from between plastic bags filled with burger rolls. I gave an involuntary shiver and pushed on to the door at the far end. I opened the door and looked at the stairs. Not good. Hastily put together a long time ago and not maintained. A couple of boards were at odd angles and obviously loose. I switched the Maglite on and carefully went down first. At the bottom of the stairs, a long, yellowed string hung down from a bare lightbulb. I gave it a pull and the room lit up enough to show your typical ugly basement. The floor was packed dirt and there were thick cobwebs in every corner. Grandma and Potts followed me down. Grandma went to a crude wooden door on the far side of the cellar. It had a large rusted-out metal padlock and ring handle.

"I have a good feeling about this. Let's get this baby open and find my treasure," Grandma said. She pulled her .45 long barrel out of her purse and aimed it at the lock. "Stand back. I've seen this work on TV. There's usually a lot of splintering."

Potts looked worried. "I don't do well with splinters. I once had one that took two weeks to work its way out. I almost fainted every time I looked at it."

Grandma unloaded a couple of rounds into the wood door, and we all froze. Our eyes focused on the cellar ceiling. We didn't hear anyone screaming about shots fired or feet stampeding to the front door. It was business as usual in the café.

Potts put his finger in one ear and then the other. "Check

one. Check two. Sibilance. Sibilance," he said. "I have delicate eardrums. I hope I didn't rupture one when Grandma shot the gun."

I gave the door a kick, the lock popped off, and the door swung open revealing the tunnel. It was almost identical to the one attached to the Mole Hole.

I aimed the Maglite down the tunnel to my right. I could see the entrance to the passage where the cave-in happened. The tunnel to our left seemed clear, but in a state of neglect and decay. At least the wooden braces weren't charred, but water dripped between boards that were supposedly supporting the tunnel ceiling. The floor of the tunnel was muck.

"This doesn't look safe," Potts said. "I can feel my sinuses clogging. I think I smell mold."

Mold was the least of our problems. The tunnel reeked of sewer gas and animal rot.

"I'll go first," Grandma said, taking the Maglite and forging ahead. "I'm already too old to die young."

I scrambled to keep up with her, sliding on the sludge, ducking around the worst of the drips. I could hear Potts humming behind me. I had no reception on my cell phone and my worst fear was that the batteries would fail on the Maglite.

"Are you looking for etchings and symbols on the walls?" Potts called to Grandma. "Are there street signs down here? Where are we?"

"I think we gotta be going to Philadelphia," Grandma said. "I'm leading the way so you're in charge of the symbols."

"I'll take pictures," Potts said.

CHAPTER NINETEEN

"**I** don't like this tunnel," Potts said, twenty minutes in. "I'm cold and wet and muddy. I'm going to have to take zinc and vitamin C when I get home. My mother is going to yell at me when she sees my sneakers."

Grandma's flashlight beam caught a shadowy figure some distance in front of us. It was a black-clad woman, and the silver studs on her boots bounced the light back at us. Gabriela.

"Follow her," I said to Grandma. "Don't lose her."

My hope was that Gabriela knew what she was doing, because we sure as hell didn't. My fear was that we'd wander forever in the dark until we face-planted in the muck and someone found our bones ten years from now.

An instant later Gabriela disappeared. It took me a beat to figure it out. There had to be a bend in the tunnel. We hurried after her as best we could, sliding in the muck. We rounded the bend, I caught sight of Gabriela, and then she was gone again.

"How is she finding her way without a light?" Grandma asked.

"Probably has night-vision goggles," Potts said. "Or maybe she's like a cat woman."

"Do you think she knows we're following her?" Grandma asked.

"I'm sure she can see the Maglite," I said.

Impossible to know if she was leading us somewhere or running from us. Also, impossible to assess the danger level. She could turn around and shoot us all dead. I didn't think a Chardonnay drinker would do this, but you never know.

Grandma picked up the pace and forged ahead. I struggled to keep my footing and stay close to her.

"Be careful to not fall down in the mud," I said.

Seconds after I said it, Potts went down.

"Don't worry about me," he called out. "Keep going. I'll probably only get worms or a rash. I hope there aren't any leeches."

I pulled Potts to his feet and we sloshed on until we came to a fork.

"Now what?" Grandma asked.

I took the flashlight from her and aimed the light at the tunnel floor. The sludge was too deep to see footprints.

"Go left," Potts said. "I've been keeping track of a symbol that looks like a bird wing. I can see one on the beam to the left.

"Works for me," I said. "I'll take over the lead."

After five minutes of trudging in the dark, the tunnel widened slightly and there were rotting wood planks overhead.

"It looks like we're under something," Grandma said. "It looks like we got a floor over us. Maybe this is it. We could be under the room that has the safe."

The wood ran for about ten feet and then the dirt tunnel continued. I rapped the beams with my Maglite and some of the wood splintered off.

"This wood couldn't hold a safe," I said.

I rapped the ceiling again and punched a hole through to the other side. A couple of boards broke apart and fell into the tunnel. I heard some squealing and high-pitched chirping sounds and suddenly the air was filled with bats escaping from the hole I'd created.

"*Bats!*" Potts yelled. "*I hate bats!!*"

We all ducked down, and the bats chirped and flapped and swirled around us and took off down the tunnel. The bats were followed by rats. They tumbled out of the hole, squealing and splatting when they landed in the mud.

"*Rats!*" Potts yelled. "*I hate rats!!*"

The rats kept coming, piling up three-deep in front of us, jumping and climbing over each other, trying to get out of the muck. I had myself plastered against the tunnel wall. I had my eyes closed tight, but I could feel the rats running over my feet. Think happy thoughts, I told myself. Don't panic. What was the line from *Ratatouille*? *Only the fearless can be great. Only the fearless can be great.* Crap. Not working. I wasn't fearless.

I opened my eyes to see the last few rat stragglers hauling ass down the tunnel.

"I think I have rabies," Potts said. "Am I foaming at the mouth? Don't anyone get near me."

I directed the flashlight beam into the hole in the overhead flooring. Water was trickling out.

"It looks like a large culvert," I said. "Maybe part of the sewer system. We can try to climb into it or we can continue down the tunnel."

"The bats and the rats all went down the part of the tunnel we just traveled," Potts said. "I don't want to go that way."

"Okay, let's go a little further in the other direction," I said. "We can always turn around and try the culvert."

We walked for a couple of minutes and came to a dead end. A ladder had been built into the wall, and two stories above the floor of the tunnel I could see what looked like a round manhole cover that was slightly ajar. A sliver of light outlined part of the opening.

"I'm going to climb up," I said. "Stay down here until I see what's up there."

I got to the top and had a moment of panic when I had to take a hand off the ladder to push the manhole cover away. Don't look down, I thought. Channel your inner Indy.

I gave the heavy metal lid a shove, flipped it back, and light flooded into the tunnel. I hauled myself up through the small round opening and crawled out onto a concrete walkway that led to a fountain. I'd come out in Liberty Park. I went flat on my stomach and looked down the hole at Grandma and Potts.

"Can you make it up the ladder?" I asked. "Or would you like me to get help?"

"I can do it," Grandma said.

"Me, too," Potts said.

Grandma came first. I grabbed her when she got to the top, and I pulled her out. Potts came next.

"Liberty Park," Grandma said, looking around. "There used to be a statue of Betsy Ross in the fountain, but the pigeon situation got out of hand. They moved Betsy to a park near the river."

"Betsy Ross was from Philadelphia," Potts said. "Along with cheesesteaks, Tastykakes, and Rocky Balboa. Do you think that's the Philadelphia part of the clues?"

"Maybe," I said, "but it doesn't feel right to me. If the treasure is in Liberty Park, the question is where?"

"It's not a big park," Grandma said. "There's not much to it. Mostly just the fountain that's seen better days."

I looked at the area around the manhole cover and the concrete walkway. It was splattered with mud from Grandma, Potts, and me, but there were also muddy footprints leading down the path to the street. Gabriela had exited the tunnel here, and I wondered if she'd deliberately left the cover ajar, so we would see it.

"My feet feel squishy," Potts said.

"I'm not looking too good, either," Grandma said. "There was a lot of mud down there."

"We're two blocks from Lucky Lucy and my car," I said. "I think we need to call it a day."

My instincts told me we were working too hard to make the

clues fit Liberty Park. Lucky Lucy seemed to have the *Ace* tie-in, but I was pretty sure it was just a coincidence.

———

I took Grandma home and waited until she was safely inside.

"Are you staying with your friend tonight?" Potts asked.

"Yes."

It was a fib. I was going back to my apartment. I needed to spend some time with my own things. My couch, my television, my hamster running on his wheel in the kitchen. If I told this to Potts he'd be camped out in front of my door and it would diminish the enjoyment of being in my own space.

I stopped in front of his house and turned to face him. "Thanks for helping me with my shopping today. I would never have found all those clothes on my own. I wanted to reinvent myself and I didn't know where to begin."

"Everyone wants to be a better version of themselves," he said. "It's easy for you because you just needed a new jacket. For some other people the job is more complicated."

———

I carried my shopping bags into my apartment and set them down in the kitchen. Rex was already busy with his nocturnal wheel spinning. I said hello and gave him a peanut. I got a beer from the fridge and drank half of it leaning against the counter.

Potts's last words were stuck in my brain. Everyone wants to be a better version of themselves. That was true for me. I was looking for a passion that would spin my life in a new direction. It was probably true for Potts as well, but Potts was a disaster of such proportions that I suspect he had given up looking for his better self. At least temporarily.

I took my bags into my bedroom and left them sitting on the floor with the tags still attached to the clothes. I went to the bathroom and looked at myself in the mirror.

"Who are you?" I asked the reflection.

CHAPTER TWENTY

My alarm went off at seven thirty. I rolled out of bed and came face-to-face with the shopping bags. Mental head-slap. What the heck was I thinking?

I showered, toweled off, and stared at myself in the mirror. I had a lot of curly wet hair. And it was short. If I let it dry naturally at this length, I'd look like a Chia Pet. After spending twenty minutes with the hair dryer, my hair somewhat resembled what Philip created. I had to admit, it was pretty, but it was too short for a ponytail. And a ponytail had its place in my life. A ponytail was easy.

I bypassed the bags and got dressed in my usual jeans, stretchy scoop-neck T-shirt, and sneakers. I put my coffee in a to-go mug and grabbed a strawberry Pop-Tart, my hooded sweatshirt, and my messenger bag.

Potts was pacing in front of the office when I drove up and parked.

"Lula is here," he said. "She had her tooth replaced. Connie is here, too. She's been on the phone nonstop. There's a lot of talk going on about the dead woman."

"Carla Skootch."

"Yes. She's going to be in Slumber Room #1. That's a big deal."

Connie got off the phone when Potts and I walked into the office. "This viewing is going to be a monster," she said. "Sid Rubenstein is making book on whether Shine or Salgusta will show."

"I'm sure they won't show," I said. "They'll get arrested."

"That would be a bad thing for you," Potts said. "If the police get them before you do, you won't have a chance to squeeze them for their clues."

He was right. On the other hand, they would be in jail and not able to kidnap, torture, and kill Grandma and me.

"Are you going?" I asked Connie.

"Yes. I'm taking my mom."

"How about you?" I asked Lula.

"I'm not ordinarily big on this sort of thing, but I might make an exception here."

"Did your mom have any more news about the La-Z-Boys?" I asked Connie.

"Only that Benny is pissed off because Shine got rid of the chairs and remodeled the room. Apparently, he didn't consult Benny before doing it."

This could work in my favor. If Benny is mad enough, he might throw in with Grandma and me. It would mean access to one more clue. And Benny knew Jimmy for a long time. He knew where the bodies were buried, and he probably knew a lot of other things about Jimmy. Like a second home somewhere. Or ownership of a commercial property where a safe could be stashed. Just because he never felt compelled to go after the treasure doesn't mean he has no idea where it might be located.

I went to the coffee station to refill my mug and Grandma called.

"You have to come over here," she said. "We made a casserole for the reception and I need a ride to Benny's house to drop it off. If you don't give me a ride your mother will drive me, and that will ruin everything. This is my opportunity to sweet-talk Benny into handing over his clue. I don't want your mother tagging along."

"I'm at the office," I said. "I'll be there in five minutes."

I hung up and took a moment to convince myself the visit was a good idea.

"I have to go to my parents' house," I said to Lula, Connie, and Potts. "Grandma needs a ride."

"I'll go with you," Potts said.

"No! Wait for me in the office. I won't be long."

"You always say that, and then people try to shoot you."

"No one is going to shoot me at my parents' house."

Truth is, I didn't know that for sure. And there was a decent possibility that someone would try to kidnap Grandma and me anytime, anywhere. Did this make me nervous? Yes. And fearful? Yes. Did I want to run away and hide somewhere? Yes. Was I going to run away and hide somewhere? No.

I was raised to have a strong sense of responsibility to my

family, my church, and my country. I wasn't raised to run away and hide. When the going got tough or scary I was expected to dig in and soldier on, because I came from a long line of survivors. War, famine, pestilence didn't stop my relatives from moving forward one foot in front of the other. They were good solid plodders without grandiose expectations. And that's the legacy they left me. The ability to plod forward, no matter the circumstances. I realize plodding isn't glamorous, but there are times when it serves a purpose.

———

Grandma was at the front door when I pulled into the driveway. She had her purse in the crook of her arm and a casserole dish in her hands. I jumped out and helped her into the SUV.

"This is good," Grandma said. "We can tag-team Benny. Do I look okay? I decided on this navy dress because it's solemn but not sad. I usually dress it up with a pink scarf, but the scarf seemed to convey too much happiness for delivering a bereavement casserole."

"The dress is perfect," I said. "What's in the casserole?"

"Baked ziti."

"The recipe with the gooey cheese sauce?"

"Yep. It's the best. And it has Italian sausage from the butcher at Giovichinni's."

"It smells fantastic."

"It just came out of the oven."

Two cars were parked in front of Benny's house.

"Drive around the block," Grandma said. "The one car belongs to Dori Klausen. She won't be in there long. She's only dropping off. The other car belongs to the woman Benny hired to help Carla. She's probably going to help with the reception after the burial."

I did a lap around the block and parked in the space just vacated by Dori. We walked to the front door and rang the bell and the caretaker answered.

"We're here to give our condolences to Benny," Grandma said.

"Much appreciated," the caregiver said, reaching for the casserole.

Grandma tightened her grip on the dish. "I gotta give this to him personally," she said, pushing her way in, past the caregiver. "You understand."

"He might not be up to visitors right now," the woman said.

"I'm not just anyone," Grandma said. "I was married to Jimmy Rosolli. I even got his La-Z-Boy. Benny gave it to me."

"Who's there?" Benny yelled from a distance.

"It's Edna Rosolli," Grandma said. "I brought you a casserole. Baked ziti with special sausage and cheese sauce. It's for tomorrow."

"Screw tomorrow," Benny said, "bring me the casserole and a fork. I'm starving back here. All I ever get is a protein shake."

"He's supposed to lose weight," the caregiver said.

"You're killing me," Benny yelled at the caregiver. "You're fucking killing me. Excuse my language."

"He's in the den in the back," she said. "I'll bring him a fork."

I led Grandma through the house to the tacked-on den. Benny was in the big comfy chair this time and the cat was in a donut-type bed by his feet.

"How's it going?" I asked him.

"My wife died," Benny said. "It's not going so good."

"I'm sorry," I said.

"God's will," Grandma said.

Benny blew a raspberry at God's will.

Grandma made the sign of the cross and looked up at the ceiling where I suppose God was lurking. "I had nothing to do with that," she said to the ceiling.

"No offense," Benny said. "You know I'm as good a Catholic as anyone else, but I'm not getting a lot of comfort from God."

"That's why we brought you this casserole," Grandma said. "If God don't come through, you can count on sausage from Giovichinni's butcher."

"You're a smart woman, Edna," Benny said. "I can see why Jimmy married you, should he rest in peace."

Grandma put the casserole on a tray table by Benny and took the cover off the dish.

"Oh, man," Benny said. "This is a work of art. It smells amazing. And the cheese!"

"It's all hand grated," Grandma said.

"*Fork!*" Benny yelled. "Where's my fork?"

The caregiver appeared with the fork. She rolled her eyes at Grandma and me, handed the fork over to Benny, and left.

Benny dug in and made a lot of appreciative sounds while he ate.

"You want a beer with that?" Grandma asked him.

He stopped eating and looked at Grandma. "You got a beer?"

Grandma pulled a cold bottle of beer out of her purse. "I usually carry my gun in this purse, but I thought a bottle of beer would be better today."

"After I observe the appropriate period of mourning, I'm going to marry you," Benny said.

"It might be worth it just to get your clue," Grandma said.

"Maybe we can make a deal," Benny said. "I'm pissed off at Shine, and Salgusta is nuts. Maybe I'll show you mine if you show me yours."

"And what happens when we find the treasure?" I asked.

"We split it," Benny said. "Trust me. There's enough for both of us to be happy."

"What have you got besides the one clue?" I asked him.

"I know two more clues," he said. "And by the way, I like your hair. It's real cute. I liked the ponytail, too, but this short cut is real cute."

"Thanks," I said. "I'm getting used to it. Are you talking about the clues in the Mole Hole safe?"

"Yeah."

"We already have those clues," I told him.

"Boy," he said, "you're sneaky. How'd you get into the safe?"

"We know people with skills," I said.

Benny chugged half the bottle of beer. "I bet."

"So, what else do you have?" I asked him.

"I know the treasure, and I've been thinking about a way to fence it that might be safe, but I'm not giving that up right away. What have you got besides the clues? You got the keys, right?"

"Maybe, but we're not giving that up right away," I said.

"Ha!" Benny said. "Wiseass." He looked over at Grandma. "Did you teach her that?"

"She's way ahead of me," Grandma said.

"The two clues in the safe aren't helping us," I said. "Is your clue worth anything?"

"Not to me," Benny said. "I'm not good at this sort of stuff. Every day I try to do the Jumble and I never get it."

"What's your clue?" Grandma asked. "Maybe we can figure it out."

"It's *pink*," Benny said. "It's the number four clue and it's *pink*."

"*Ace it, Philadelphia*, and *pink*," I said.

"The six of us were real close when we thought this scheme up about the clues and the keys," Benny said. "We weren't all sick and crazy and dead."

"Let's start with Philadelphia," I said to Benny. "You knew Jimmy for a long time. Did he have any Philadelphia ties? A second home there? Business property?"

Benny shook his head. "Not that I know. Jimmy didn't go across the river a lot. He was more a south Jersey guy. He liked the shore. Wildwood, Cape May, Atlantic City. He liked the slots. Sometimes he played the poker table."

"Did he have any properties there?"

"He used to have a house in Cape May, but that was years ago. Back in the day when the mob was big and there were lots of occasions for us to use our special talents, we all had real estate. We were living high back then, spending money like water. When the contracts started to dry up, to use a fancy term, we liquidated our holdings. It's not like any of us got poor, it's more we got careful with our lifestyles. Except for Shine. He always has a couple girls on the side. Still likes a new pinky ring once in a while."

"What about *Ace It*?" Grandma asked Benny. "If Jimmy liked to play poker maybe that's the tie-in. Did he have a special casino?"

"He would go to the Hard Rock sometimes. Sometimes Tropicana."

"I went to the Hard Rock with him once," Grandma said. "We only played the slots. We didn't go to the tables."

"Did Jimmy have any aliases?" I asked Benny.

"Sure. We all did. His favorite was Mickey Gooley. Sometimes he used Mickey Fast. He probably had others, too. I can't remember them all. I can't even remember all of my own aliases." Benny shoveled more ziti into his mouth. "I don't suppose you have more beer in your purse?" he asked Grandma.

"I could only fit the one bottle," Grandma said. "You don't want to drink too much anyway. You got a viewing tonight."

"I want to do what's right for Carla," Benny said. "And I know she deserves a nice viewing, but I'm not looking forward to this. Everybody and their brother's going to come out tonight. Half of the people would put a knife in my back if I didn't sit against the wall."

"That's not true," Grandma said. "You're well-liked."

"Not by everyone. I made a lot of enemies in my time."

"Most of them are dead," Grandma said.

Benny nodded. "Good point."

"I guess we should be moving along," Grandma said. "We'll see you tonight."

"Are you coming to the viewing?"

"Of course," Grandma said. "I wouldn't miss Carla's viewing."

CHAPTER TWENTY-ONE

Everyone looked relieved when I returned to the office.

"You didn't have to be so worried," I said. "We just delivered a casserole."

"What kind of casserole?" Lula asked.

"Baked ziti with cheese and sausage."

"I might go to the after-funeral party to get some of that," Lula said.

"Too late. Benny ate it."

"Now all I can think of is ziti and melty cheese," Lula said. "We should order from Pino's."

"I'll go for the Vodka Rig," Connie said.

"Make that two," Lula said.

"Order me something without dairy or tomatoes or gluten," Potts said.

"That would be the paper napkins," Lula said. "Are you sure you have all those allergies?"

"I have a nervous stomach from the PTSD," Potts said. "It's hard to tell what's an allergy and what's irritable bowel syndrome. All I know is I get the poops a lot."

"Bummer," Lula said. "In the beginning I just thought you were weird and annoying, but now I'm starting to see you're okay. It's just that you've got a lot of problems. Even if they aren't real, I guess they're still problems if they give you the poops."

"That's profound," Potts said.

"You bet your ass," Lula said. "There's more to me than meets the eye."

"Call the order in to Pino's, and get a vodka rig for me, too," I told Connie. "I'll pick it up. I want to drive by some addresses anyway."

Lula and Potts followed me out of the office, and everyone piled into my SUV.

"You know what this is like?" Potts said. "This is like we're a posse. I've never been part of a posse before. This is so cool."

"Where'd you come up with that one?" Lula asked him.

"I was watching television last night and they had a rerun of *Entourage*. Remember that? It was a television show and then it was a movie? And this guy Vince had a posse. And I was thinking that's like us. We're a posse."

"I remember that show," Lula said. "Vince was hot. He didn't have as much muscle as I like but he had good hair."

My first drive-by was Cluck-in-a-Bucket. I wanted to check on Arnold Rugalowski. It was lunchtime and he should be working the fry station. I thought it wouldn't hurt to see if he wanted to get a new court date. A polite inquiry.

I turned into the lot and parked and told everyone to stay in the car. Lula was happy to do this, and Potts didn't put up much of a fight. They were getting worn down by failure and getting syringed and shot at. I wasn't that smart. I kept pushing forward. Nothing stopped me. I was like RoboStephanie.

I cut the line at the counter and went straight to the front. "I'd like to talk to Arnold," I said.

"He isn't here," the girl working the counter said. "He quit yesterday."

"Did he get another job?"

"I don't know," she said. "He just left."

"Well?" Lula asked when I got back behind the wheel.

"He wasn't there. He quit yesterday."

"Where did he go?"

I shrugged. "Don't know."

The next address on my list was the Mole Hole. It was in the opposite direction from Pino's, but I had time to kill before our food was ready. I crossed over the train tracks and wound my way past the train station to the Mole Hole. I cruised through the lot and noted that the blue pickup and black Escalade were parked close to the entrance. Shine's henchmen were on-site.

I drove past the Margo and Carlotta's Bakery. I didn't see Shine lurking in either of these locations. There were cars parked in front of the bakery, but nothing that had Shine's name on it. I drove around the block and headed for Pino's.

"I think there's a big black car following us," Potts said. "When you drove past the Mole Hole just now, it came out of the lot. It's hard to tell, but I think the two guys in front are the ones who shot at us."

I pulled up my back camera and saw the Escalade was two car lengths behind me. So much for being hidden in Ranger's stealth Honda. I turned toward the center of the city, where I knew I could count on traffic and lights. The Escalade turned with me. I right-turned into heavy traffic and they had to drop back by four or five cars. I ran a yellow light and they were stopped on the red.

"Hah!" Lula said. "Amateurs."

They weren't amateurs. They were unlucky. And they weren't tailing me for surveillance. They would have rammed me from behind or passed me and cut me off. And then when I was stopped, they would have yanked me out at gunpoint.

I turned right and a block later I turned right again and made my way to Pino's. I arrived just as my order came out of the kitchen. Lunchtime and late at night, Pino's was a cop hangout, but I didn't see anyone I knew today. Just as well, since I was feeling awkward walking in with my posse. It wasn't as if we were going to eat at a table. This was three people coming in to carry out one bag.

––––––––

I ate my lunch at the office, finishing it in record time. "I'm off the clock," I said. "I have things to do?"

"What kind of things?" Potts asked. "What are we going to do?"

"*We* are not doing anything," I said. "I have things to do. And

I imagine you have things to do. You're probably way behind on your game with Mugman's princess."

"Do you want me to guard your door?"

"No. Thank you for offering, though."

"What about the viewing tonight?"

"I'm going with Grandma and I'll be perfectly safe because I'm sure she'll be packing. Besides, no one hardly ever gets shot at a viewing. That's usually reserved for the funeral."

"You don't want to go to the viewing, anyway," Lula said to Potts. "You'll have an attack from the lilies."

"That's true," Potts said.

"Do you want me to drop you off someplace?" I asked him.

"No," he said. "I'm going to stay here and read Lula's new *STAR* magazine. I can walk home."

I drove back to my apartment building, watching for a tail, thinking about the three clues. I did a slow ride around my parking lot, making sure no one was hiding behind or sitting in a car. No blue pickup and no black Escalade. I marched into the building, took the stairs, and peeked into my hallway. Empty. Yay. I let myself into my apartment and listened. No heavy breathing. No clothes rustling. That was a good sign. I threw the bolt on my door and did a fast walk-through. No monsters lurking under the bed. No zombies in the closet. I went back to the kitchen and looked in on Rex.

"This is no way to live," I said to Rex. "I'm starting to understand Potts . . . waiting for diarrhea to strike."

I went to my dining room table and opened my laptop. Since the clues began with a card reference, I ran a search for casinos in Philadelphia. Two racetrack casinos. One stand-alone casino, one hotel resort casino. Plus, slot machines in more locations. I reviewed what I knew. *Ace it.* Missing clue. *Philadelphia. Pink.* Two more were missing clues. I stared at a map of Philadelphia that marked out all the casinos. Nothing. I was blank brained. There was nothing that shouted out *pink.* I needed the rest of the clues.

I called Ranger. "Howdy," I said.

"Babe."

"Here's my problem. There are some rumors that Salgusta or Shine might try to attend Carla's funeral or show up at her viewing. I'm sure there will be police presence, but I wouldn't mind additional security for Grandma."

"No problem," Ranger said.

"Thanks. I hate to keep asking you for help, but I can't do this alone."

"I file this under entertainment," Ranger said. "And the help will come with a price. I'm running a tab for you."

Oh boy.

———

I fluffed up my hair, added an extra coat to my mascara, and swiped on some lip gloss. I left the bathroom and confronted the bags that were on my bedroom floor. A half hour later, the bags were empty. Everything had been put away in drawers or hung on hangers. I was dressed in new skinny black slacks, black flats, a royal blue and black striped sweater, and a short black jacket that matched the slacks. I was pretty sure I looked amazing. I thought about taking my gun but decided against it. The gun wouldn't fit in my new little cross-body bag. Plus, I didn't have any bullets and I didn't want to shoot anyone.

Grandma was ready to go when I got to my parents' house. My mother was at the door with her.

"Don't let her out of your sight," my mother said to me. "She's got it into her head that Lou Salgusta will be at the viewing and she's going to take him down."

"I said he *might* be there," Grandma said.

"This is why I drink," my mother said.

"As good a reason as any," Grandma said, already on the move to my SUV.

———

The funeral home is a five-minute drive from my parents' house. We arrived fifteen minutes before it opened, and all the parking places were already taken. The lot was full, and cars were parked on both sides of Hamilton as far as the eye could see. A crush of people filled the front porch and spilled down the steps onto the sidewalk.

"Go around the block," Grandma said. "You can park in front of Lena Kriswicki's house and we can cut through her yard. She's right behind the funeral home."

I parked in front of Lena's house and followed Grandma. She walked past Lena's dining room window and a dog started barking.

"That's Lena's Scotty," Grandma said. "He's a snappy one."

Lena's back door opened, and Lena stepped out just as we were rounding the corner of her house. She tagged Grandma in a flashlight beam.

"Edna, is that you?" Lena asked.

"There's no parking places left for the viewing tonight," Grandma said. "We parked in front of your house."

"No problem," Lena said. "Just be careful. I hear Lou and Benny are feuding, and since Lou is crazy, anything could happen."

"I'll keep my eyes open," Grandma said.

We walked through Lena's backyard, bushwhacked through a six-foot hedge, and skirted the funeral home's garage.

"We can go in through the back door," Grandma said. "That way we'll beat the crowd and I can get a good seat up front."

"Are you sure that's okay?"

"Sure. Lena and I do it all the time. I know the key code."

"How do you know the key code?"

"Lena told me. She helps out doing makeup on the deceased sometimes. She knows all about blending foundation to get just the right skin tone. She used to work the Estée Lauder counter at Macy's."

Grandma punched the code into the door lock, and we walked down the long hallway to the public area. A door was open just past the hospitality kitchen. It was the side door to Slumber Room #1. I looked in and saw that Benny was sitting at the head of the open casket. He was sitting on a straight chair that was too small for him and he was oozing over the sides of the seat. Two young wiseguys in training stood behind him. I knew them from previous experiences with Benny, and I knew their primary function was making food runs and getting Benny out of his chair.

Benny saw us standing in the doorway and waved us into the room. "Sit," he said. "They're gonna open the doors right away and it's gonna be a cattle stampede."

Grandma took a front-row seat, I sat down beside her, and I got a text from Lula.

Where are you? Lula wanted to know.

Front row left. Right in front of the casket, I texted back.

Save me a seat, Lula texted. *And save seats for Connie and her mother. We're all together in a big jam-up in the lobby.*

The doors crashed open and people rushed in, some sitting, some filing past the deceased. Benny accepted condolences with a nod of his head. Lula sat next to me, and Connie sat next to Lula. Connie's mom was somewhere in the casket viewing line.

"The satellite television truck is outside," Lula said. "And I think half the police force is in here. I saw Morelli at the back of the room. He's looking hot. He's wearing a tweedy jacket with jeans. And he's got a five o'clock shadow and his hair is overdue for a cut and sort of waving over his ears. I wanted to take a bite out of him."

"Is he alone?" I asked.

"He's with Schmidt. Schmidt isn't looking all that hot. Schmidt needs to lay off the donuts."

"Did you see Ranger?"

"No, but Potts is outside. He can't come in because of his allergies. He said to tell you he's there if you need him."

Connie leaned across Lula. "My mom said there's talk about how Lou has gone completely off the rails. Total postal. Word is he's completely obsessed with you and Grandma. Marie Georgio said she was driving home, and she spotted him in front of your parents' house two nights ago. She said he was crouched behind a parked car and he had his flamethrower with him. She blew her horn at him and he skulked away."

"That's the Golden Years for you," Grandma said. "One minute you're doing good, retired from your day job of whacking people, and then out of the blue you get an aneurysm and next thing you've got your flamethrower out and you're setting cats on fire."

"I can't sit here," Lula said. "I'm getting the creepy crawlies. I'm going out to the cookie table."

"I'll go with you," I said. "I want to look around."

Mostly I wanted to look around for Charlie Shine and his flunkies. Probably I didn't need to look for Lou Salgusta, since the police would notice an old guy carrying a flamethrower.

"Follow me," Lula said. "I'll muscle us through the folks who are sweating it out in the lobby. It wasn't pretty when we were stuck in the middle of them. I thought they were never going to open the doors to the viewing room." She nudged a couple of people out of her way. "Coming through. S'cuse us. We got an emergency here."

We reached the cookie table in the lobby. I took an Oreo and told Lula I was going off on my own.

"Okay," she said, "but don't get kidnapped or anything."

I inched my way through the crowd, scanning the room. I reached the far side of the lobby and someone wrapped an arm around me and pulled me aside. It was Morelli.

"I almost didn't recognize you," he said. "No ponytail."

"It's job related. Uncooperative FTA."

"Did you make the capture?"

"Yes."

That got a full-on smile. "You look pretty. How's the treasure hunt going?"

"It's going slow."

"I never thanked you for walking Bob. Maybe I could thank you over dinner tomorrow," Morelli said.

"Bob looked like a sissy dog."

"He rolled in something disgusting. I put him under the hose, but it didn't help, so I had to take him to a groomer."

Duh. I should have thought of that instead of jumping to conclusions. Not sure Morelli being all smiley and chatty with Gabriela would be so easy to explain away.

"I imagine you and forty other cops will be at the funeral tomorrow," I said.

"You got that right. We're hoping Shine will be dumb enough to show. And Benny still has a few enemies. Most of them have cataracts, but Benny is a big, slow-moving target."

"He has his wise guys with him."

"Dumb and Dumber," Morelli said.

"Shine has some of his own."

"They aren't as dumb. Two of them are seasoned soldiers."

He still had his arm around me, and I was having conflicting feelings. The contact felt warm and comforting and delicious, but at the same time there was the knowledge that it wasn't especially healthy.

"I should be getting back to Grandma," I said.

"About dinner?"

"I was under the impression that you had other dinner partners."

Morelli looked at me for a long moment. "Do you really want to have a dinner partner discussion right now?"

I looked over his shoulder and saw Ranger watching from a distance. "No," I said. "You make a good point. I'd like a rain check on the dinner. I have a lot going on."

What went unsaid was that we had a conflict of interest on several fronts . . . romantic, professional, and personal.

I stopped at the cookie table, filled a to-go cardboard coffee cup with cookies, and made my way back to the front row. I gave the cup of cookies to Benny, and he looked like he was going to burst into tears.

"You're an angel," he said, shoving the cookies into his mouth. "God bless you."

"You missed Gabriela," Lula said when I sat down. "She was wearing a black Akris two-piece with Mikimoto pearls on her ears. She gave Benny her condolences and kissed him on his cheek."

"How'd the kiss go over?" I asked.

"Not nearly as well as your cookies."

I turned toward the back of the room and caught a glimpse of Morelli looking cozy with Gabriela. They were standing too close together for my comfort. Not touching. Not exchanging spit. Just too close. She was too pretty. Too slick. Too at ease.

"My life is such a mess," I said to Lula.

"Maybe," she said, "but your hair looks good."

CHAPTER TWENTY-TWO

I was counting down the minutes to the end of the viewing. Benny was still accepting condolences, but the end of the line was in sight. Lula left at eight thirty. Grandma and Connie and her mom were hanging with me until we all got kicked out at nine o'clock.

I had my head down, checking my text messages, and Grandma nudged me.

"It's them!" she said. "It's the men who shot at us. They're standing in line behind Ruth Kuleski."

Ruth moved up to the casket and Charlie Shine's goons held back. Waiting their turn. Appropriately solemn. No eye contact made with me or Grandma. Ruth moved on and Ed Gruman and Chick Rizer stepped up to Benny and told him they were sorry for his loss, and Mr. Shine regrets not being able to attend but sends his sincere condolences.

"Communicate to him my appreciation of his sympathies," Benny said.

The men moved on and Benny looked at me and mouthed *fuck him*.

When the last person in line passed by Benny and headed for the lobby, the four of us went forward and paid our respects to Carla. Benny leaned in when I walked past.

"Partners," Benny said.

"Partners," I replied.

Benny had a moral flexibility that I didn't share, and being partners with him, even at a limited capacity, made my stomach knot. I was appalled at his chosen profession, and if I thought too hard about the details of his skills, I wouldn't be able to sleep tonight.

"That was a real successful viewing for Carla," Grandma said as we inched our way to the door. "She had a good showing of people."

"They ran out of Italian cookies," Connie's mother said. "They should buy more from the bakery and not so many of those cookies that come in a bag."

We reached the lobby and I saw Ranger watching from across the room. He nodded at me and I nodded back. Obviously, no one snagged Shine tonight. I moved out of the building with the mass of humanity, onto the porch and down the stairs. I searched the area for Potts but didn't see him.

"We have to walk around the block to Lena's house," Grandma said. "Good thing it's a nice night for a walk."

"We can give you a ride," Connie said. "I'm parked across the street in Mo Bernardi's driveway."

A text message buzzed on my phone and I checked the screen. It was a picture of Potts with his eyes as big as saucers and a gag in his mouth. He was in a fetal position, hands cuffed behind his back. It looked to me like he was in the trunk of a car. The message attached was that we might want to trade some information and items of interest for Potts's safe return. It was suggested that they would start chopping off minor body parts in twelve hours if I didn't cooperate.

"Bad news?" Connie asked me.

This wasn't anything I wanted to share with Grandma. And I for sure didn't want it getting back to my mom.

"Not bad," I said. "Just unexpected. Ranger would like to talk to me about something. Can you take Grandma home for me?"

"Sure," Connie said. "No problem."

I texted Ranger and told him to meet me in front of the funeral home. Grandma, Connie, and Connie's mom crossed the street, and minutes later, Ranger pulled to the curb in his Porsche 911.

"Drive around the corner so you can park for a moment," I said. "I want to show you something."

He made a right turn into the Burg and parked in the middle of the block. I accessed the text message and passed my phone to him.

"George Potts," he said.

"Yes. He has allergies so he couldn't come inside, but Lula said he was outside in case I needed protection."

"And he got snatched."

"Yes. I imagine Gruman and Rizer ran into him when they left the viewing. He would have been an easy mark."

"And you would prefer that they don't use a bolt cutter on his fingers and toes."

"Yes."

Ranger called his control room, requested two backup cars, and gave them the address of the house in Ewing. He called his second in command, Tank, and told him to take a couple of men to the Mole Hole.

"Since we're going to Ewing, I'm guessing you think Potts has been taken there," I said.

"It's a place to start looking," Ranger said.

Even under these circumstances, or maybe especially under these circumstances, riding next to Ranger in his Porsche, in the dark, is a provocative, sensual experience. The 911 is a sexy, powerful, perfectly engineered machine. The same is true for Ranger. When you put the two of them together there's a good potential for orgasm . . . or, at the very least, teeth-gnashing desire. It was hard to judge my current level of desire because it was mingled with an adrenaline surge over concern for Potts and the fear that we were about to be involved in a shootout.

———

The Rangeman cars were already in place when we reached the house in Ewing. They were parked one house down, across the street. Ranger parked behind them, removed a gun from the glove compartment, and handed it to me.

Lights were on in the house, but the shades were drawn. The faint flicker of a television could be seen through the front room shade. The blue pickup and the Escalade were in the driveway.

The four men in the Rangeman cars met us on the sidewalk. They were in Rangeman black uniforms, wearing full utility belts, sidearms strapped to their legs.

"There are at least four men and possibly one hostage in the house," Ranger told them. "I'll take point. We don't want to use excessive force. I want Baker, Sanchez, and Stephanie behind me and Rodriguez and Jake at the back door. My team will go in at nine fifty-five. Rodriguez and Jake will enter one minute later."

I trailed behind Ranger and his two backups when we crossed the street at nine fifty-three. Ranger went to the door, tried the doorknob, found it to be locked, and crashed the door open with a single kick. Obviously kicking a door down didn't count as excessive force.

Gruman, Rizer, Kenny Farmer, and a fourth guy were in the living room, watching television. They all jumped to their feet when the door flew open. Gruman lunged at Ranger. Ranger grabbed him and threw him halfway across the room. Gruman hit the wall and slid to the floor like a sack of sand. Rizer spun around, ran for the back door, and slammed into Rodriguez. Rodriguez stands six feet six inches tall and looks like he could pull a freight train. Rizer bounced back a couple of feet, went for his gun, and thought better of it. He was late to the party.

"Piece-of-shit safe house," Rizer said. "Busted in less than an hour."

"Uncle Charlie is going to be pissed," Farmer said.

Ranger dragged Gruman to his feet and cuffed him. "Uncle Charlie is the least of your worries," Ranger said. "We have your text message, and this takedown on body cam. You can face jail time for kidnapping, or you can return to Miami and never come back."

"I miss my girlfriend anyway," Farmer said.

"Where's Potts," I asked Gruman.

"Who?"

"The guy you kidnapped."

"He's not in the house," Jake said. "I just did a run-through."

Gruman looked at Farmer. "You were supposed to put him in the back bedroom."

"You said *we* would put him in the back bedroom," Farmer said. "I didn't know you meant *me*. You didn't specifically say that I should put him there."

Gruman cut his eyes to Ranger. "The nephew is an idiot. I'm guessing Potts is still in the car."

"You have a pickup and an Escalade in the driveway," Ranger said. "He wasn't in either of those."

"There's a white Taurus in the garage," Gruman said.

Ranger and I went to the garage and flipped the light on. Ranger popped the trunk and Potts looked up at us. He was red and sweating and his eyes were huge. His hands and feet were bound with duct tape. He had duct tape across his mouth. I ripped the duct tape off his mouth, and Ranger cut the tape binding his hands and ankles. We hauled him out of the trunk and got him standing. He was shaking and gasping for air. He pulled an emergency inhaler out of his pocket and took a hit.

"F-f-f-fudge," he said.

Ranger and I walked Potts out of the garage and through the house to the living room. All four men were cuffed and standing by the front door.

"Take these four to the airport," Ranger said to Rodriguez. "Take both cars. Make sure they get on a flight to Miami. I'll tend to the hostage."

"I was k-k-kidnapped," Potts said to Ranger. "They put me in their t-t-trunk. I guess you already know that."

"You were in the wrong place at the wrong time," Ranger said. "I want to make a more thorough search of the house and the car in the garage. Stay here."

"Did they hurt you?" I asked Potts.

"No. They just scared me."

"We'll take you home after Ranger searches the house."

"Is he the guy you sleep with sometimes?"

"Yes."

"Wow," Potts said.

I nodded in agreement.

Ranger returned after five minutes. "The house is empty," he said. "Tank is on his way. He'll take George home."

"What about the doors?" I asked.

"They'll close, but they won't lock. Not my problem."

"I was surprised they both got knocked open so easily."

"I checked out the locks when I was here last time. I knew they wouldn't hold," Ranger said. "They didn't put a lot of quality into these ranches when this neighborhood was developed. And this one hasn't been renovated beyond carpet and a couple appliances."

"Boy," Potts said to Ranger, "you know a lot of stuff. I know a lot of stuff, too, but none of it is useful. For instance, I can whistle like a canary."

"Something to remember," Ranger said.

"And I can hum just about anything, but it all comes out sounding the same."

Tank arrived shortly after the cars left. We loaded Potts into Tank's SUV. And Ranger and I drove off in the Porsche.

Ranger stopped at a cross street, then leaned over and kissed me. His hand slipped under my sweater and found my breast. His thumb brushed across my nipple and the kiss deepened.

Nothing like a semi-violent takedown to put a person in the mood.

"Maybe we should get a room," I said.

CHAPTER TWENTY-THREE

What seemed like a good idea in the middle of the night now was a logistical nightmare. My car was still in front of Lena Kriswicki's house. My funeral clothes were in my apartment. And thanks to my new short hair I needed at least a half hour, probably more, with a hair dryer. Not to mention hair product and makeup. I was supposed to pick Grandma up at eight thirty to take her to the church for the service. It was now seven o'clock and I was still in Ranger's bed. Ranger was long gone.

I grabbed my phone and called him. "Hey!" I said. "Where are you?"

"In my office on the fifth floor."

"I need help. I overslept and it's all your fault. I should have gone home last night. I have a funeral this morning. I'm supposed to take Grandma."

"Babe, you were the one who said we should get a room."

"Yes, but that was all because of your thumb and your tongue and other things."

"Where are we going with this?"

"My car is at Lena's house. I'm sure you already know this because you can track it. My clothes are in my apartment along with my hair stuff and my makeup."

"Do you really need the hair stuff and makeup?"

"Yes! This short hair doesn't happen all by itself."

"Take my 911. The keys are in it. I'll take your Honda to the service and funeral. We can swap later."

I picked my clothes up off the floor, put them on, and ran through Ranger's apartment to the elevator. Half an hour later I was in my apartment. I rushed through the shower and hair and did an abbreviated makeup job. I looked at my hair in the mirror and decided it was lacking. I spritzed it with styling lotion that was supposed to be a de-frizzer and wrapped my hair around big Velcro rollers. I blasted it all with the hair dryer and brushed it out. Better. I was going to be late for Grandma but that was okay. The church was only ten minutes from my parents' house. I got dressed in black flats, a slim gray skirt, and an orange and gray striped sweater. I grabbed my little purse and ran to Ranger's Porsche 911.

Grandma was waiting at the curb when I got to my parents' house.

"You shouldn't be standing out here," I said. "It's dangerous."

Although the danger level was temporarily diminished now that Shine's goons were on a plane flying back to Florida.

"I'm good," Grandma said. "I'm packing and I got pepper spray as a backup. How about you?"

My little purse was lying on the console. "Lipstick, a comb, keys, phone, and a credit card holder."

I also had Ranger's gun in a compartment under my seat, plus God knows what else was stashed in the car.

"This is a hot car," Grandma said. "I bet Ranger gave it to you."

"It's a loaner for this morning."

"I'm going to be the talk of the Burg riding in the funeral procession in this car. I'm glad I got a new dress."

I parked in the car line and Grandma and I went inside the church and found seats. I did a fast scan and found Gabriela sitting four rows behind me and to the left. Morelli was close to the front on the aisle. Ranger was standing behind the last pew.

"It looks like they're doing a Requiem Mass," Grandma said.

A Requiem Mass was long, and it included Holy Communion. I didn't usually take communion, but I was starving, and communion would get me a cracker. Something to look forward to.

Forty minutes later I inched my way down the aisle in the communion line and caught Morelli's attention. He shook his head at me, and looked down at the missal in his lap, making an effort not to laugh out loud. He knew I was only after the cracker.

When the ceremony was over, Benny moved down the aisle with impressive speed for a man of his size. I figured the single communion cracker wasn't doing it for him and he was on a mission to get home to the buffet and booze.

The graveside ceremony was relatively short and without incident. No one was shot, punched, cursed out, or stabbed. The police in attendance looked disappointed. The local TV sat-news truck packed up and rolled to Benny's house, hoping for better luck with the reception. The mourners scrambled to their cars.

"I always wanted to drive a Porsche," Grandma said. "Would it be okay if I just drove it to the gate?"

"You don't have a license."

"Yes, but this is private property. I could drive here. And everyone's only going two miles an hour. And you could take a picture of me behind the wheel."

"Okay," I said, "but only to the gate."

Grandma got behind the wheel, I took her picture, and we joined the traffic jam slowly making its way to the cemetery exit. It was a large cemetery with gentle sloping hills. The newer section had acres of flat headstones and easy-to-mow grass. The older section where Carla had been laid to rest had large elaborate headstones. Some family plots had life-size marble sculptures and aboveground crypts. There was the occasional mature tree, clump of shrubs, and cluster of colorful plastic flowers.

We were creeping along through the older section when I caught a glimpse of Lou Salgusta. He was partially hidden behind a large winged angel. He was easy to spot because he was holding his flamethrower.

Grandma saw him, too. "It's Lou!" she said. "He's behind the angel on the Rigollini plot."

The car line to the road was dotted with police, including Morelli. Plus, Ranger was somewhere behind me. I got my phone out to call Ranger, and Grandma jerked the wheel to the right and stomped on the gas pedal.

"I got him in my sights," she said, leaving the road and bumping over the grass. "He's thrown his last flame."

"No!" I yelled. "No, no, no! Stop. Let Ranger go after him."

"No time," Grandma said, dodging headstones, hurtling down

a small hill. "I'm gonna run over that little weasel. Get my gun out of my purse just in case we have to shoot him."

Salgusta had moved from behind the angel and taken up a position behind a granite crypt. I looked over my shoulder and saw a couple of cars peel off the road after us. One looked like it might be Ranger in the Honda.

"This is an expensive sports car," I said to Grandma. "It doesn't do off-road."

"It does now," Grandma said. "Get ready to shoot him when I come around the crypt."

I powered the window down and two-handed the long-barrel, but we were bouncing around so much that chances of me hitting Salgusta were zero to none. Even without the bouncing they weren't all that good. I wasn't exactly a marksman.

We came around the corner of the crypt and Grandma shouted, "Shoot him! Shoot him!"

Salgusta launched a forty-foot stream of fire that swept across the hood of the 911, and I answered with a shot that hit nothing. Grandma clipped a headstone and the Porsche jerked to a stop. Another burst of fire hit the car.

Morelli's SUV slid to a stop on the driver's side of the flaming Porsche. He hit the ground running and pulled Grandma out and away from the 911. I was out on my side and sprinting for cover. Ranger roared past me in the Honda. He stopped, jumped out of the car, and ran Salgusta down on foot. The Porsche was engulfed in flames and my vision was obscured by clouds of black smoke. I moved away from the fire and saw that Morelli had pulled his car to a safe distance and Grandma was sitting in it. A couple of unmarked cop cars had driven up and the guys were standing hands on hips, watching the bonfire. Two of them had fire extinguishers in case the fire started to spread.

Morelli crossed over to where I was standing and hugged me hard against him. Neither of us said anything for a full minute. He was the first to speak.

"Thank God you're okay," he said. "I saw that car go up in flames and my heart stopped."

I was beyond words. I had my eyes closed and I was pressed against his chest.

"I have to tell you, I was surprised to find Grandma behind the wheel," Morelli said.

"I'll tell you about it when we do the thank-you dinner," I said. "Right now, I'm trying to erase the last five minutes from my brain. Why do these things keep happening to me?"

"You have a knack," Morelli said.

Ranger walked through the smoke, tugging Salgusta after him. He turned him over to the plainclothes guys and joined Morelli and me. He did a guy fist-bump thing with Morelli and turned his attention to what was left of the Porsche. Mostly a smoldering lump of blackened twisted metal and charred, melted car guts.

"Babe," Ranger said. "You never disappoint."

I blew out a sigh. "Sorry about your car."

"This might rival the time you got my Porsche flattened by a garbage truck."

I nodded. "Hard to top that one."

"While you two are walking down memory lane I'm going to check on Salgusta," Morelli said.

I looked over at Grandma, waiting in Morelli's SUV. "And then we need to get to the reception," I said to Morelli.

———

Grandma had a few black smudges on her dress, but aside from that she was fine. I'd exited the car through fire and smoke. I had some singed hair, and soot smudges everywhere. Fortunately, I had no burns.

Morelli dropped us off at the house and went in search of parking. Grandma and I worked our way through the crush of people and found Benny hiding in his den.

"Get in," he said. "Close the door behind you. It's a mob scene out there. I got some meatballs in red sauce and pasta, and I got a couple casseroles in here. I don't know what's in them. And there's potato salad and those little hot dogs in tiny dough wrappers. They didn't fit on the dining room table, so they stuck them in here. Help yourself."

Grandma held back but I went for the hot dogs.

"You smell smoky," he said. "What's up?"

"Lou set Stephanie's car on fire," Grandma told him. "He was hanging out in the cemetery and we chased him down and he flamethrowered our car. We were lucky to get out."

Benny's eyes got wide. "Are you shitting me? He was in the cemetery? Where is he now?"

"In police custody," I said.

"Well, at least he made an effort to come to the cemetery," Benny said. "I appreciate that."

"He tried to kill us," I said.

"Yeah," Benny said. "He shouldn't have done that, but you know how it is—old habits die hard."

"Have you thought any more about where the treasure might be?" I asked him.

"Jimmy was a shore guy. He liked the salt air. And he could sit on a bench on the boardwalk and look at the waves for hours. If he didn't hide the stuff in Trenton, I'm guessing it's somewhere in south Jersey. One of the shore towns."

"*The stuff*," I said. "What exactly is *the stuff*?"

"I might as well tell you," Benny said. "You should know what you're looking for, right?" He closed his eyes. "Just give me a minute. I'm not feeling so good. Something I ate."

"Maybe *everything* you ate," Grandma said. "There's only three meatballs left, and half of the casseroles are gone. Did you eat all that?"

"I'm a big guy," Benny said. "It takes a lot to keep me going. And the funeral was a downer. I'm one of them comfort eaters."

"You don't look good," Grandma said to him. "You're pale as a ghost and you're sweating."

"It's gas," he said. "I get indigestion. Jeez, I feel like there's an elephant sitting on my chest."

I grabbed my phone and called for an EMT. I went out of the den into the main part of the house and yelled for a doctor or nurse. Two first responders and a nurse came forward. I sent them in to Benny. Grandma stayed with Benny and I guarded the door to keep the curious out. A fire truck and an EMT angle-parked in front of the house. I let them into the den, and Grandma came out.

"How is he?" I asked.

"Dead," Grandma said.

My heart contracted. "Dead? Are you sure?"

"Trust me, I know dead when I see it, and he's dead. I don't know where they're going to get a casket to fit that man. It's going to have to be a custom."

I took a step back, away from the door, and I bumped into Ranger.

"Benny's dead," I said to Ranger. "Most likely a heart attack. Grandma and I were with him when it happened."

"Are you okay?"

"I think my hair got burned in the car fire."

"Is that all?"

"Yes," I said, and a tear leaked out of my eye.

Ranger wiped the tear away. "We need to get out of here. Can you leave?"

"Yes." I turned to Grandma. "Are you okay with leaving now?"

"I am," Grandma said. "I want to go home and watch some television. I'm worn out."

Ranger herded us through the crowded house and out the front door. A shiny black Mercedes sedan was idling in the middle of the street, guarded by a uniformed Rangeman.

"It's good to be you," I said to Ranger.

"Sometimes," Ranger said.

He drove to my parents' house and I walked Grandma to the front door and gave her a hug.

"I love you," I said to Grandma.

"I love you, too," Grandma said. "Maybe that's why God gave us death. So, we remember to love what's alive."

I returned to Ranger and he handed me a worn-out black leather wallet and some keys.

"I took these off Salgusta before I handed him over to the police," he said. "One of the keys is for a Ford Escape rental. I found it parked on a side road in the cemetery. The rental papers were in the glove compartment, listing the renter as Lou Balou. The address he gave is fake, but we ran a search and found a Lou Balou owning a row house on Sedge Street."

"That's by the button factory."

"Yes. Eventually the police will discover it, and I want to get there first."

"He could have stolen the identity," I said.

"It doesn't look like stolen identity. It looks like an alias for a safe house. There's no history for Lou Balou. He's owned the house for almost twenty years. No mortgage."

"What about the wallet? Anything helpful in there?"

"Expired driver's license and seven dollars."

CHAPTER TWENTY-FOUR

The button factory was on the other side of town, and Sedge Street was part of a rabbit warren of what used to be company housing. Ranger parked one house down from the small single-story house Lou Balou owned. We watched the area for five minutes and went to the door. No one answered Ranger's knock, so he opened the door with one of the keys he took from Salgusta.

The living room was small with worn-out, dated furniture. An overstuffed couch and chair. An ancient television. A dark, threadbare Oriental rug. A couple of side tables. A pair of men's sneakers with Velcro latches in place of laces had been kicked off and left by the couch. The dining room table was scarred with scratches and rings from glasses. Four side chairs. Clutter on the table. Used paper plates. Crumpled to-go bags from fast-food places. Newspapers. Benzene canisters. A laptop computer. A jumble of pliers, hammers, knives, and drills. Some were beginning to show signs of rust.

Ranger pulled on gloves and powered up the computer.

"Without taking the time to recover deleted files or comb through his browser history, I'm not seeing a whole lot on this computer," Ranger said.

He shut the computer and we moved into the kitchen. Old appliances. Not especially clean. Mold in the refrigerator plus some deli ham, a loaf of bread, a bottle of vodka. Junk in the junk drawer. Silverware in the silverware drawer. Mismatched glasses and plates in the above-counter cupboards. Some inexpensive pots and pans that looked fifty years old. A bag of Chips Ahoy! on the counter. No slips of paper with cryptic messages that might be a clue.

"Did you ask him about the clue when you took him down?" I asked Ranger.

"Yes, but he was babbling nonsense."

"What about his house in the Burg?"

"His sister is living in it. I had a team go through it when she was out, and it was clean. Nothing that could be a clue or indicate he had other properties. We went through Charlie Shine's house too, when his wife was gone."

We searched the bedroom and bathroom and didn't find anything.

"Maybe he didn't keep the paper," Ranger said. "He could have committed it to memory."

"Benny said it was a ritual to put the paper in the safe when someone died. I think Salgusta would have kept the paper."

"We've already been through the Mole Hole, but we can take another look," Ranger said.

We were on our way out of the house and I stopped short. "His La-Z-Boy chair! If he hid it anywhere in the Mole Hole it would be in his chair, and the chair is gone. Shine redecorated."

We buckled ourselves into the Mercedes and Ranger called Tank.

"Find out what Shine did with the La-Z-Boy chairs when he redecorated," Ranger told Tank. "Maybe the bartender knows."

I leaned back in the cushy leather seat and closed my eyes. "I need to go home," I said. "I'm tired of smelling like cooked Porsche Turbo. I want to take a shower and change my clothes."

And I wanted to have four or five peanut butter sandwiches and a beer. Stick a fork in me.

———

Potts was slouched against the wall by my door.

"I can't believe you're here," I said.

He stood straight and shoved his hands into his pockets. "Yeah, me, either."

I opened the door and we went inside.

"You're all smudgy," he said.

"Long story short, there was a car fire, but I got out okay."

"That had to be scary."

"I'm getting used to scary."

"Really?" he asked.

"No," I said. "Not even a little."

I took my cross-body bag off and removed my phone, happy that I'd been wearing the bag when I jumped out of the flaming Porsche.

"I'm having a late lunch," I said to Potts. "Do you want something to eat?"

"No thanks. I had a gluten-free granola bar a little while ago."

"Beer?"

"There's gluten in beer."

I made myself a peanut butter sandwich on bread that had extra gluten added to it. I gave a little piece to Rex and I cracked open a beer. I put the television on for Potts and I took the sandwich and beer into the bathroom with me.

My hair was singed on one side, but it wasn't as bad as I feared. I showered and did the whole glam hair thing. I got dressed in my old jeans and T-shirt and felt pretty good. Benny had died but Grandma and Potts were okay. And truth is, Benny's death was sad and unfortunate, but wasn't unexpected.

I went to the living room to check on Potts and Ranger called.

"Tank talked to the bartender at the Mole Hole," Ranger said. "The chairs went to a consignment store. We're tracking them down. Tank also found out that Shine brought in more soldiers. Supposedly some very bad guys. So be careful. Your Honda has been detailed and is parked in your lot."

"Now what?" Potts asked when I pocketed my phone.

"Now we go to the office."

I was vigilant leaving my apartment and getting into the Honda. I drove to the office with an eye on my rearview mirror. I parked directly in front of the large plate-glass office window, and I could see Connie and Lula look out when I pulled to the curb.

"If you didn't show up in the next ten minutes, I was going to call you," Connie said when we walked in. "I heard about Benny. They're saying it was a heart attack."

"Grandma and I were with him when it happened," I said. "The house was jammed with people and he was hiding in his den. He said he didn't feel well and then he was gone."

"Mom and I went to the service," Connie said, "but we passed on the burial and the reception. I knew the reception would be impossible in his house."

"Did you hear about the fire at the funeral?"

"Fire at the funeral?" Lula asked. "What fire? What did I miss?"

"Grandma and I were in the car line leaving the grave site and we saw Salgusta hanging out by the Rigollini plot. We took off after him, and he caught us with the flamethrower, setting the car on fire. The good part is that Ranger ran him down and turned him over to the police, so he's off the street. One less crazy killer to worry about."

"That leaves Shine," Lula said. "Crazy in his own way."

"For his entire adult life, Shine's made money and stayed out of jail by intimidating people and making them disappear," I said. "He has no reason to believe it won't work now."

"Yeah, but your Honda is at the curb," Lula said. "What about the car fire?"

"We were in Ranger's Porsche."

"If I had a quarter for every Ranger car you destroyed, I'd be rich," Lula said.

Connie turned her attention to the front window. "We have company," she said.

We went to the window and looked out. The black Mercedes

sports car was parked behind mine. It pulled into traffic and drove away when we went to the window.

"Gabriela again," I said.

"I see her in your parking lot sometimes," Potts said. "One time I asked her what she was doing there, and she said she was hanging out. That it was a quiet place to think."

"Did she say anything else?" I asked him.

"She wanted to know what I was doing there, and I told her about you and how I was protecting you."

"And?"

"She said she thought that was wonderful and that I was heroic."

"Did she ever have anyone with her?" Connie asked.

"No," Potts said. "She's always alone."

"Did you happen to notice her handbag? Was it Fendi?" Lula asked Potts.

"I didn't notice," Potts said. "One time she had a gun laying out on the passenger seat. It was partly hidden by a laptop, but I could still see it."

"And she has no history?" I asked Connie.

"None that I can find," Connie said. "All we have is Gabriela. No last name. I ran the plate on the Mercedes but didn't come up with much. It's a New York plate registered to an LLC that has no history. No corporate officers listed. I'm sure the information can be found somewhere, but my search programs aren't designed to go there."

I could probably get her last name from Morelli, but I had to be careful how I went about it. I didn't want to embarrass myself by admitting I was spying on him.

I placed the call and got a stomach flutter when he answered. "Hey," I said.

"Where are you?"

"At the office."

"You rushed out of Benny's house before I had a chance to reconnect with you," Morelli said.

"Ranger had a lead that we wanted to chase."

"Speaking of Ranger, he turned Salgusta over to Manny Bartok, one of the other cops on the scene, and Manny said Salgusta didn't have a wallet or keys on him. I don't suppose you know anything about that?"

"Maybe they fell out of his pocket when Ranger took him down. Did Manny look around for them?"

"I'll pass your suggestion on to Manny."

"I'm being sort of stalked by a woman we only know as Gabriela. No last name. I saw you talking to her at the viewing."

"Gabriela Rose," Morelli said. "She carries credentials from a bank in Switzerland and supposedly she's investigating some illegal accounts, but I'm not sure I buy it."

I took that in for a beat. "What's your opinion of her?"

"She'd eat her young. If she's following you around, you want to be careful and not let her get close."

"Jeez."

"Are we still on for dinner?"

"Sure."

"I'll pick you up at six o'clock," Morelli said.

"How'd that go?" Lula asked when I put my phone away.

"Good," I said. "Her name is Gabriela Rose and she told Morelli she's investigating some illegal Swiss bank accounts."

Connie typed Gabriela Rose into her search program.

"Nothing," Connie said. "No history for Gabriela Rose. Either it's a new alias or it's been scrubbed. Maybe both."

Ranger called. "We found the chairs, and we have the clue," he said.

"Let me guess," I said. "Under the seat cushion."

"Yes. Do you want the clue over the phone, or do you want the paper?"

"Over the phone is good."

"Fifty. The number fifty. And it's the second clue."

"What about the other chairs? Any more clues?"

"No more clues, but we found a party favor condom and some loose change."

"Do you have any ideas?" I asked him.

"Only that these clues are directions, like a map. The six men probably knew Jimmy well enough to be able to follow the clues when they were all put together."

"I agree."

"Babe," Ranger said. And he disconnected.

———

"I hate to bring this up," Connie said, "but you have Arnold Rugalowski outstanding. I ran a credit check on him today just for giggles and discovered a car loan."

"Local?"

"Yeah. I followed through on it and it looks like he bought a food truck."

"Maybe he's selling fried roaches," Lula said. "It could be a new specialty being that his chicken nuts were lacking."

"I don't have any more information other than his loan application," Connie said.

"Did it say where he was buying the truck?"

"Steve's Used and Abused," Connie said.

"I know where that is," Lula said. "It's across from the pawnshop in Hamilton Township. It's right on the highway."

"I tried calling but I got a machine and no call back," Connie said.

"Okay," I said. "We'll check it out."

Lula and Potts got into my Honda and I drove to Steve's. I kept one eye on the rearview mirror, and every now and then I would get a flash of a black sports car that was four or five cars behind me. I turned into Steve's lot and lost sight of the black car.

"You can let me handle this one," Lula said. "I'm wearing my ultra-voluptuous spandex dress today. And I got a way with used car salesmen and their sort."

Lula got out of the Honda and sashayed off to the sales hut.

Five minutes later, Lula walked out of the sales hut, adjusting her girls on the way to the car. She slid onto the passenger seat and buckled in.

"Steve wasn't there but his assistant Louis said Arnold is looking to cruise the area by the government buildings on the river," Lula said.

"Did Louis say anything else about Arnold?"

"Only that he bought a beast of a truck. I don't exactly know what he meant by that. I was on my way out by then."

I took Nottingham to Clinton and headed for the capitol buildings. It was late afternoon and there would be end-of-workday traffic in town. I wasn't sure how this translated into food truck sales. I reached State Street and rolled past a taco truck and a donut truck. Neither truck looked like a beast and we didn't see Arnold in either truck.

"Holy cow," Lula said. "I think that's gotta be the truck up ahead, parked on the corner. That's a seriously ugly truck. That's a beast truck."

"Are you sure it's a food truck?" I asked.

"There are a couple of people standing by it and they're eating something," Lula said. "And in between all the graffiti on the side, I think it says *chicken nuts and bull balls.*"

"It looks like it used to be an EMT truck or a police truck," Potts said. "About a hundred years ago. Or maybe it got caught in a riot."

"Looks like a giant Hummer that got a nose job," Lula said. "So how are we going to do this since we know he's a dangerous armed felon?"

"We aren't going to provoke him," I said. "I'm going to ask him if he's reconsidered and wants to reschedule. If he says no, we'll leave and come back tomorrow. And we'll continue to come back until he says *yes.*"

"What if he never says *yes?*" Lula asked.

"We'll go to plan B."

"What's plan B?"

"I'm working on it."

"You don't have a plan B," Lula said. "We all know you don't have a plan B. The man is out here selling bull balls to people and we don't have a plan B."

"Bull balls might be okay if they're cooked properly," Potts said. "I would be reluctant to eat them, but I could see where they might have some nutritional value."

"I'm pretty sure they aren't really bull's balls," Lula said. "Bull's balls might be hard to come by. It's not like they sell them in the supermarket. I never saw bull's balls in the meat section."

I parked behind the truck and we all got out. A window had been carved out of the side of the truck, and Arnold was handing someone a cardboard bucket of something.

Lula and Potts stood back, and I stepped up to the window. "Hey, Arnold," I said. "How's it going?"

"Long time no see," Arnold said.

"Nice truck you've got here."

"It's a beast," Arnold said.

"Appropriate for selling bull balls."

Arnold grinned. "Yeah. I like your hair. You got it cut short. It's pretty."

"Thank you! I was wondering if you wanted to reschedule your court date."

"I've been thinking about it," Arnold said. "I just re-up, right?"

"Right. We bond you out a second time with a new date."

"Now that I got my new business going and I'm my own boss, I guess I could do that."

"Close up and we'll give you a ride."

"I can't do that. I can't leave my truck here. They'll tow it. I'll close up and follow you."

"That don't sound like a good idea," Lula said to me. "I

don't trust him. He threw chicken nuts at me and he shot at me."

"Yeah, sorry about that," Arnold said. "I was having a rough day."

Okay, so plan A wasn't perfect. Turns out there's some unfounded trust involved. Unfortunately, I didn't have a lot of options. As long as he was in the truck and I was standing on the sidewalk I couldn't pull a sneak attack with my stun gun. I wasn't going to instigate another gunfight. And even with the three of us combined I didn't think we could wrestle him down to the ground and cuff him.

"It's just a couple blocks through town," I said to Lula.

I gave him a thumbs-up and we all went back to the Honda. After a couple of minutes he waved at me from his driver's-side window and I pulled in front of him. He followed me for two blocks. I stopped for a light and he didn't. He gave me a gentle bump on my back bumper and inched me forward into a school bus.

Potts turned in his seat and waved at Arnold.

"He's laughing," Potts said. "And he gave me the finger."

The school bus was pushed forward slightly by my Honda but was stuck behind a long line of cars.

"I think he's going to smush us!" Potts said, shouting over the sounds of crunching metal and fiberglass.

The Honda hood buckled and popped open and Arnold kept pushing.

"Everyone out," I said. "He's not stopping. He's insane."

We all jumped out. Arnold tooted his horn, gave us a little

finger wave, and backed up. He made a U-turn over the curb and sidewalk and drove away.

"It's not so bad," Potts said, looking at the crumpled Honda. "You could probably straighten it out."

"It's two feet shorter than it used to be," Lula said.

I called Ranger.

CHAPTER TWENTY-FIVE

Ranger and Tank were standing hands on hips, looking at the Honda. Ranger had changed out of the suit he wore for the funeral, and he and Tank were wearing the usual uniform of Rangeman black cargo pants and insignia shirt. Very badass.

"Let me get this straight," Ranger said. "Arnold said he was going to follow you to the municipal building."

"Yes."

"And when you stopped for a light, he pushed you into the school bus."

"Yes."

"And then he drove away."

"Yes."

"In a food truck."

"Yes."

Potts and Lula were next to me.

"He was laughing, and he gave us the finger," Potts said. "I think he wanted to squish us."

"He's evil," Lula said. "He's a evil person and he can't cook neither."

Ranger looked at me.

"Yes," I said.

"Would you like me to take charge here so you might have a word with Arnold?" Tank asked Ranger.

"It's all yours," Ranger said. "Make sure Lula and Potts have a ride home. I'm taking your SUV. Call for another car."

Ranger turned to me. "Does this guy have an address?"

"He gave 43 South Clinton Street as his address on his bond application, but that turned out to be bogus. He had to give an address when he got the loan and registered his truck, so maybe Connie can pull that for us. I knew where he was hanging with the food truck so that's where I went."

"Where was the food truck."

"A couple blocks down, across from the government buildings."

"Hard to believe he'd go back there. Have Connie get a home address."

I called Connie while Ranger drove down State Street. We passed several food trucks but not Arnold's. We got to the end of the government complex and Connie texted me an address.

"North Trenton," I said to Ranger. "Lester Street."

Ranger turned off State, and I called Morelli.

"I'm going to have to cancel dinner," I said. "Business."

"Treasure business?" Morelli asked.

"Arnold Rugalowski business. He's the Cluck-in-a-Bucket cook who fed fried roaches to his ex-wife. He's FTA."

"Do you have someone watching your back? Word on the street is that Shine brought in more reinforcements and they aren't nice guys."

"I'm covered. I'll call later to reschedule."

I disconnected and Ranger glanced over at me. "I don't care about the Honda or my Porsche," he said, "but I'm starting to worry about your car karma."

"My bad car karma is the tip of the iceberg."

———

Lester Street is a slightly shabby street in a perfectly respectable section of North Trenton. The tiny front lawns are neglected. The paint has faded and has begun to peel on many of the houses. The cars in front of the houses are splotched with Bondo and rust patches. With the exception of the car in front of 207 Lester. The car in front of 207 Lester was a grossly ugly food truck.

"This is it," I said to Ranger.

He idled alongside the truck and read the writing that was almost hidden behind graffiti.

"Chicken Nuts and Bull Balls?"

"His specialty," I said.

Ranger parked, and we went to Arnold's door and rang the bell.

The door was wrenched open, and Arnold glared out at us. "What?"

I showed Arnold my fake badge. "Bond enforcement."

Arnold stood half a head taller than Ranger, had him outweighed by about a hundred pounds, and was holding an eight-inch chef's knife. He was wearing a sleeveless gray T-shirt and gray sweatpants, and he looked like Sasquatch on a bad hair day.

"Get lost," Arnold said. "Go away or I'll gut you like a fish."

Ranger told Arnold to put the knife down, Arnold lunged at Ranger, and Ranger stepped aside and tagged Arnold with a stun gun. Arnold dropped the knife and looked a little confused, but he didn't go down.

"Your turn," Ranger said to me. "Go for it."

I didn't have any weapons, so I kicked Arnold in the knee.

"Ow," Arnold said. "Now I'm going to have to kill you."

Ranger stomped on Arnold's sneakered foot, and when Arnold looked down, Ranger sucker-punched him with an uppercut that snapped his head back. Arnold shook his head to clear the cobwebs, and Ranger cuffed him.

"Nice move with the foot stomp and uppercut," I said to Ranger.

"Classic Three Stooges," Ranger said. "I learn from the best of them."

Ranger tugged Arnold toward the door, and Arnold sat down on the floor.

"I'm not going," Arnold said. "You can't make me."

Ranger raised the charge on his stun gun, pressed it against Arnold's neck, and Arnold flopped onto his back.

"You reached a couple neurons on that one," I said to Ranger.

"I gave him enough volts to take down an elephant. Grab a foot."

We dragged Arnold out of the house and wrangled him into the rear cargo space of the fleet SUV, then Ranger secured Arnold's ankles with shackles that were bolted to the floor.

By the time we got to the police station Arnold was on a rant, thrashing around as best he could, moaning and yelling obscenities. Ranger didn't seem to notice. I had the beginnings of a headache.

Half an hour later, Ranger and I were back in the SUV, and I had my body receipt tucked into my bag.

"Now what?" Ranger asked.

"Home. This has been a long day. Long enough to feel like it's been four or five days."

The sun was low in the sky when Ranger drove into my building's parking lot. He paused at the back of the lot and looked at the cars already parked.

"You know most of the tenants here," he said. "Does anyone drive a black Escalade?"

"No."

"There's an Escalade a couple rows in front of us. It looks like there are two men in it. One might be texting."

"And you think they're waiting for me?"

"I think they're waiting for *someone*. There are several options. I can go up to them and ask if they're waiting for you. I can walk you to your door and deal with them on my way out. Or you can come home with me."

"I'm going to pass on all those options, and have you drop me at my parents' house. I can't keep destroying your cars and having you do my job for me. And as much as I love sleeping with you, I can't keep doing that, either. Your life path is clear to you. I need to find some clarity about mine."

"Understood," Ranger said, "but I'm going to keep you under GPS surveillance. You're a walking disaster, and you're my only source of fun."

"Understood," I said.

I called Potts and asked if he was in front of my door.

"Yes," he said. "Are you coming home soon?"

"I'm not staying in my apartment tonight. How did you get there?"

"The Rangeman guy dropped me off."

"Come out the front door and I'll give you a ride home," I said. "Do *not* go out the back door that goes to the parking lot."

———

My father was in his favorite chair in front of the television, sleeping off dinner. I found my mom and Grandma tidying up the kitchen.

"Look who's here!" my mom said. "We just finished dinner, but there's lots of leftovers."

I dropped my messenger bag on the floor by the kitchen table. "Leftovers sound wonderful. Don't fuss. I can help myself."

"It's no fuss," she said. "We had pot roast and mashed potatoes, and everything is still warm. I'll just heat up the gravy."

I fixed a plate for myself and took it to the table. "I thought I would stay here tonight, if that's okay," I said. "The pest control guy sprayed my apartment building today and it smells like insecticide."

Better to fib than to tell my mom about the two hit men waiting to kidnap me.

My mother brought the hot gravy, and I poured it over everything.

"When you were a little girl you used to pour gravy on your dessert," Grandma said. "Cupcakes, ice cream, apple pie."

"I was a strange child," I said.

"I liked to think of you as uniquely creative," Grandma said. "For a while there, you were convinced you could fly. And you always wanted to be a superhero. If we couldn't find a bath towel, we knew you were probably wearing it as a cape."

"And here I am today," I said. "Normal, boring Stephanie."

"For goodness' sakes, Stephanie, you're a bounty hunter. You track down killers and other horrible people. That's not normal. Normal daughters work in banks and button factories. They get married. They have children. They don't destroy cars once a week. They don't get their apartments and their parents' house firebombed. They don't go on crazy treasure hunts. They go on vacations down the shore."

"She's right," Grandma said to me. "You aren't normal."

Another piece has been fitted into the puzzle. I'm not normal.

"On the subject of the treasure hunt, have you thought any more about the clues?" I asked Grandma.

"*ACE it, 50, Philadelphia, pink*. And clues number five and six are missing," Grandma said. "I think about them all the time and I can't come up with anything. I've looked at maps of Philadelphia and I can't figure it out. I'm not sure the last two clues would even help."

I had the same thought, but I wasn't going to say it out loud. And I was worried about the last clue. This was Jimmy's clue, and we didn't have much hope of finding it. If Benny was right and Jimmy's clue was the safe combination, that was a game changer.

Either we abandoned the treasure or else a safe specialist was going to risk their life trying to open the safe.

I finished eating and I took my place on the couch. Grandma sat beside me with a glass of sherry. My mother sat beside Grandma and worked on her Jack Daniel's big gulp. My father woke up and clicked the television on to a rerun of *Jeopardy!* We watched a couple of game shows, an hour of the shopping network, and we all went to bed.

There are three small bedrooms and a communal bathroom upstairs. Grandma has taken over my sister Valerie's room, but my room is still untouched. It's precisely as I left it when I graduated from college and moved out of the house. T-shirts from high school and college are still in my bureau drawers. Some underwear. Some socks. A couple of pairs of jeans. Clothes I didn't want at the time and still don't want. The bed was made, and the room was spotlessly clean. My mom and Grandma couldn't have it any other way.

I found pajamas with red hearts and was about to get ready for bed when Grandma came in and closed the door behind her.

"I think I might have figured something out," she said. "I didn't want to tell you in front of your mother. She's all in a dither about this treasure hunt. And she probably would think I'm being silly and jumping to conclusions."

"What is it?"

"When your husband passes, one of the customs is to move your wedding band from your left hand to your right hand. I got two dead husbands, so I'm wearing both rings. Truth is, it doesn't feel right to have them so close together on my finger. It's not like they even knew each other. Anyway, I was washing my hands this afternoon, and I took my rings off. And I was looking at the rings on the counter by the sink and wondering what I should do about them, and this idea hit me."

"And?"

"And I never said anything about this before, but the date on the inside of my band is wrong. I've been keeping Jimmy's band in a box in my underwear drawer next to the keys and his band has the wrong date, too. It's not even the same as mine."

"Didn't you get the rings together?"

"No. It was so sudden. I thought we were going to the Bahamas to have a couple of nights of sin, but when we got there, he had it arranged to get married."

"And?"

"Maybe the numbers are his clue," Grandma said. "The La-Z-Boys think he gave his clue to me, and the wedding bands are all I've got from him."

"Wow."

"Yeah," Grandma said. "Do you think that's crazy?"

"I don't know. What are the numbers? Do they make any sense to you?"

"That's the thing. They're just numbers."

Grandma took her ring off and handed it to me. The numbers inscribed on the inside were 2/5/20.

"And here's Jimmy's ring," she said, handing me a second ring. His numbers were 11/7/20.

"The safe most likely needs numbers to go with the two keys," I said. "Maybe this is the safe combination."

"That would do us a lot of good if we knew where the safe was," Grandma said.

CHAPTER TWENTY-SIX

The house was quiet when I got up. My mom and Grandma were at church, and my dad was at his lodge doing whatever men do at lodges. The coffee was still hot and there was half an Entenmann's coffee cake on the kitchen table. I had coffee and cake, and I wrote a note to my mom that I was borrowing the Buick and returning to my apartment.

Twenty minutes later I chugged into my building's parking lot and did a fast scan for unfamiliar cars. I'd had a restless night, thinking about Grandma's rings. She'd been accused of possessing not only the keys but also a clue and now it might turn out to be true.

I took a shower and got dressed in *old* Stephanie clothes. Ratty T-shirt, worn-out jeans, sloppy gray hooded sweatshirt. It was Sunday and the bonds office was closed, so I was going used car shopping. I've found that it's best not to look successful when you shop for a used car.

Uncle Matt's Used Car Lot was ten minutes away and opened at noon on Sunday. I wanted a car that was unremarkable. Not too flashy. Not too shabby. Not too big and not too small. And it had to have good juju. Since I didn't seem to have a lot of good car karma, it would help if I could offset it with a car with good juju.

I grabbed my messenger bag and headed out. The sky was blue, and the air was a perfect seventy-five degrees. I was parked toward the back of the lot, and the bulbous powder blue and white Buick was clearly visible when I stepped out of my apartment building. I walked past the first row of cars and two men came out of nowhere.

"Mr. Shine would like to talk to you," one of them said.

My heart did a little flip and it took a couple of beats for me to find my voice. "I would love to talk to Mr. Shine," I told him. "I can meet him at the bail bonds office anytime tomorrow."

"He wants to talk to you now," he said.

I stepped to the side and moved in the direction of the Buick. "Now isn't convenient."

On the outside I was putting up a pretty good show of you-don't-scare-me nonchalance. On the inside I was a mess. Rapid heartbeat and scramble-brain. We were the only ones in the lot, and I doubted anyone would hear me if I started screaming. My phone was in the front pocket of my messenger bag. I reached for the phone and he yanked the bag off my shoulder.

"Hey!" I said. "Give it back."

He dangled it in front of me. "Make me."

He was in his late twenties and bulked up like a gym monkey in too-tight dress slacks and a three-button, collared knit shirt that was bursting at the seams over his pecs and biceps. The other guy was my height with no apparent muscle, wearing a slim-fit navy suit with a tapered leg. He had a jagged scar running from the outer corner of his eye to the bottom of his chin. The gun on his hip was too large for the cut of the suit. Neither of the men was attractive. Both of them looked like they were enjoying tormenting dumb little me.

"We're going to take you for a ride now, Sweetie Pie," the gym monkey said. "You can come with us nice and easy or Sanchez can stun-gun you."

"Nice and easy," I said.

He smiled and relaxed a little, and I sucker-punched him in the throat. I hit him square in the Adam's apple, and his eyes almost popped out of his head. Truth is, I was as shocked as he was. My self-defense skills are sadly lacking, and I'd acted out of terrified desperation. I thought it was a miracle that I made contact, much less with such precision.

He was gasping and choking, and before Sanchez could grab me, I was off and running. I couldn't get into the Buick because I didn't have my messenger bag with the key. I couldn't get into my building because they were between me and the building, so I ran across the lot toward a residential area. I could hear Sanchez running after me, but I had a head start and I was motivated. I reached the edge of the lot, crossed the street, and ran for the nearest house. I ran up to the front door and hammered my fist on the door and yelled "*Help!*"

Sanchez caught up to me and reached out with the stun gun.

I stumbled trying to get away from him and knocked us both off the small concrete and brick porch. I rolled away from him, tried to get to my feet, and he grabbed my ankle. I went into blind panic mode, screaming and thrashing around, trying to get free, and somehow managed to kick him in the face. Blood gushed out of his nose or maybe his mouth. I didn't hang around long enough to find out which. I was on my feet and running again.

I ran between two houses and cut across two backyards. I had no idea if he was following me or not. My heart was pounding so hard and my breathing was so labored, I couldn't hear a stampeding herd of buffalo if they were on my heels. I hid behind a detached single-car garage and bent at the waist to catch my breath. I peeked out and didn't see him. I stayed there until I no longer felt like throwing up and then I ventured out. I heard a car cruise down the street. It didn't stop. I didn't hear any footsteps. No heavy breathing.

I took the long way back to my apartment building, going one block over and coming into the lot from the service entrance. I paused behind an SUV and looked and listened. There weren't a lot of cars parked. Residents were out doing weekend things. This is good, I thought. Fewer places for the bad guys to hide. I could see my messenger bag lying on the ground by the Buick. I ventured out and was almost at the Buick when Sanchez and the gym monkey appeared from behind Mr. Mullen's ancient Lincoln Town Car.

"No more fun time," gym monkey said. "You run this time and Sanchez is going to shoot you."

Sanchez had a wad of tissues stuffed into his nose, and even at a short distance the nose looked crooked and his eyes were beginning to bruise and swell.

"I'm a crack shot," Sanchez said, "and I'm not going to shoot to kill. I'm going to shoot you someplace real painful, and then when we bring you to Mr. Shine, you're going to be cooperative. And maybe he'll let us play with you when he's done."

I'd skinned my knee when I fell off the porch and I didn't know how much more running I had in me. I thought I might be able to dodge around a couple of cars and make it to my building's back door. If luck was with me Sanchez wouldn't be a crack shot with a broken nose and swollen eyes.

I ran for the nearest car, ducked down behind it, and Sanchez got off a shot that zinged over my head. I ran to another car, ducked down, and in my peripheral vision I caught a flash of black. It was Gabriela in the Mercedes. She sped past me and drove straight for Sanchez. He uttered something in Spanish and pointed the gun at the Mercedes. Gabriela slammed into him before he could get a shot off, punting him at least twenty feet. She skidded to a stop, put the car into reverse, and took down gym monkey. He went down with a cell phone in one hand and a gun in the other. Gabriela put the Mercedes into drive and ran over him a second time.

I worried that I might be next, but she drove out of the lot and didn't look back.

Sanchez wasn't moving. Gym monkey was moaning a little, and there was what looked like leg bone sticking out of a tear in his trousers. I retrieved my messenger bag, ran into the building, and locked myself in my apartment. I walked to the window on shaky legs, looked down at the parking lot, and dialed 911. I told dispatch that a hit-and-run had occurred, but I hadn't gotten a good look at the car.

I wasn't sure what to do about identifying Gabriela. She probably saved my life. *Why* was the big question.

While I was on the line with 911, the blue pickup raced into the lot. A couple of young guys in jeans and T-shirts got out, scooped up Sanchez and gym monkey, and took off.

"Hold on a minute," I said to dispatch. "The two hit-and-run victims just left. Sorry for the false alarm."

I stood at the window for a couple of minutes, staring down at the empty pavement. Good thing my jeans were torn, and my knee was bleeding, because otherwise I might think I hallucinated the entire episode.

I went into the kitchen and searched for something comforting, settling on a handful of Froot Loops and a spoonful of peanut butter.

"My life is crap," I said to Rex. "On the other hand, I didn't just get run over by a car, twice. And I think my hair still looks good. Even Arnold Rugalowski thought it was pretty."

No comments from Rex.

I put a huge Band-Aid on my knee, changed into new jeans, and went back to the kitchen for more peanut butter. I was contemplating washing the peanut butter down with a beer, and I heard something bump against my front door. I looked out my peephole and saw the back of Potts's head.

"I had a feeling you were home," he said when I opened the door. "It was one of those telepathic things. So, what are we doing today?"

"I need to find Shine."

"That might be difficult."

"And I wouldn't mind talking to Gabriela."

"Sometimes she parks by the dumpster. She kind of hides behind it in her little car. It's like the stealth car."

"Was she there when you got here?"

"No. I didn't see her."

I thought she was probably getting the dents taken out of the Mercedes and having it detailed to get rid of the blood.

I called Connie and asked if her mother had any thoughts on where Shine might be hiding.

"Mom isn't here," Connie said. "She's with Benny's sister. They're making the funeral arrangements. I'll ask if she's heard anything when she comes home."

"I had two of Shine's men try to kidnap me just now. Young. Late twenties. One was bulked up with muscle and the other was thin. The thin one was named Sanchez and had a scar running the length of his face. They were trying to shoot me in my parking lot, and Gabriela came out of nowhere in her Mercedes and ran them over."

"For real?"

"Yeah. For real. Sanchez ended up a crumpled heap on the pavement and the muscle guy had a compound fracture of his right leg. Probably a bunch of other body parts were also broken, but I couldn't see those. I was calling 911 when a blue pickup drove into the lot, scooped them both up, and drove off. You have a lot of nurse contacts. Could you call around and see if they checked into any of the hospitals or clinics?"

"I'm on it," Connie said.

"Wow," Potts said when I hung up. "You didn't tell me any of that. I must have just missed it. Were they really shooting at you in the parking lot?"

"Only one of them."

"So, you're going to try to track down these guys and get them to tell you where to find Shine?"

"Yes. While Connie is checking hospitals and clinics, I'm going to check on the house in Ewing."

"Do you think we should be doing this all by ourselves?" Potts asked. "Maybe we should get Lula. She has a gun."

I wasn't interested in Lula's gun. Half the time she couldn't find it in her massive purse. And if she did find it, chances of her hitting what she aimed at were zip, and that was usually a good thing. *However*, I could use her car. Her Firebird stood out, but it didn't shout *Stephanie Plum* like the Buick.

CHAPTER TWENTY-SEVEN

Lula was on the sidewalk in front of her apartment when I drove up. I parked the Buick, and Potts and I got out and transferred over to the Firebird.

"I was surprised when you called," Lula said. "I thought you'd be taking a day off after the funeral and the car squashing. And it sounded to me like you were at another dead end."

I told her about Shine's two thugs and Gabriela.

"So, you're ramping up the Shine search? Are you sure you don't just want to move to Santa Fe? I hear it's real nice there. You could get some kick-ass snakeskin cowboy boots."

"The cowboy boots have some appeal," I said, "but I'm a Jersey girl. And Jersey girls always get their man."

"Fuckin' A," Lula said. "Let's do it. Where are we going?"

I gave Lula the address, she pulled away from the curb, and

Potts started his nervous humming. He had a right to be nervous. He'd been punctured, shot at, and kidnapped. And in spite of all that, he was sticking with me. That took guts. There was strength of character buried under all his weirdness. Unfortunately, that didn't make him any less annoying.

"If you don't stop humming, you're gonna have to ride on the roof," Lula said to Potts.

"Is this going to be dangerous?" Potts asked. "I need to prepare myself if it's going to be dangerous."

"How are you going to prepare?" Lula asked him.

"I might take a pill," Potts said. "I have Xanax, Imodium, a multivitamin, Benadryl, lithium, and a couple orange pills that aren't entirely legal."

"I'd go with the multivitamin," Lula said. "It's a good start."

"Yep," I said. "Definitely the multivitamin."

We got to the house and did a slow drive-by. There were no vehicles in the driveway. No activity on the street. Lula parked a couple of houses down and we sat for ten minutes.

"Okay," I said. "I'm going to take a look around."

"I'll go with you," Lula said.

"Me, too," Potts said.

"No. It'll attract too much attention with all of us creeping around," I said. "I'll signal you if I need backup."

"What's the signal going to be?" Potts asked. "You could do a special bird whistle. Can you whistle?"

"I was thinking about waving my hand," I said.

"Okay," Potts said, "but if this gets made into a movie or a video game, we'll need something better."

I walked down the street to the safe house, went to the door, and rang the bell. No answer. The shades were open on the front windows. No one walking around. No television playing. I went to the backyard and looked in the kitchen window. No mess. No lights on. No dishes in the sink. The back door was locked. I returned to the car.

"It looks empty," I said. "I couldn't see in the garage or in any of the bedrooms, but the downstairs is clean."

"I could open a door for you, if you want," Lula said. "I'm real good with a screwdriver and a hammer."

"You have a screwdriver and a hammer?" I asked.

"Of course, I have a screwdriver and a hammer," Lula said. "Who doesn't carry a screwdriver and a hammer? Actually, it's not a big hammer. It's more like a mini hammer, but it works fine if you put some muscle into it."

We left Potts in the car and Lula and I walked around to the back of the house. We banged on the door and when no one answered, Lula did her thing and popped the new door lock open.

"You're right about it being clean," Lula said, looking in the refrigerator. "Nothing much in here. Some mustard and ketchup."

We did a fast search of the rest of the house and found nothing. Closets were empty. No car in the garage. Trash had all been taken out.

"They must have had one of those maid services come in here yesterday," Lula said. "There's little points on the toilet paper like you see in a hotel. It doesn't look like the new guys were staying here. How many houses does Shine have?"

"Maybe the new guys don't need a house. Maybe they're local. Jersey or Pennsylvania. Hopefully Connie gets a hit at one of the hospitals. They got scooped up and tossed into a blue pickup. I didn't get a chance to check the plate, but it looked like the same truck Shine's nephew was driving."

"Are you sure one of them wasn't the nephew?" Lula asked.

I shook my head. "They were new."

We returned to the car and Lula drove out of the neighborhood. "Now what?" she asked.

"The Mole Hole," I said.

Potts started humming, caught himself, and stopped.

"Isn't that like walking into the hornets' nest?" Lula asked.

"Yes," I said. "That's exactly what it is."

"Okay," Lula said. "I'm in."

"Me, too," Potts said.

———

There were only a handful of vehicles in the Mole Hole parking lot and none of them was a blue pickup, a white Taurus, a black Escalade, or a Mercedes sports car. It was midafternoon and the dining area was empty when we walked in. The bar was half full and a rhythm-challenged woman was on the pole.

I went to the bar and the bartender came over.

"You again," he said.

I nodded. "Nice to see you, too. Guess who I'm looking for?"

"Someone alive?"

"Yes."

"That eliminates a bunch of people."

"Do you know where he is?"

"I know where he isn't. He isn't here."

"Suppose I wanted to talk to him. Where would I find him?"

"I'm a bartender. I don't know these things. Are you going to order, or what?"

"Is anyone in the back room?"

"No. They're all out extorting money and killing people."

"Do you know when they'll stop by?"

"When they get hungry."

I returned to Lula and Potts, and Morelli called.

"Someone just dumped two bodies behind the bail bonds office," he said. "One of them has a broken leg. I thought you might want to take a look at this."

"Are they dead?"

"Yes."

"I don't want to look."

"Let me state this another way. I'm the principal on this and I suspect you have information I would want."

"Why would you suspect that?"

"You called a hit-and-run in this morning for two men, one of them having a broken leg. One of these men has a broken leg plus tire tracks on his trousers."

Crap.

"I'm out with Lula. I'm about a half hour away."

"I'm not going anywhere. This is going to take a while. I'm waiting for the photographer and the medical examiner."

"I need to go to a crime scene," I said to Lula. "Take me back to the Buick."

———

Potts and I transferred over to the Buick and waved adios to Lula. I dropped Potts off at his parents' house and drove to the bail bonds office. Morelli was standing inside the yellow tape when I got there. He motioned me over, and I ducked under the tape.

"Sorry I had to make you do this," he said. "I need the backstory. They aren't carrying any ID."

Both men were on their backs, sprawled at awkward angles. Shot once in the head and once in the chest. From the lack of blood at the scene I was guessing they were shot somewhere else, and then probably pitched off the pickup.

"They tried to kidnap me this morning when I came out of my apartment building," I said. "They said Shine wanted to talk to me. I declined the invitation, they chased me around the neighborhood, and finally they pinned me down when I tried to return to my parking lot. The guy in the suit is named Sanchez. I don't know any more than that. He got off a shot at me, a car came out of nowhere and ran him over, and then ran the other guy over. The car sped off and I went to my apartment and called 911. I was looking out the window, talking to dispatch, when a blue pickup drove into the lot, scooped both guys up, and drove away with them."

The medical examiner arrived, and Morelli and I moved away from the taped-off area.

"This is a classic Shine hit," Morelli said. "Once in the head and once in the chest. If we can retrieve a bullet, I'm guessing it'll match the one we recovered from the dead hooker you found. Alice Smuther. Schmidt interviewed her neighbor across the hall. He said Shine was living with Smuther for a short time. He heard them arguing and he assumed Shine moved out. He didn't see Smuther after that."

"Why would Shine kill her?"

"I can only speculate, but possibly Shine killed Smuther for the same reason he killed these two. Shine has a reputation for getting rid of loose ends. Dead men tell no tales. They can't give you up to cop a plea bargain. In the case here, if he hadn't killed them, they would be getting medical attention. I'm taking a wild guess, but you probably have Connie calling around to find them. And after you had a heart-to-heart with them you would have turned them over to us, right?"

"Right."

"And one more wild guess," Morelli said. "You know the driver of the hit-and-run car."

"It wasn't Ranger."

"And?"

"It was moving fast. All I can tell you is that it was black, and it was small. Not an SUV."

"That narrows it down," Morelli said.

I left Morelli, walked around the block to the front of the building where my car was parked, and I called Connie.

"Your men didn't check in at any of the clinics or hospitals," Connie said.

"That's because they're dead," I said. "Shot Shine execution-style and dumped behind the office. I'm there now."

"A bullet in the head and another in the chest?" Connie asked.

"Yes."

"You'd think Shine would change it up once in a while."

"Is your mom home? Did she hear anything helpful?"

"Jimmy's sister said Shine is in Atlantic City. He comes to Trenton when he has to, but mostly his crew goes to him."

"Did she say where in Atlantic City?"

"She only knew that he was staying in someone's home. She said she heard it was one of his buddies from the old days. He was well connected when he was younger, and he had a lot of friends. If you wanted a liquor license or a pizza at three in the morning for your pregnant wife or demanding girlfriend, Shine could make it happen."

"Start collecting a list of his friends," I said. "You make the phone calls and give me the names. I'll run the real estate searches."

"Do you have those programs?"

"No. I'm on my way home. Send me links to whatever I need."

I was back in the Buick. If Shine's henchmen came after me, I'd deal with it. If necessary, I could mow them down. If Gabriela could do it in a Mercedes sports car, I could for sure do it with the Buick.

I had a few butterflies in my stomach when I pulled into my parking lot. That's okay, I thought. It's a reminder to be cautious. And it's good to be cautious. It's not good to be fearful. Fear isn't a productive emotion.

I found a parking place close to the back door and three minutes later I was in my apartment with the door locked. Cautious but not afraid, I told myself. My new mantra.

I grabbed a granola bar and a bottle of water, took them to the dining room table, and opened my MacBook. I downloaded the search programs from Connie plus three names. I researched the three names and eliminated them. No real estate in Atlantic City. Four more names came in from Connie. I ran them through the system. Nothing.

It was nine o'clock at night when I received the last batch of names from Connie. It was as if she'd downloaded the entire

Trenton phone book and sent it to me. Out of all those names, I found two with Atlantic City residences. In both cases they were second residences. One was a condo in a low-rise building. The other was a modest house in Pleasantville. I'd take a road trip in the morning.

CHAPTER TWENTY-EIGHT

I opened the door to my apartment and Potts tumbled in.

"Sorry," he said. "I was sitting with my back to your door, and I guess I fell asleep."

"It's eight thirty in the morning. How long have you been out here?"

"Not that long," he said. "An hour maybe." He got to his feet. "Where are you going? Are you going to the office?"

"Briefly. I need to see if Connie has anything new for me, and then I'm going to check out a couple of addresses."

I locked my door and took the stairs to the lobby with Potts tagging along. I had my gun tucked into my messenger bag, but it wasn't loaded. I didn't have any ammo. Probably I could get some from Connie. Just in case.

Connie was at her desk and Lula was texting when I walked in with Potts.

"I got two possible addresses from your list," I said to Connie. "I'm going to check them out this morning."

"Me, too," Potts said.

"Me, too," Lula said. "Where are we going?"

"Atlantic City," I said.

"I'm all about Atlantic City," Lula said. "Maybe we should bring Grandma with us. She's like my lucky charm. You got Grandma behind you at a craps table and you can't lose."

"We aren't going to a casino," I said. "I'm checking out two residences."

"Yeah, but after that we might need something to eat and we could at least do some slots. I mean, we're going all that way," Lula said. "I'll call Grandma and see if she's up for it."

I handed my gun over to Connie. "Do you have any bullets that fit this?" I asked. "I thought I should start carrying it. Just in case."

"Just in case is a good possibility," Connie said.

She went to the storeroom and returned with a box of rounds. She loaded my .38, spun the cylinder, and handed it back to me.

"Grandma's not answering her phone," Lula said.

I called my mother. No answer there, either. There were hundreds of reasons why they weren't answering their phone, but the worst stuck in my mind.

"We can stop at the house on our way out of town," I said.

I parked in my parents' driveway and noticed that the front door was slightly ajar. I hit the ground running and entered the house with my gun in hand. I stopped in the foyer and listened.

Silence. I cautiously walked through the living room and dining room, and into the kitchen. One of the chairs by the kitchen table was overturned, and the cast-iron fry pan was on the floor. I ran upstairs and looked in the bedrooms and the bathroom. They had all been searched. Drawers were open. Clothes were dumped on the floor. The keys were missing from Grandma's underwear drawer. The ring was still there, in its box. They didn't know to take the ring.

Lula was behind me. "What do you think?" she asked.

"I think they have Grandma."

"That's what I'm thinking, too," Lula said.

I pocketed the ring, and we went downstairs. Grandma was standing in the foyer, holding a grocery bag.

"This is a nice surprise," Grandma said. "We already had breakfast but there's some Entenmann's crumb cake left."

"Where were you?" I asked.

"It's such a beautiful morning, I thought I'd walk to the deli and pick up some fresh rolls and potato salad for lunch."

"Where's Mom?" I asked.

"Isn't she in the house? Maybe she stepped next door."

I called her cell phone, and I could hear it ringing in the kitchen. We went to the kitchen and Grandma set the bag on the counter.

"Did you knock the chair over?" she asked.

"No. It was like that when we got here." I picked the fry pan up and set it on the stove. "I just went upstairs, and the rooms have been searched and the keys are missing."

"We figured the bad guys snatched you," Lula said, "but now I'm thinking they took Mrs. P."

"Why would they do that?" Grandma asked.

"You weren't home," I said. "Maybe they didn't want to leave empty-handed."

"Maybe they aren't smart, and they took the wrong woman," Potts said. "Maybe they thought they were taking Grandma."

"That could be it," Grandma said. "I'm real young looking for my age. It's an easy mistake to make."

There was a slim possibility that my mom was at church or somewhere in the neighborhood. And there was a slim possibility that she'd forgotten to take her phone. And if I went with this scenario, the house got searched while she was away. I couldn't explain the overturned chair and the fry pan. I also couldn't get rid of the hollow feeling in my stomach.

"Where's Dad?" I asked Grandma.

"He's fishing with Johnny Lucca. They went to Belmar early this morning. I'm worried about this," Grandma said. "I don't like thinking your mother got kidnapped."

I was breathless. This was my mother. The woman who endured twenty-two hours of hideous labor to bring me into the world. She welcomed me home when my marriage failed. She welcomed Grandma into her home when Grandpa passed. When my sister Valerie and I turned out not to be perfect, my mother made it clear that her love wasn't dependent on perfection. She was the voice of reason. She accepted the role of Practical Pig because someone had to be Practical Pig. I know that someday there will be life without my mother, but right now I couldn't imagine such a thing.

I called Morelli and explained the situation.

"I'll put out an alert," Morelli said. "Have you contacted Ranger?"

"He's next on my list."

"Tell him to keep me in the loop."

I hung up and called Ranger. "I'm following a couple of leads," I said. "I'll be back in touch."

Grandma put the potato salad in the fridge. "There's no Entenmann's in here," she said. "And it's not on the counter or on the table. I think it got taken along with the keys."

"That's sick," Lula said. "What kind of person steals a crumb cake?"

"We have two leads," I said. "To save time I think we should split up. I'll take Potts with me. We'll go to the shore house in Pleasantville. Lula and Grandma, you can go to the condo in Atlantic City. Don't put yourself in jeopardy. If it looks like Shine has been using the condo, call me and I'll bring Ranger in."

I dropped Lula and Grandma at Lula's car at the office, and I drove off with Potts riding shotgun.

"I have the route all mapped out on my phone," Potts said. "You take 206 to the New Jersey Turnpike."

I knew the way to Atlantic City, but I was happy to let Potts navigate if it occupied him enough to keep him from humming.

"In the movies it only takes a few seconds for Indiana Jones to fly from the States to Istanbul," Potts said. "This road to Atlantic City feels like forever."

Tell me about it. I was trying hard to push away horrible thoughts of my mother at the hands of Shine's thugs, but my stomach was sick, and my palms were sweating on the steering wheel.

"Okay," he said. "We're coming up to the Jersey Turnpike. You want to go south."

Good deal, I thought. I could make time on the turnpike. Going north on the turnpike from Trenton was a nightmare. Going south was usually open road.

I connected with the turnpike and pushed the Buick up to 85 mph. It was like driving a nuclear-powered tank with bad brakes. It was terrifying. Potts had his hands braced against the dash, and he was humming loud enough to be heard over the roar of the engine.

"Exit eleven!" Potts yelled. "*Exit 11!*"

I slowed the tank and peeled off onto the Garden State Parkway. I got up to speed and Potts was watching the exit signs fly by.

"This next one is it," he said. "The A-C-E is coming up at exit 38."

"The *what*?"

"The A-C-E. Atlantic City Expressway."

There was dead silence in the car for a beat.

"Holy smokes, Batman," Potts said. "It's the first clue, isn't it?"

"Yes! It wasn't *Ace it*. It was *Atlantic City Expressway*. ACE. Initials. The La-Z-Boys would have known that. *I* should have known that."

"The next clue is 50, right? Maybe there's a Route 50." Potts went to his phone. "Route 50 is exit 17. West Egg Harbor."

I had a choice to make. I could go to the Pleasantville house or I could follow the clues to the treasure. I chose the Pleasantville house.

"Stay on the expressway," Potts said. "We want to get off on North New Road."

I hit the North New Road exit ramp and stomped on the brake. Slowing the Buick down was like slowing down a freight train.

I took the E-ZPass lane and cruised onto North New Road.

"You're going to turn left in about a half mile," Potts said.

Minutes later we were in front of the house. It was a two-story frame that was probably built in the fifties. Very plain but well maintained. It was on a street with mature trees and shrubs. It had a driveway but no garage. There were no cars parked in front of the house. A small center-console boat was trailered in the driveway. No vehicle attached to the trailer.

"It doesn't look like anyone's here," Potts said.

I didn't waste time with the usual sit-and-observe routine. I got out of the Buick, ran to the door, and rang the bell. No answer. I ran around to the back door and looked inside. No lights on. No one visible. The door was locked. I banged on the door. No answer. I broke the glass in the door with my gun butt and let myself in. Potts was on my heels.

I did a fast search to make sure my mom wasn't in the house. I didn't find her, but I found clothes in one of the bedrooms. The clothes looked like they belonged to Shine. A couple of pinkie rings had been left on the bedroom dresser. I returned to the kitchen. There was food in the fridge. The Entenmann's crumb cake box was in the trash. Plus, a crumpled wad of bloody paper towels.

I froze for a moment, telling myself to breathe, to push the panic away. I had to stay calm and focused. I had to be able to think clearly. I didn't have the luxury of unproductive emotion.

There was no sign of struggle in the house. No bloodstains other than the paper towels. I told myself that was a good sign, but truth is, I wasn't sure.

"We missed them," I said to Potts.

"Maybe they know the treasure location," Potts said.

In seconds we were in the Buick.

"You need to get back on the expressway," Potts said. "It's the fastest way to Route 50."

I returned to the expressway and got the Buick up to eighty.

"You should hum," Potts said to me.

"What?"

"Hum. It's very calming. You look like you need calming."

He was dead-on. I was having a hard time pulling myself together.

"What should I hum?" I asked him.

"Anything."

I started humming "Happy Birthday." It was the only song in my head.

"That's a good choice," Potts said. "I hum that song a lot."

We hummed "Happy Birthday" together all the way to exit 17 and for a couple of minutes on Route 50.

"Speed limit," Potts said. "It will slow us down if we get stopped by the police or hit a cow or something."

"There's a fork in the road."

"Stay to the right on Route 50. Route 50 just turned into Philadelphia."

"That's the third clue. *Philadelphia.* I thought Jimmy made this treasure hunt impossibly difficult, but he made it ridiculously easy. Benny's clue number four is *pink.*"

We traveled Route 50 through the town of Egg Harbor, looking for something pink. We left the town and drove through a residential area. Philadelphia Avenue continued on past churches, over a creek, and past a lake.

From time to time I checked my rear mirror for a Rangeman car. I knew Ranger would have someone following me when they saw that I left Trenton. And he was probably coordinating with Morelli, and I suspected that Morelli was also following me.

CHAPTER TWENTY-NINE

I pulled to the side of the road. "We must have missed it," I said. "We've been on Philadelphia for a long time and there isn't anything out here."

Potts went back to his phone and tapped in a satellite map of Philadelphia Avenue.

"I see it," he said. "There are some pink buildings about a mile up the road."

I put the Buick in gear and in a couple of minutes we came to a driveway leading into Bowman Storage. Two acres of single-story, pink concrete block storage units with roll-up garage doors.

"This is it," Potts whispered.

I no longer wanted the treasure. I wanted my mom. I wanted her safe and unharmed. If she wasn't already here, I knew they would be bringing her here soon. I wanted to ride around and look for the black Escalade or the blue pickup, but I was driving a big, stupid powder blue and white Buick Roadmaster. It wasn't quiet and it never went unnoticed.

"I'm afraid to go any further in this car," I said to Potts. "We'll be instantly recognized if Shine and his men are roaming around."

I scanned the area. There weren't many places to hide a Buick. A small office with its own parking was attached to the first row of garage-size lockers. The office looked closed and unoccupied. Two large dumpsters had been placed off to the side of the office.

I drove behind the dumpsters and parked. It wasn't ideal, but it was the best I could do. The Buick would only be visible to someone depositing trash. We walked past one row of storage units and didn't see any cars. A tan Honda sedan was parked in front of the first unit on the second row. I looked past the Honda and spotted the black Escalade and a white Taurus at the other end of the building. The door was down on the unit. Two men stood beside the Escalade.

"There's a car coming," Potts said.

We ducked down and wedged ourselves halfway under the Honda. A black Mercedes sedan rolled past us and parked by the other cars. Shine got out of the Mercedes. The door to the storage unit rolled up and Shine went in.

My sick stomach was back, and my heart thumped in my chest. I wondered if this happened to Indy. Probably not. He had a lot of *Oh crap* moments, but I couldn't remember him looking nauseous. Probably because no one ever kidnapped his mother.

"I'm going to circle around this building so I can get close without the two men seeing me," I said to Potts.

"Then what?" he asked.

"I don't know. One step at a time."

I honestly didn't know what I would do. I had no idea what was going on inside the concrete bunker, and I didn't want to make things worse for my mom if she was in there. If I made a move to rescue her and failed it would be horrible for both of us.

I turned to go, and the garage door opened at the end of the row. Potts and I crouched behind the Honda and watched everyone come out of the storage unit.

Shine stormed out first. He was waving his arms, and even from this distance, I could see that his face was red.

"Idiots!" he yelled at the two men behind him. "Fucking idiots. I can't believe you screwed this up. This was a no-brainer. Get the old lady and bring her to the locker."

"We knocked on the door like you told us," one of the men said. "Polite. And we asked her if she was a grandma. And she said, yes."

"She's not the *right* grandma," Shine said.

"We didn't know that."

"And then you brought her to the house in Pleasantville instead of the locker," Shine said.

"She hit Andy with the frying pan and he had a big gash on his cheek. So, we stopped at the house for a Band-Aid. We figured there wouldn't be any Band-Aids here."

"Now she knows about the house," Shine said.

"She wasn't in the house," the guy said. "She was in the trunk. I figure it doesn't matter because we're gonna kill her anyway."

"We still need the old lady," Shine said. "The *right* Grandma. She has the last clue. She has the numbers to get into the safe."

Two more men walked out of the storage locker, bookending

my mother. Her hands were bound. Her walk was steady and unassisted. She looked okay.

"Follow me to the safe house," Shine said. "We'll stick her there and use her to get the old lady."

Shine got into the Mercedes. My mom was placed in the backseat of the Escalade with the two men. One of the men standing watch on the outside of the unit got behind the wheel. The fourth man shut the garage door and got into the Taurus.

"They've got your mom and they're leaving," Potts said.

"We need to get to the Buick."

"Indy would take *this* car," Potts said.

"This Honda?"

"The owner is in the storage unit behind us," Potts said. "I can hear him rummaging around in there. And he left his car unlocked with the key fob in the cup holder."

"That's car theft."

The three cars drove single file around the end of the building, with the Mercedes leading the way.

"They won't know it's us in this car," Potts said. "And it's here!"

He opened the door, got behind the wheel, and started the car. I ran around the car and jumped in.

"This is a nice car," Potts said, rounding the end of the row. "The owner keeps it clean inside. It smells nice. After I got the job delivering pizza my car always smelled like pizza."

"I've never seen your car."

"I traded it for a PlayStation 4Pro."

"You traded a car for a gaming console?"

"It wasn't much of a car, and the 4 Pro is awesome."

Shine turned right onto Philadelphia and the two cars followed him. We gave them a good lead before we exited the storage facility.

I called Lula. "It's not necessary for you to look at the condo," I said. "Go to Egg Harbor and wait for me to get back to you."

"Did you find your mom?" she asked.

"Yes, but it's complicated. I can't talk now. Just wait in Egg Harbor."

An occasional bungalow hugged the side of the road but mostly we were driving through scrubby pine intermingled with heavier forested areas. After two miles the Mercedes led the other two cars onto a gravel driveway and disappeared into the woods.

Potts pulled to the side of the road and cut the engine. I slid the window down and listened. Car doors slamming shut. Men talking. And then quiet.

"This is where we abandon the car," Potts said.

"I get the feeling you've done this before."

"Mostly in video games. Usually there's a high-speed chase involved. I'm awesome at the high-speed chase. Especially if it's an obstacle course."

We walked the length of the driveway and moved into the woods to look at the house. It was a small ranch. Probably three bedrooms. The yellow paint was peeling, and the yard was mostly dirt and weeds. No garage. Everyone was inside.

"Now what?" Potts asked.

"Everyone is inside, and the shades are down. That means they can't see out. I'm going to the back of the house and try to determine where they're keeping my mom. I'm guessing they'll stash her in a bedroom." I sent Morelli's and Ranger's phone numbers to Potts's cell phone. "You stay here and call Joe Morelli and Ranger. Fill them in and give them our location."

I slipped my phone into my back pocket and tucked my .38 into the waistband of my jeans. I left my messenger bag with Potts and instructed him to guard it with his life.

New mantra, I told myself. From here on out it was *balls to the wall*. I moved across the yard with as much stealth as possible. I hugged the side of the house and listened at a living room window. I could hear men talking. I couldn't make out what they were saying. I had a half-inch view of the room where the shade didn't meet the window frame. I knew there had been five men in the cars. I could see three of them in the room. I didn't see my mom, and I didn't hear her voice. A fourth man crossed the room and disappeared from view. I crept around to the back and peeked in a kitchen window. No one there.

I got lucky at the far end of the house. I found a bedroom window with the shade half closed, and I could see my mom duct-taped to a straight-back chair. I caught her attention and made a sign not to talk. I tried opening the window. Locked. Breaking the window could draw the attention of the men in the living room but I saw no other option. I didn't want a SWAT team arriving and my mom inside as a bargaining chip. I was about to smash the glass with my gun butt when Gabriela tapped me on the shoulder and scared the bejeezus out of me. I would have instinctively shot her, but I was holding the wrong end of my gun.

"I'm here to help," she whispered.

"How did you get here?"

"I followed you, of course." She held up a glass cutting tool.

"Do you always carry a glass cutting tool?"

"Tools of the trade," she said, fixing a suction cup to the window.

"What trade is that?" I asked.

"It depends on the moment," Gabriela said. "By my count there are five men in the house. Another car with two more men just arrived and the men are standing watch outside. We're going to take your mom out the window. Cross the backyard and go straight into the woods. I'll cover you."

My mom's eyes were as big as saucers. I gave her a thumbs-up, and she did an eye roll so huge that it almost tipped her chair over. Thirty seconds later Gabriela removed a circle of glass from the window, reached in, and opened the lock. The window was up, and Gabriela crawled in. She cut my mom free and passed her out of the window to me. Gabriela followed.

"Is your grandmother okay?" my mom asked me.

"Yes," I said. "She's with Lula."

"She won't be okay when I get done with her," my mom said. "I'm going to put her in assisted living somewhere far away. Georgia or Texas or Slovakia. I told her to give the keys to Benny and she wouldn't do it. And you're no better. You went along with it all. And look what happened. I got kidnapped. They put me in the trunk of a car."

"I know. I'm sorry but we need to discuss this later."

"*In the trunk of a car!*"

"Not now, Mom. We need to get out of here."

I grabbed her arm and pulled her toward the tree line. We were halfway across the hardscrabble yard when one of the men walked around the side of the house. He shouted to his partner and fired a shot over our heads.

Gabriela turned and fired two shots, hitting the gunman on the second. He went down to the ground, and we ran into the woods. Gabriela caught up to us and turned us in another direction.

"We want to circle around the house and go toward the road," she said. "Slow down and try not to make noise. There's a rusted-out Airstream camper just past the house. We can use it for cover, and I can try to pick them off one by one."

We bushwhacked through the undergrowth, listening to the men shouting to each other back at the house and in the woods behind us. Gabriela was leading the way. She looked like she knew what she was doing, and she was dressed for the job. Camo cargo pants, a formfitting V-neck olive drab T-shirt, and thick-soled, spike-studded boots. Small camo backpack. Olive drab utility gun belt sized for a woman.

Gabriela held her hand up and we all stopped and listened. Someone was stalking us. Dried leaves and twigs were crackling under his footstep. I could see a sliver of silver peeking out of the thick vegetation in front of us. It was the Airstream.

Gabriela motioned for us to go. We covered half the distance to the camper and a man burst out of the woods in front of us, holding us at gunpoint. Without a moment of hesitation, I pulled a Potts. I staggered sideways a little, rolled my eyes back in my head, and did an Academy Award–winning faint, grabbing hold of my mom and pulling her down with me.

The instant we hit the ground, Gabriela went airborne, looking like G.I. Ninja. She planted her boot to the man's chest, he let out a whoosh of air, and the gun dropped out of his hand. Gabriela kicked him hard in the crotch with her toe spikes. He went to his knees and rolled into a fetal position.

"He was the one who locked me in the trunk," my mom said, getting to her feet. "Asshole," she yelled at the guy, and she kicked him in the vicinity of a kidney.

Another thug came out of the woods and went for Gabriela. I rushed over and yelled "Hey!" He turned to look at me, and I smashed him in the face with my gun butt. Blood gushed out of his nose and I hit him again.

"Ow," Gabriela said. "Nicely done."

A police chopper flew low over the yellow ranch house. Red and blue lights flashed on the driveway. We could see parts of the house through the trees. It was surrounded by men in black SWAT gear. I recognized them as Rangemen. We walked out of the woods, and by the time we reached the house the yard was filled with cars. Local cop cars, Rangeman SUVs, and two EMTs. The last car down the driveway was Lula with Potts and Grandma.

Lula, Grandma, and Potts parked and hurried over to us. Grandma grabbed my mom and hugged her close. "Are you okay?" she asked. "Are you okay?"

"I don't know," my mom said. "I think so. I was really scared. They locked me in the trunk of a car. And they put duct tape across my mouth."

"They did that to me, too," Potts said. "It was uncomfortable. I don't want to have that happen anymore."

My mom turned to me. "Thank you for rescuing me, but you could have been killed. I saw your face in the window and I had such a mix of emotions. Relief that I might be able to escape and horror that you might be captured or worse. Those men were terrible. No respect for anything. And then Charlie Shine showed up. I never liked him. All those gaudy pinkie rings. And everyone knew he abused women."

"It looks like we missed all the good stuff," Lula said. "And I see Gabriela standing over there all by herself. What's she doing here?"

"She followed me," I said. "And she helped with the rescue."

"She shot someone," my mom said to Lula. "And she flew through the air and wiped out one of the bad guys like you see on television. And then Stephanie smashed her gun into another bad guy's face."

"And you kicked one of them," I said. "It was a good kick, too. Right in the kidney."

"I got carried away," my mom said. She looked around. "There are a lot of people here."

"I called Joe Morelli and Ranger," Potts said. "They were already on their way. Ranger was right behind us. I think Morelli must have notified the local police." He looked at me. "Lula and your Grandma were waiting in Egg Harbor and I told them to come here. I hope that was okay."

He had my messenger bag hung cross-body. I took the bag from him and told him he did great.

"It's like I'm in a video game," he said, grinning. "Freaking awesome . . . now that it's over."

Ranger walked over, raised the flap on my messenger bag, and dropped the two safe keys into the bag. "I found these on Shine when we went inside ahead of the police. Don't let them get away from you. I need to send some of my men back to Trenton. I'll catch up with you later."

A police transport truck and a third ambulance parked in the front yard. Morelli drove in and went to the transport truck. He turned midway, stopped, and looked at me for a long moment. I gave him a thumbs-up, he nodded acknowledgment and continued on to the truck.

"It's almost here," Grandma said. "Treasure time. We just need to go get it."

CHAPTER THIRTY

It was close to four o'clock when we assembled at the storage facility. Grandma, Lula, Potts, my mom, Morelli, Ranger, and Ramone, Ranger's safecracking specialist. Gabriela was there as well, keeping to herself.

Ranger unlocked the door to the storage unit, rolled the door up, and we all peeked inside. The unit was the size of a single-car garage. It was concrete block on the inside just like it was concrete block on the outside. It was lit by two fluorescent ceiling fixtures. The unit contained a brown leather, slightly used La-Z-Boy recliner, and a large safe. The garage door was the only exit.

Ramone stepped forward with a backpack. "I know this style safe," he said. "This should not be a problem."

"Did you tell him about Hiroshima?" I asked Ranger.

"Yes," Ranger said. "He knows about Hiroshima."

I gave the two keys and the two wedding bands to Ramone, he walked to the safe, and set his backpack on the floor. Everyone moved away from the unit.

"How long will this take?" I asked Ranger.

"Not long," he said. "One way or the other."

"Do you think we're far enough away?" Lula asked. "Hiroshima is big."

Potts moved behind Lula, as if that would protect him from nuclear disaster. Morelli wasn't saying anything. He was looking on with his cop face in place. Gabriela was silent. Grandma was leaning forward in anticipation, her eyes focused like lasers on the safe.

I was a half step behind Grandma. We'd been through a lot to reach this point, and now that the nightmare of worrying about everyone's safety was over, I was getting excited about the treasure. My excitement had less to do with how I was going to spend it, as what exactly was this treasure? Bars of gold? A priceless relic? What had we been chasing?

The minutes ticked on. It seemed like a lifetime, but it was only four minutes on my watch when Ramone finally stepped away from the safe. The door was open, and there was a collective sigh of relief that we hadn't all been blown to bits.

We rushed into the storage unit and stared at the inside of the safe. It was as if all of the air had been sucked out of the room and no one moved. Everyone was frozen in stunned silence.

"It's empty," Grandma finally said. "There's nothing in it but some comic books. It looks to me like Jimmy used to come here to sit in his La-Z-Boy and read comics. How could this be? Where's the treasure?"

"Superman and Uncle Scrooge," Potts said. "Excellent choice of comics but not worth much in their present condition."

"This here's a bummer," Lula said. "I almost got blown up for nothing."

"There was no charge attached to it," Ramone said. "There was no chance of Hiroshima."

Lula was hands on hips. "Well, what about those tunnels with the rats and the fire and the crazy-ass old assassin? What about that?"

"All in a day's work," I said.

Morelli was standing next to me. He looked over at me. Quizzical.

I shrugged. Truth is, it could have turned out a lot worse. My mother and my grandmother could have been horribly hurt or killed. I could have been horribly hurt or killed. Those possibilities had been laid to rest.

"The La-Z-Boys were sure there was a treasure in here. There were clues. There were keys," Grandma said. "They were willing to kidnap and kill for it. What happened to it?"

"In this video game I play there's a princess. And a dragon took her treasure. It was in a chest in the tower room and the dragon flew away with it," Potts said.

"I like it," Lula said. "Some hot-shot dragon flew away with the princess's treasure."

"I guess it could happen," Grandma said. "Did the princess get her treasure back?"

"I'm working on it," Potts said.

"I can't think about this anymore," my mom said. "I'm exhausted. Look at the time. I need to get dinner going."

"I need some selfies for Facebook and Instagram," Grandma

said, standing in front of the safe. "I bet I could be a sensation. And if nobody minds, I'm going to take the comic books."

"I'm gonna snap some selfies, too," Lula said. "I might be able to add in a dragon to mine."

Gabriela hadn't moved forward with everyone else. She'd stood in place. Her expression throughout was thoughtful. Ranger was back on his heels with the same thoughtful expression.

I knew what they were thinking because I was thinking the same thing. This wasn't done. There was more.

Morelli's phone buzzed, and he checked the screen. "I have to go," he said to me. "I don't want to lose sight of Shine. And I have paperwork to do. I'll call you later."

I turned to Lula when Morelli walked away. "Can you take everyone home? I want to stay and talk to Ranger and Gabriela."

"No problem," Lula said. "I might even let Potts hum. He told me he stole a car so you could sneak up on the bad guys. He's coming along."

I waved them off, and I walked back to the safe. Ranger and Gabriela joined me.

"What was supposed to be in here?" I asked Gabriela.

"Diamonds," she said. "D color and flawless. I represent the legal owner of the diamonds, and I've been empowered to claim them and have them tested and ultimately returned to my employer."

"I assume you have documentation for this," I said to Gabriela.

"I do," she said. "Morelli has seen it, and it's been filed with the court and the appropriate agencies."

"Why were you following me?" I asked her. "Why didn't you just go after the diamonds?"

"You and I have something in common," Gabriela said. "Tenacity. Beyond that our talents are miles apart. You have no skills whatsoever, but you have dumb luck and uncanny instinct. I have skills, but I don't always have luck. And as they say, it's better to be lucky than good. At least some of the time. I realized in this instance, I was better advised to follow you around and let you find the diamonds than for me to do my own investigation. All I had to do was keep you alive. That in itself is a full-time job."

I shifted my attention to Ranger. "Did you know?"

"No," he said. "I was concentrating on keeping you in cars."

"None of the La-Z-Boys took the diamonds," I said. "I'm sure Jimmy has them stashed somewhere, either for himself or as part of the clue system. Shine had the last clue. Number nine. That was the number on the storage locker. The wedding bands had the safe combination, but maybe that wasn't Jimmy's clue."

"You know the location of the clue," Gabriela said.

I nodded. "I have a suspicion. Look under the La-Z-Boy seat cushion."

Ranger lifted the cushion and found a folded piece of paper and a key ring with some age-worn keys on it.

Ranger pocketed the keys on the key ring and opened the paper. "RIP, Anthony."

I called Connie. "Did Jimmy Rosolli have a relative named Anthony?"

"His grandfather," Connie said. "Anthony Rosolli."

"Do you know where he's buried?"

"Hold on," Connie said. "I'll ask my mom."

Connie came back on the line a minute later. "She thinks it's Saint John's. It's outside of Egg Harbor. Anthony was a big deal.

He immigrated from Sicily, and he was made. I guess he was like Godfather or something. Mom said she was a little girl when she visited the cemetery, but she remembers that Anthony Rosolli had a house there."

"A house in the cemetery?"

"She said it was probably a little chapel or maybe a monument, but she remembers it as a house. I already heard there was no treasure. Sorry about that."

"It's okay," I said. "Life goes on."

I hung up and looked at Ranger and Gabriela. "Saint John's Cemetery."

"Let's check it out," Ranger said. "Ramone has already gone back to Trenton, but I have the keys and the wedding bands."

Gabriela had the cemetery pulled up on her smartphone. "It's about twenty minutes from here. Follow me."

———

Saint John's Cemetery was on the northwest side of Egg Harbor. It was a small, ancient-looking graveyard attached to a small, ancient-looking Catholic church. We parked on a dirt road that ran parallel to the church lot, crossed over some scrub vegetation, and passed through the elaborate wrought-iron gate that led to the graves. We read the names on the weathered tombstones as we walked. Gianchinni, Mancuso, Salerno, Capaletti. Obelisks, crosses, statues of the Virgin marked the graves of the wealthy. Others had simple granite markers. A badly maintained small stone and granite chapel had been erected on a patch of flat ground in the middle of the cemetery. There was a peaked roof on the one story, windowless building and two Corinthian-style

columns on either side of the door. The entire building was
decorated with reliefs of angels, cherubs, Madonnas, and horse-
drawn chariots. The name carved into granite above the door was
Rosolli.

"I think we found the house of Rosolli," I said.

Ranger tried the door. Locked. He looked at the three keys on
the key ring he found in the La-Z-Boy chair and selected one. He
turned the key in the lock and the door opened. He switched the
light on and nothing happened. No electricity. We stepped inside
and Ranger and Gabriela powered up their Maglites.

The walls were covered with religious paintings. Some were in
the form of murals, others were on velvet. An occasional cobweb
clung to the velvet. Two rows of ornately carved pews that could
have seated no more than four people were on either side of a
center aisle. A small altar holding a cross and a bunch of burned-
out votives was at the front of the room. There was a tiny cast-
iron staircase behind the altar.

I saw Ranger scan the room, looking for security cameras.

"See anything?" I asked him.

"No," he said. "I think this chapel no longer plays an important
role in the spiritual life of the Rosolli family."

We followed Gabriela to the staircase and descended single file
to the underground room.

"A crypt," Gabriela said.

There were twelve niches in the room. Six on each side. The
walls, ceiling, and floor were concrete. Hammered copper doors
sealed each of the niches. Names of the interred were on the
doors. Sarah Rosolli, Salvatore Rosolli, Manfred Rosolli, Joseph
Rosolli, Anthony Rosolli.

Gabriela stood in front of Anthony Rosolli. "Hello, Anthony," she said.

Ranger looked at Gabriela's camo backpack. "Do you have anything useful in there?" he asked her.

Gabriela removed a screwdriver and handed it to Ranger.

Ranger pried the copper door off the wall and exposed the casket. "Usually there's a second shutter here," he said. "The copper shutter I just removed is decorative. There should be a heavier metal shutter that actually seals the tomb."

"Pull him out," Gabriela said. "There's a reason he wasn't sealed in."

Ranger slid a mahogany casket out of the niche and Gabriela and I helped lower it to the floor. Ranger slipped the brass latch on the lid and raised the lid.

"It's not locked, and it's not sealed," he said. "And it's empty."

Gabriela and I looked inside. The satin lining wasn't in great shape, but the casket had obviously never been used. Or maybe only used for a short time.

"Where's Anthony?" I asked.

"Probably bunking with someone," Ranger said. "Probably with Mrs. Rosolli."

Ranger flicked the beam of his flashlight into the niche. "Looks like the niche opens to a tunnel."

I did a mental head slap. "What's with these guys and their tunnels? It's like they had a tunnel obsession."

"Escape routes," Ranger said.

"Places to hide stolen treasures and bootleg whiskey," Gabriela said, flashing the Maglite beam around the space, crawling into the niche. "I came across something similar in Nepal when I was hired to find a stolen carving of Birupakshya from the Pashupatinath Temple in Kathmandu. I thought for sure it was in that tunnel. Turned out it was filled with vipers. Let's hope this goes better. Truly, what are the chances of that happening twice?"

Considering my recent tunnel experiences, I thought the odds weren't in my favor. I followed Gabriela into the niche and Ranger followed me. The tunnel was dirt and supported by chunky, crude timbers. It was a couple of feet wide and not quite six feet high. Ranger had to duck slightly when standing. After about fifty feet we came to a Y intersection.

"Go to the right," I said.

"Intuition?" Gabriela asked.

"There's a symbol burned onto the timber. I've seen it in the La-Z-Boys' tunnels. Potts was the first to notice it. I have pictures."

We turned toward the symbol and came to another fork. Again, a symbol told us to go right.

The right-hand tunnel curved, and we came to a heavy metal fire door. Ranger selected a second key on the key ring and opened the door to a small concrete room with a safe embedded in the concrete. A second metal fire door was on the far wall.

"Interesting," Gabriela said. "This takes mob paranoia to a new level."

Ranger opened the door with the third key on the ring. Beyond the door was a short dirt tunnel that ended with a ladder going to a manhole cover. This was almost identical to the escape hatch opening to Liberty Park.

Ranger climbed the ladder and put his hand to the heavy cover.

"If it's like the Liberty Park cover it has two steel pins that need to be pulled out," Gabriela said.

Ranger felt around, found the pins, pulled them out, and moved the cover to the side.

"What do you see?" I asked.

"A field," Ranger said. "A road in the distance. The cemetery and church in the opposite direction."

He dropped to the floor and walked to the safe. "This looks familiar," he said.

"Looks identical," Gabriela said. "The only difference is that this safe is set into the concrete wall."

I was excited at the thought of opening the safe in the storage locker. I was filled with dread over the opening of this safe.

"I have a bad feeling," I said. "I think we should get Ramone."

"It's your treasure," Ranger said to Gabriela. "What's your call?"

"I'm willing to roll the dice," Gabriela said. "Give me Grandma's keys and the wedding rings. I was watching Ramone. He started with the numbers on Grandma's ring."

"I'm not so sure," I said. "He had both rings in his hand, and we were standing at a distance. And he was using some gizmo to help him hear the tumblers. If you start with the wrong number, you'll blow us up."

"I can feel the tumblers on this without a gizmo," Gabriela said. "The only thing unusual about this safe is that it has two keys instead of one. The rest is basic. I opened a number of safes just like this in Portugal when I was looking for some stolen Patek Phillipe watches."

"Did you find them?" I asked.

"Yes, but not in those safes. Those safes were filled with drugs, compromising pictures, and one had an entire Iberian ham leg."

"Must have been a big safe," I said.

"Average," Gabriela said. "It was a relatively small pig."

Ranger gave her the keys and the rings, and I backed away toward the ladder. "I might need some fresh air," I said.

Gabriela inserted the keys. "They fit," she said.

Ranger was behind her, focused.

"Grandma's sequence starts with the number two," Gabriela said. She carefully turned the dial to the number two.

"Oops," Gabriela said, when it didn't tumble. "Shit."

Ranger yanked her away from the safe and shoved her through the open doorway. He jumped into the tunnel after her and slammed the fire door shut. I was already halfway up the ladder. Gabriela and Ranger were close behind me.

Bang. The first explosion blew the fire door off just as we bolted out of the manhole. The ground shook, throwing me off balance, knocking me to my knees. Ranger jerked me to my feet, and we ran across the field until the second explosion sent us to the ground. The second explosion shot fire out of the manhole and blew a crater in the roof of the concrete bunker. Chunks of sod and concrete shot into the air and plummeted to the earth. Scraps of blue velvet floated down, and diamonds glinted in the sunlight like it was raining fairy dust. The ground rolled and rumbled, and a third explosion blasted the Rosolli chapel into nothing more than a memory.

"Hiroshima," I said.

Gabriela nodded. "My bad. I shouldn't have taken the risk."

The first responders all went to the smoking rubble of the chapel. That left us to pick diamonds out of the scrub grass in the field.

"How many were there?" I asked Gabriela.

"One hundred and seventy-four, lovingly stored in four blue velvet cases."

"Oh boy."

After an hour, we had collected eighty-seven and we had attracted the attention of a couple of the men at the chapel site.

"Time to go," Ranger said. "Gabriela can continue to search for the diamonds later today or tomorrow."

We crossed the field, picking up a few more diamonds on the way. We reached our cars and Gabriela tossed her backpack onto the Mercedes's passenger-side seat.

"Good luck with the diamonds," I said to her. "It's been interesting."

"All in a day's work," she said.

Ranger drove into my apartment building's lot and parked next to Grandma Mazur's Buick.

"You didn't destroy any cars today," Ranger said, "but you blew up a chapel, so your day wasn't a complete bust."

"Technically Gabriela blew up the chapel."

"She chose poorly," Ranger said.

"It's amazing that she was able to retrieve so many diamonds. I don't imagine she'll find all of them."

"I can guarantee it," Ranger said, taking my hand and placing a diamond in it. "I thought you deserved a finder's fee. You might not ever be able to cash this in, but you can put it in your underwear drawer with all your other treasures."

"I don't have any other treasures."

"Not yet," Ranger said.

CHAPTER THIRTY-ONE

Morelli knocked on my door at nine o'clock. He had a bottle of wine and a box of cupcakes.

"Is this a celebration?" I asked him.

"I thought we'd see how it goes."

He opened the bottle, and we took the wine and cupcakes into the living room.

"This has been a busy day for you," I said. "I heard Shine took a plea bargain on the kidnapping."

"We brought him in, and he went off on a rant. His lawyer was sitting next to him and he couldn't stop Shine from talking."

"Anything you can share with me?"

"I'm going to share everything with you. It's going to all come out anyway. You can't keep a secret in the Burg.

"Eighteen years ago, a guy named Paulie Valenti was working

as a tech for a security company. On one of his jobs he got to see the interior of a vault in a pricey Manhattan brownstone. The vault held racks of gemstones. Mostly diamonds. Paulie mentions this to his cousin, who mentions it to his wife, who mentions it to Jimmy's wife, who mentions it to Jimmy, who tells the La-Z-Boys. The La-Z-Boys get friendly with Paulie, and before Paulie knows it, he's deep in their pocket and providing them with security codes to all his accounts. Two weeks later, the La-Z-Boys, armed with safecracking tools and the security code, break into the Manhattan brownstone and make off with $30 million worth of diamonds. They grab four boxes indiscriminately, choosing them by their unique blue velvet cases.

"It turns out the diamonds weren't the largest or most valuable. They were the owner's private collection. They were the diamonds that were never supposed to be sold. The owner goes gonzo and offers a sixty-million-dollar reward for the capture of the thieves and the return of the diamonds. This is double the value of the diamonds."

"He took it personally."

"Big time."

"Let me guess the fate of Paulie," I said.

"We did some digging in old police reports and Paulie's fate wasn't good. A shallow grave in Far Rockaway."

"So, they took the diamonds and hid them away until they weren't so hot."

"Yes, but it's more than that. All diamonds are unique. They have their own distinct fingerprint that identifies them under x-ray or with the use of a laser. The owner distributed the fingerprints of his diamonds to every law enforcement agency, every jeweler, every pawnshop, every black-market fence worldwide. The La-Z-Boys had no choice but to hide them away for a long time."

"If they're all perfectly hidden away, how did Gabriela track them to Trenton?"

"One of the smaller diamonds surfaced. Jimmy brought it to a trader in New York's diamond district. Jimmy told him it was his wife's, but his wife had passed some time ago, and now he was going to get married, and he needed money for his honeymoon."

"Omigod!"

Morelli was grinning. "I know. It gets better and better. Anyway, the trader lasered the diamond and checked the list and knew it was hot. He bought it from Jimmy because he knew the reward was a lot more than the money he shelled out for the stone. Unfortunately for the trader, he walked into a bullet when he was closing up shop that night. I feel comfortable assuming Jimmy was the shooter. Unfortunately for the La-Z-Boys, the trader had already sent an email to the diamond's legal owner. And the owner hired Gabriela to retrieve the diamonds. My understanding is that Gabriela is an expert at treasure retrieval."

"Did Shine say anything about how he found the safe location?"

"He followed Jimmy way back when Jimmy first hid the treasure. Shine always knew where the safe was located, but he didn't know how to get in without setting off the explosion."

"As it turns out, the treasure wasn't in the safe anyway," I said.

Morelli topped off our wine. "You were surprisingly mellow when the safe turned out to be empty."

"In the end, it was the journey and not the destination for me. I am upset that you knew about Gabriela and didn't tell me."

"I couldn't."

"One of those cop things."

"Yes."

Morelli cut his eyes to the cupcake box. "Are you going to eat the chocolate one with the sprinkles?"

"I might have been thinking about it."

"What would it take to bargain it away from you?"

"What have you got to offer?"

Morelli smiled. "Something a lot better than a cupcake."

I knew this to be true.

Here's a sneak peek at
Janet Evanovich's next irresistible
thriller, *The Recovery Agent*,
coming in July 2021.

Gabriela Rose was standing in a small clearing that led to a rope and board footbridge, which was swaying in the wind. The narrow bridge spanned a gorge that was a hundred feet deep and almost as wide. Rapids rushed over enormous boulders at the bottom of the gorge, but Gabriela couldn't see the water, because it was raining buckets and she could barely make out the far side.

She was celebrating her thirtieth birthday deep in the Ecuadorian rainforest. The birthday wasn't important to her. She was all about the job. Her long dark brown hair was hidden under her Australian safari hat, its brim shading her exotic almond-shaped brown eyes. She was 5'6" and slim. She kept in shape for the job but also because she liked pretty clothes. And pretty clothes didn't always come in size fourteen.

She was with two local guides, Jorge and Cuckoo. She guessed they were somewhere between forty and sixty years old, and she was pretty sure that they thought she was an idiot.

"Is this bridge safe?" Gabriela asked.

"Yes, sometimes safe," Jorge said.

"And it's the only way?"

Jorge shrugged.

She looked at Cuckoo.

Cuckoo shrugged.

"You first," she said to Jorge.

Jorge did another shrug and murmured something in Spanish that Gabriela was pretty sure translated to "chickenshit woman." *Let it slide,* Gabriela thought. Sometimes it gave you an advantage to be underestimated. If things turned ugly, she was almost certain she could kick his ass. And if that didn't work out, she could shoot him. Nothing fatal. Maybe take off a toe.

It had been raining when she landed in Quito two days ago. It was still raining when she took the twenty-five-minute flight to Caco and boarded a Napo River ferry to Nuevo Rocfuerte. And it was raining when she met her guides at daybreak and settled into their motorized canoe for the six-hour trip down a narrow, winding river with no name. Just before noon, they'd pulled up at a crude campground hacked out of the jungle. Four hours on foot after that, following a trail that barely existed. All in the pouring rain.

She'd been hired to find Henry Dodge and retrieve a ring he was carrying. Not a lot of information on the ring or Dodge. Just that he couldn't leave his job site, and he'd requested that someone come to get the ring. Seemed reasonable, since Dodge was an archeologist doing research on a lost civilization in a previously unexplored part of the Amazon rainforest. The payoff for Gabriela was a big bag of money, but that wasn't what convinced her to take the job. She was a treasure hunter. For profit and for pleasure. She was an amateur anthropologist, a descendent of Blackbeard, a history buff, and a collector of pirate plunder. The opportunity to visit a lost-cities site was irresistible.

"How much further?" she asked Jorge.

"Not far," he said. "Just on the other side of the bridge."

Ten minutes later, Gabriela set foot on the dig site. She'd been on other digs, and this wasn't what she'd expected. There was some partially exposed rubble that might have been a wall at one time. A couple of tables with benches under a tarp. A kitchen area that was also under a tarp. A stack of wooden crates. A trampled area that suggested several tents had been recently used and recently abandoned. Only one small tent was left standing.

There were no people to see except for one waterlogged and slightly bloated dead man lying on the ground by the rubble, and a weary-looking man sitting nearby on a camp chair.

"This is not good," Jorge said. "One of these men is very dead, and something has eaten his leg."

"Panther," the man in the chair said. "You can hear them prowling past your tent at night. This site is a hellhole. Were you folks just out for a stroll in the rain?"

"I was sent to get a ring from Henry Dodge," Gabriela said. "I believe I was expected."

The man nodded to the corpse. "That's Henry. Had some bad luck."

"What happened?"

"He was checking on an excavation in the rain first thing this morning, fell off the wall and smashed his head on the rocks. Then a panther came and ate his leg before we could scare it away. Everyone packed up and left after that. Too many bad things happening here."

"But you stayed," Gabriela said.

"They couldn't carry everything out in one trip. I stayed with some of the remaining crates and the body. Cameron said he would be back with help before it got dark."

"Do you know where Henry kept the ring?" Gabriela asked.

"It's on his finger," the man said. "He felt it was the safest place."

Gabriela looked at the dead man's hand. It was grotesquely swollen and clenched in a fist. The ring was barely visible.

"Someone needs to get the ring off his finger," Gabriela said.

No one volunteered.

Gabriela flicked a centipede off her sleeve. Could the day get any worse? She was wet clear through to her La Perla panties, her boots and camo cargo pants were covered with mud, and she had bug bites everywhere. *All part of the jungle experience,* she told herself. The dead man with the swollen hand was not. The question now was, how bad did she want the ring? The lost-cities site had turned out to be a bust, but there was still a payday attached to the ring. So, the answer to the question was that she wanted the ring pretty damn bad. Without the ring, there would be no big bag of money. And she needed the money to finance her own treasure hunt. She'd recently found a three-hundred-year-old map that had been lost in her family for fifteen generations. It was a treasure map signed by Blackbeard, and she had it on good authority that it was real.

"I've come this far," she said. "I'm not going back without the ring." She looked at the man in the chair. "I need to pry Dodge's hand open and work the ring off his finger. I need gloves and a baggie. I know all archeological sites have them."

The man shrugged his shoulders as an apology. "They were all packed out. Truth is, we were shutting down before Henry happened. Henry was the holdout. He found the ring, and he thought there was more here. The rest of us didn't care."

"We need to leave now," Jorge said. "It will be bad to be in this jungle after sunset. Hard to find the way, and panthers will be hunting at night. We have maybe five hours of daylight left."

"I'm not leaving without the ring," Gabriela said.

Cuckoo took his machete out of its sheath and *whack!* He chopped Henry Dodge's hand off at the wrist.

"I suppose that's one way to go," Gabriela said. "I would have preferred to try my way first."

"He's dead," Cuckoo said. "He doesn't need the hand."

He picked the hand up by the thumb, grabbed Gabriela's daypack and dropped the hand in.

"Problem is solved," Jorge said.

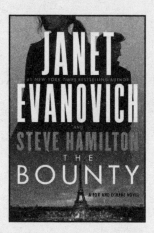